FALSE

VICTIM

What a fascinating story! Talk about suspense! This book has it all.

Kathie Truitt has crafted a taut, suspenseful page-turner. High drama comes to suburban DC.

Kathie Truitt has written a fascinating true-to-life story that is practically impossible to put down. That what she describes could happen in America is difficult to believe but unfortunately true.

Kathie Truitt captures emotions and uncertainty...Wait and see what happens next. I just couldn't put the book down.

FALSE

VICTIM

BASED ON A TRUE STORY

FALSE
VICTIM

KATHIE TRUITT

Enixus Publishing Company

Author photo by Lucy Krodell

Formatting by Daniel J. Mawhinney
40DayPublishing.com

Cover design by Jonna Feavel
40DayGraphics.com

Published by Enixus Publishing Company

Printed in the United States of America

ACKNOWLEDGMENTS

To my parents, Bill and Lynda Bishop, who have always loved me unconditionally and encouraged me in all I've ever sought.

My brother, Chuck Bishop, who always knows how to make me laugh. (Thank you for letting me use your name for one of my characters.)

The Dale City Church of Christ in Woodbridge, Virginia, thank you for praying with me and for me. I love each and every one of you.

Bob and Amy Flenniken and Blanche Robinson for being brave enough to tell the truth, even when you knew there might be repercussions. You three were literally a Godsend.

A special thank you to my editors and consultants Darlene Shortridge and Dan Mawhinney—none of this would be happening without you.

A HUGE thank you to my very talented graphic artist Jonna Feavel!

To Rachael & Dino and Gabby & William and grandchildren, Sophia, Jay, Max and Jason—you make life worth living—

And last but not least, Jay, the love of my life—
we lived this story and by the grace of God were
delivered from it—

PROLOGUE

Julie Patterson caught a glimpse of her face in the mirror as she slipped her arms into her coat. Something was missing. Ah, lipstick. Mama had always taught her that no self-respecting Southern lady would ever step foot outside her house without lipstick no matter how dire the circumstances.

Wondering if a five-year prison sentence was dire enough, Julie paused long enough to do what she had done every morning since she was sixteen years old. Trying to hold her shaky hands steady, she carefully lined her lips with a deep red lip pencil and then filled in with a shade of matching ruby lipstick. Running her fingers through her shoulder-length blonde hair, she coiled it into a chignon at the nape of her long neck and secured it with a couple of bobby pins taken from the pocket of her coat.

Julie glanced at the clock. Six fifteen. There was still time. She needed just one last look at the children before she left. They were still sleeping. The night before had been rough, especially for William, who didn't understand why his mother was more than likely going away. Olivia was trying to stay strong, but Julie could see the fear in her eyes. And why wouldn't she be afraid? Just thirty days ago, she was starting her junior year at Mississippi State University. Now, she would be moving all the way across the country to be a part-time student at a tiny local college nearby and help her father raise her little brother. She prayed that Olivia wouldn't become bitter for all that she'd given up, and she prayed that they both wouldn't hate her for the embarrassment when word got out that their mom was in prison.

She took off her heels and quietly tiptoed down the stairs. Reaching the bottom, she bent over to put her shoes back on. When she stood up, she was staring straight into the periwinkle blue eyes of a young girl—herself at twenty years old. It was the night she'd been crowned Miss Mississippi. Half of her hometown of Portman, population 725, had been there to cheer her on.

The next frame held a photo of Tom's college graduation, followed by Julie at hers a year later. They'd both graduated with honors at Mississippi State, he with a degree in political science, she with a degree in journalism. Their wedding picture was followed by a photo of her pregnant with Olivia and then pictures of all of Olivia's firsts—first tooth, first ballet recital, first day of school.

Next to that set was baby Samuel, their only photo of him, thanks to a sweet, thoughtful nurse who'd had the insight to know his parents would want one to remember him by. The nurse had wrapped him in a blanket and placed him in his father's arms. He looked like he was sleeping but, in fact, had been stillborn. That photo had consoled them so many, many times through the years. There were days after that when Julie wondered if Samuel had really existed or if it had all just been a bad dream. All she had to do was look at that picture to be reminded that he was indeed a real child, and he was loved.

William. The pictures of him always made her smile. After Samuel, they had tried for years to have another child, and it had just never happened. He was born seven years after they'd lost Samuel and two days before Olivia's eleventh birthday. What a wonderful, joyous surprise he had been!

She stopped at the final collage, taken a few weeks before they'd relocated to the Washington DC metro area. Each shot had successfully captured the excitement in their expressions. Tom had planned and worked hard for a long time to get to this point in his career. Julie clearly remembered what they were thinking that day just four years ago; the move they'd waited their whole married life for was finally, *finally* happening!

Tears stung Julie's eyes when she got to the last set. In one, she was giving a big thumbs-up in front of the sold sign at the old house in Jackson. There were pictures of the going-away party their neighbors had thrown for them. And one last poignant family photo by the fireplace before they embarked on their new adventure. She had been so full of happiness, hope, and anticipation.

She wiped the tears from her eyes, wanting to focus, to study every photo, to etch every minute detail into her memory. It might be years before she would be home again. If that was the case she would only be able to see Tom and the children once a month when they came to visit and maybe not even that often, depending on where she was sent.

The thought of being separated from her family shook her to the core, and as she gasped for air, she felt Tom's gentle touch on her shoulder. She jumped.

"It's time to go," he said, barely whispering.

She gently traced the image of her face in the photo and without looking at Tom spoke, "I look at her and she is so happy. I want to tell her to *stay*, to *stay there*. Don't move *here*! Don't come here—it will ruin your life!"

She dissolved into tears.

Tom tried to hold her, but she pushed him away.

"Come on, Julie. Honey, don't do this to yourself. Let's just try to get through today."

She sobbed, still pointing, forcing him to look at the pictures, images of a happy, smiling Julie—a Julie that no longer existed.

"Look at her, Tom. *Look at her!* What happened to this girl? What could she have possibly done to deserve this? What did she do? What did I do to *deserve this*? Please tell me!"

Tom brushed at the tears that were now flowing down his cheeks. The fact was he'd asked himself those same questions at least a dozen times.

CHAPTER I

Three years earlier
Woodbridge, Virginia

"Thanks for everything, guys," Julie told the movers as she signed the receipt confirming that the furniture had arrived safe and sound. They'd given her three days to file a claim if when she started unpacking boxes something had been damaged. The supervisor tore off her copy and handed it to her as the three other men wiped sweat from their faces and filed into the air-conditioned truck cab.

She was too distracted to be bothered by the heat and too overwhelmed to give in to the gnawing hunger she felt as a result of skipping both breakfast and lunch. Instead, she was wondering how in the world she was going to get everything done that needed to be done in the allotted time frame.

Tom had always prepared the family for the fact that his job would one day send him to Washington DC. Even in high school he had made his plans known to her that he wanted more than good-ole-boy

Magnolia state politics. He'd worked hard and sacrificed many weekends at the firm in Jackson. It was no surprise when the time came to promote someone to the head of the legislative offices in DC that it would be Tom. He had earned it, and no one was more proud or excited than Julie.

As soon as he accepted the promotion, the firm had paid for them to make several trips to the District to scout out neighborhoods, to find a place where Julie would feel comfortable raising their children.

Finding a home in a safe neighborhood with good schools wasn't as easy as the Pattersons had expected. The search had been a long and painful one. After three months of coming up with nothing, they finally found what they were looking for, only to be outbid by fifty thousand dollars over the asking price. Several weeks and forty houses later, they found another one. This time they were outbid by sixty-five thousand dollars. Completely frustrated and fed up with the process, Julie suggested to Tom that maybe he should follow in the footsteps of some of his colleagues and commute on weekends while she stayed with the children in Mississippi. Tom was having none of that. He would keep his family together at all costs. He promised her that the right house would come along. And it did.

The white, two-story colonial, still very new, had looked very grand from the street. Standing tall and proud on a slight hill in Woodbridge, Virginia, it reminded Julie of the historical antebellum homes she had grown up with in the South, with four large columns and double doors waiting so graciously to welcome them in.

The family stood on the front porch as the realtor, Mrs. Shea, fumbled for the key to open the door. Julie waited with baited breath as the older woman finally found it and unlocked the doors to let them in.

Julie gasped at the terrible odor that slapped them in the face as they entered the foyer.

"What in the world?" She gagged as she cupped one hand over her nose.

Six-year-old William, oblivious to his mother's reaction as well as the stench, ran straight through the house, dodging various mounds of garbage and debris to check out the backyard.

"Wow! This is so cool! Look at the woods in the backyard, Mom. I'll betcha there are millions of snakes and frogs, maybe even a creek! I'm gonna go look!"

"Whoa, son. Let's back up a sec. I'm sorry for wasting your time, Mrs. Shea, but this isn't..."

Tom looked slightly nauseated.

"Wait," Julie said. "Let's take a closer look. Even though it's a mess, it is practically new, so it should be sturdy. Let's just take a deep breath—okay, not too deep—but let's finish going through before we write it off."

"Mom, are you kidding?" cried Olivia. She put both hands over her nose to protect herself from the smell but made no attempt to brush away the tears rolling down her cheeks. "This is the most disgusting house I have ever seen in my life. I can't believe you'd even *consider* living here. I just saw a field mouse run through the yard, which hasn't even been mowed in this century!"

The move had been hardest on Olivia. Voted "most likable" by her peers at her former high school, she was also a straight-A honor student, on the cheerleading squad, and active in her church youth group. Tom and Julie's decision to uproot the family was best financially, but as a mother, she knew it would be devastating for Olivia to leave behind friends she'd had since grade school. Seventeen was a difficult age even without the added stress of a cross-country move.

She sighed as she turned her attention back to the house. The walls still had the basic, colorless contractors' paint. Crayon marks at knee-high level indicated a toddler had been living there, as well as a cat or two from the smell and stains on the carpet. Both conclusions were confirmed as they moved from room to room, stepping over toys, trash, and a litter box that obviously hadn't been changed in weeks.

Knowing how much Julie hated a dark house, Tom quickly pulled back the heavy brocade drapes. What was meant to be a thoughtful gesture only highlighted more of what was wrong, including missing light fixtures, busted wall outlets, and a broken windowpane. Julie sighed. Everywhere she looked she noticed more and more work that needed to be done. *Nope*. They'd have to keep looking. There was simply too much to deal with.

Sensing the change in what she considered the decision maker's mood, Mrs. Shea immediately kicked into sales mode.

"You simply *must* see this gorgeous sunroom." She motioned for Julie to follow as her high heels click-clicked across the hardwood floor. "Just *look* at the way the sunlight shines through this room. Wouldn't this be absolutely divine for entertaining? Why, the French doors are enough to—"

Julie put up her hand.

"Stop!" She laughed. "You had me at 'sunroom.'"

It was the most beautiful space Julie had ever seen. Strangely enough, as trashy and disgusting as the rest of the house was, this room had been decorated with painstaking detail. It was almost completely glass with a palladium window in the center. Massive amounts of sunlight filtered in, casting a warm, soothing glow throughout.

Looking outside, Julie saw the woods that William had earlier wanted to explore. The trees in the backyard were so green and lush. For a moment, she imagined what those same trees would look like in autumn when the leaves were turning their bright orange and gold and again pictured the scenery with a white blanket of snow, icicles dangling from the branches like glass. She pictured herself curled up in her wicker chair with her coffee as she sat down to write letters back home or ensconced in her morning Bible study.

"Obviously, the house does leave a lot to be desired," said Mrs. Shea. "But as you pointed out yourself, Mrs. Patterson, the home is only five years old, and the owners are very anxious to sell."

"Let's do it!" Julie giggled, walking over to Tom. "You know, I've always wanted to buy an old house and restore it, and you've always balked at that idea! This will be good for both of us. I'll get to start from scratch and add my own touches, and you won't have to worry about the roof crashing in!"

"Well, then," said Mrs. Shea, sounding triumphant and wanting to get the ball rolling before anyone could change their mind, "shall we make an offer?"

While Tom and the realtor started on the paperwork, Julie stepped outside to the deck to get a closer look at the yard. Yes, Olivia was right. The yard did look as if it hadn't been mowed in a while. Actually, it looked as if it hadn't been mowed in the five-year history of the property. Their work was definitely cut out for them. She just smiled. Tom was a master landscape artist, and he'd have this lawn in tip-top shape in no time at all.

The house itself would be Julie's responsibility. She looked around some more and wondered how on earth a house this new could have been torn apart so badly. What kind of people lived like this? She studied the rest of the neighborhood in comparison. All around were beautiful, well-kept homes with impeccable yards. Pretty flowers and bushes bloomed everywhere in sight. The homeowners on both sides would no doubt be very happy when someone moved in and started caring for this property.

The only recognizable downside was Tom's commute. Woodbridge was thirty miles away from the District of Columbia, and while that would be quite a trek for him during rush hour traffic, it would be good to have some privacy, to raise Olivia and William in this perfect, Norman Rockwell-like neighborhood.

The roaring sound of the moving truck shifting into its final gear as it pulled off onto the highway brought Julie's thoughts back to the present. She swiped her arm across her forehead to catch the trickling sweat. Bringing her other hand to her mouth, she tried to stifle a yawn.

Seven weeks of living in a tiny hotel room with every weekend spent cleaning and renovating their new home had taken its toll. She wanted nothing more than to seek solace from the hot summer sun, sip lemonade, and put her feet up on the white wicker sofa she'd just purchased for the new sunroom.

But there was no time for that. She had two days to get everything unpacked and put away before picking Olivia up at Washington/Reagan International Airport.

CHAPTER 2

Just give me sixty days," Julie said. "Sixty days and I'll have this place looking like it was ripped from the pages of *Better Homes and Gardens.*"

"Mom, even you are not that talented." Olivia was totally unconvinced that this rattrap had any kind of potential at all. The teenager had not even bothered to unpack her clothes upon their arrival. Her parents had promised her before she'd even left Mississippi that she could spend the summer back in Jackson with friends and a few days with her grandparents in Portman before starting her senior year at C.D. Hylton High School in the fall. They had agreed to such a long visit to assuage their own guilt for moving her so late in her high school years and also in hopes that she would miss the family and just be happy to be back with them regardless of where it might be.

Olivia was pensive and sulky when Julie and William picked her up at the airport. She wrapped her little brother in her arms with a big bear hug but greeted her mother with a short peck on the cheek.

"Where's Dad?" she asked as they patiently waited for her Vera Bradley bags to appear on the luggage belt.

"He's still at work. He should be home by the time we are, provided traffic cooperates."

"Wait till you see our house, Liv! It's bee-yu-te-ful!" exclaimed Will. "Dad says next summer we might even build a pool! And guess what?"

"What?" she asked in mock excitement as she got down on her knees to meet him at eye level, kissing his cheeks and tickling him as he tried to tell her about his new friends and new adventures.

Olivia was exactly eleven years older than Will. She felt like he was more her baby than her brother. She had only been three and a half when Samuel had died, but she still remembered the disappointment and confusion of those days. She remembered the times she and Dad teased Mom about morning sickness while bringing damp cloths to put on her head, and the trips to the paint store to pick out colors for the nursery. She still remembered the baby shower Mom's Bible class had given her in which the ladies also made a fuss over Olivia, showering her with gifts so she wouldn't feel left out. She remembered the last night before Samuel was born. She slept between her parents, her tiny hand on Mom's belly the whole night. The next morning, she packed her small suitcase to stay at Aunt Dot's while Mom went to the hospital to have the baby, not understanding why she came home with no tummy and no baby.

Eight years later and two days before her eleventh birthday, William was born. For the first two weeks of his life, Olivia could not get enough of him. She changed his diapers, rocked him, and only turned him over to their mother for feeding.

Julie jokingly complained that the only thing she was good for was being the milkmaid. But she loved watching them bond. It was summer, and in two weeks Olivia would be going back to school. Several relatives predicted that the new would soon rub off and the baby would be more of an annoyance to his sister than anything else. But that never happened. Even now, at seventeen and six, Olivia and Will were two peas in a pod.

"I missed you, buddy," Olivia said as she tickled his ribs. He giggled and then hugged her neck as hard as he could.

"Wow, I think you've gotten stronger since I've been gone." She playfully squeezed his upper arms. "Have you been working out?"

"No," he replied. "But I *have* been playing street hockey every day. There's three other boys that live by us, and the big kids always let us practice hitting the puck in the goal. Sometimes I even get to play a whole game with 'em. It kinda makes Jamie mad, though, because they never ask him."

'Jamie? Who's Jamie?"

"He lives on Frostman Court. He has a sister named Kayla, and his mom is friends with our mom.

Sometimes we go to the pool together. He even spent the night with us one night."

He chatted nonstop all the way home, barely stopping to take a breath. Olivia welcomed the distraction. She still wasn't quite ready to forgive her mother for moving her not only away from her home and her friends, but also for moving her to that disgusting excuse of a house.

"Well, what do you think? Notice any changes?" Julie glanced sideways at her daughter as she pulled the keys from the white Mercedes, a gift from Tom for her thirty-eighth birthday.

Olivia could not believe her eyes. Why, this wasn't even the same house, the same yard! Azaleas in their bright, pink hue graciously framed the front and sides of the home, gently blending with a honeysuckle-covered trellis. If she didn't know better, she'd swear the two weeping willows firmly planted in the ground had been there for years.

"Wait until you see inside." Julie smiled, pleased with her daughter's reaction thus far. "However, I didn't touch your room other than to clean and fumigate with the rest of the house. It's there just waiting for you to add your touch! If you want, tomorrow we'll go into Old Town Alexandria and look at drapes and furniture and buy some paint. We can start on it immediately!"

Olivia giggled in delight as she went through the front door.

"Are you sure *this* is the same place?"

"Oh yeah," Julie said as she set Olivia's bags on the floor. "I can't tell you how many days I spent getting all that trash out of here. On top of that, we had to hire a company to come get the owner's belongings out. It was so weird—they didn't want any of their furniture, dishes, anything. So, at settlement they offered to take ten thousand dollars off the price if we'd just get rid of it, so they wouldn't have to come back and take care of it.

Olivia gave her mother a strange look. "You're right. That is weird. Why would they just up and leave and not want any of their belongings?"

Julie shook her head. "Beats me. I guess when they decided to leave they packed their kids, clothes, cats, and skedaddled out of here. And what was even weirder was that they refused to come to settlement. They hired an attorney to show up and take care of business on their behalf."

"Maybe the house was haunted, and they just left in the middle of the night because they were scared," Olivia joked as she made her best ghost sound. "*Wooooo.*"

"Uh, I hate to burst your bubble, but this house is too new to be haunted," Julie answered. "Anyway, your dad found a company that hauls junk. The Goodwill came and got the furniture, and then we immediately got started on the decorating. I had to do everything really quick since I promised you I'd have it in tip-top shape by the time you got back. I take it that it meets your approval?"

"Oh yeah," Olivia embraced her mom in a big bear hug. "This is gorgeous. And it sure smells a lot better than I remember, that's for sure. Speaking of smells"—she took a deep breath—"what are you cooking?"

"Pot roast with carrots, potatoes, green beans, and your favorite, homemade sourdough bread."

"Ah, so you missed me."

"Of course, I did!" She tucked a strand of Olivia's dark brown hair behind her ear. "I missed you before you even left, Liv. You just haven't been the same. Look, I know this is hard for you. You miss your friends—so do I. It broke my heart to leave Mississippi, but your dad has worked so hard for this promotion and wanted it for so long. I owe it—*we* owe it—to him to make this work and to get on with our lives. Please, sweetheart, promise me that you'll give this place a chance, that you'll try to be happy here."

They both stared at each other for what seemed like forever. Just as Julie started to plead again, Tom burst through the front door.

"Hey! Where's my girl? I hope you didn't forget to pick her up at the airport." Putting his briefcase down, he punched William playfully on the shoulder.

"Okay, Mom," Olivia said as she turned to greet her father. "I promise I really will try."

Julie looked heavenward and mouthed, "Thank you." She had faith that once Olivia started school, began making friends, and became involved in school activities that she would adjust and maybe even be as happy here as she had been back home.

She was hoping the same thing for herself.

CHAPTER 3

There were forty-two homes in the neighborhood known as Cardinal Estates, and within the first two weeks, Julie had met almost everyone that lived there.

John and Brooke Williams, a quiet couple in their late forties, lived next door to the left of the Patterson's, along with their teenage daughters, Jennifer, and Rebecca. Within the first few days the Patterson's had moved in, John and Brooke arrived at their door with a beautiful dieffenbachia plant in a splendid ceramic container.

John was a tall, thin, soft-spoken man who wore what little hair he had left in a comb-over. Brooke, his wife, had a very petite, fit figure that she enjoyed showing off in midriff-baring tops that looked ridiculous on a woman pushing fifty. Although Brooke seemed to go to great lengths to keep her figure, once mentioning she hadn't eaten a French fry in fifteen years, it was a mystery to Julie why she neglected the rest of her grooming. Her mousy, brown, curly hair was completely unruly with no set style. Her thick pop-bottle eyeglasses did nothing to accentuate her brown eyes, and her face was completely devoid of makeup—with not even a hint of mascara or lip gloss, which was a concept that was totally foreign to Julie. Southern women were notorious for being well polished and ultra-feminine, something that women didn't seem to take too seriously here.

After all, Virginia is a southern state, she thought.

"This is NOVA—Northern Virginia," Salena Sanderson, an attractive African American woman in her early sixties explained to her. "You need to go farther south to ROVA, *Rest of Virginia*, if you want that Southern culture you're so used to."

Salena, a retired government worker, lived in the lovely brick home with the wraparound porch directly across the street. Her husband, Wendall, a retired military officer, worked at the Capitol as a security officer. They took time out the very first week to introduce themselves, commenting on the positive changes taking place at the "McKinney House," as the neighbors had dubbed it after the previous owners.

The home to the right side of the Patterson's was always busy with the hustle and bustle of the four Lopez children. Their father, Antonio, worked at Quantico Marine Base while Lisa, their mother, was a homemaker. Micah looked to be about high school age, and Julie guessed twins Kendra and Jordana to be ten or eleven. Jonathan was four. Julie knew that to be a fact because Jonathan himself had told her.

She had been painting the family room one morning when she heard this tiny little voice behind her.

"Hi. What's your name?"

Startled, she dropped the paintbrush. Quickly, she grabbed a paper towel to sop up the paint while at the same time looking to see who the voice belonged to. She smiled when she saw the most precious dark-haired, brown-eyed little boy with his face smashed against one of the sunroom window screens.

Julie properly introduced herself and asked him what his name was.

"I'm Jonathan. I'm four. Do you have any cookies?" She didn't, but from that day forward, she made sure to keep the cupboard fully stocked. Jonathan was never disappointed after that.

The Johannes lived around the corner and halfway down the block. Julie thought Mike looked like a surfing instructor, although his job as manager of Fairfax Ford was probably a bit more lucrative. Shelley, his pretty wife, reminded Julie of a shorter, slightly younger version of Sandra Bullock. The kids, Stuart, Whitney, and Robbie, all the spitting image of their dad, were avid soccer players. Will, also a soccer fan, had found a fast friend in Robbie. Will, Robbie, and Jamie, the little boy he'd told Olivia about, were inseparable, and the three always had a basketball, hockey, or soccer game going on in the neighborhood.

Anne Mumfort, Jamie's mother, lived around the corner on the opposite end of the cul-de-sac from the

Johannes. She was a tall, lanky, plain woman with a gentle smile and easy nature. Julie thought Anne had the kindest brown eyes she'd ever seen, and she admired the endless amount of patience she had with both Jamie and his older sister, Kayla. Anne and her husband, Bob, had moved from Chicago a few weeks before the Patterson's, so both ladies were starting over in a new area. Not only did they have the boys in common, but the friendship took on a whole new level when they realized they both had a passion for antiques. They spent a lot of time scouring the shops of Occoquan, a charming village known across the DC metro area for its unique cafes, boutiques, and antique stores.

The only people Julie had yet to meet were the ones who lived behind her. That was soon about to change.

The house sat on a hill with the back facing the Patterson's home. From Julie's sunroom, there was a full view of the back of the house with its spacious deck. The first morning when she was having her coffee, Julie got the uneasy feeling that someone was watching her. Sure enough, when she turned to look outside, there was a small, dark-haired woman staring at her. Julie had smiled and waved, but the lady's icy glare cut right through her. She had tried several times after that to speak to her to no avail. The "deck lady," as she came to be known, simply refused to acknowledge her.

It got to be a routine. Every morning like clockwork when Julie went out on her own deck or sat in the sunroom, this woman would follow suit, just sitting and staring at her.

It gave Olivia the creeps, but Julie didn't let it bother her. She'd heard through the neighborhood grapevine that the woman was from somewhere up north. It was common knowledge that sometimes it took Northern folks a little longer to warm up than it did Southerners. Julie figured the woman would come around in her own time. If not, well, that was okay, too. Some people just didn't like to socialize with their neighbors.

One bright, sunny morning, Julie was outside with a contractor from Silver's Pool and Spa. Tom had given the go-ahead to start measuring off the yard to build a pool. It was too late to have it finished for this summer but would definitely be ready for the next one.

"Hello!" came a high-pitched voice from the hill. Blind without her sunglasses, Julie held her hand horizontally above her eyes and squinted, trying to focus in the direction of the voice.

There was "deck lady" smiling and waving so hard that Julie thought it looked like she was going to take flight. *Hmm. She must know the pool man*, she thought.

"Is she waving at you? "Julie asked him.

"I've never seen her in my life," he answered, wiping sweat off his forehead with the back of his arm and then going back to measuring the yard.

"Someone must have slipped some happy pills in her cereal," Julie muttered under her breath.

Within the next few minutes, the woman was in Julie's yard introducing herself.

"Hi. I'm Lynn Hennessy," she said, extending her hand.

"I'm Julie Patterson. It's nice to meet you, Lynn. By the way, has anyone ever told you that you look exactly like Martina McBride?" The resemblance was amazing.

"I hear that a lot! I'm not really a country music fan, but my husband is. He thinks I look like her too— except for the eye color."

Lynn was a beautiful woman with thick, dark hair, ivory skin, and piercing black-brown eyes. She was much smaller than Julie expected, only about five feet, one inch. If her figure was any indication, she must have spent every waking hour in the gym. Her hips were accentuated by tight jeans, and the plunging white halter top showed ample cleavage. Julie thought it a tad inappropriate for a woman who looked to be her own age to show that much skin however, the pool man didn't seem to mind. Then again maybe she was just annoyed because it reminded her of that extra twenty pounds that she'd made no attempt to lose.

Julie politely invited Lynn to come inside out of the hot morning sun.

"Thank you." Lynn accepted. "I have to admit I am a bit nosy to see what you've done with the place. The outside looks absolutely amazing. Are you building a pool?"

"Yes," Julie answered nonchalantly. "Tom, my husband, promised the kids we'd find a house with a yard big enough for one."

"We've always wanted a pool," Lynn replied as she stepped into the house. "This is beautiful." She took in every detail from top to bottom. "Did you hire a decorator?"

"Oh no," said Julie. "We did it ourselves. But thank you. That's a compliment."

She wondered for a split second what prompted Lynn, after weeks of snubbing her, to finally warm up to her and pay her this visit. *Oh well*, she thought, *I guess it takes some people longer than others to come out of their shell.*

"I can't believe this is even the same house," Lynn said.

"What do you know about the McKinney's?" Julie asked, thinking maybe Lynn could give her some insight as to why the family seemed to be running from something or someone.

Lynn wrinkled her nose at the mention of the family.

"Those people were pure trash," she said. "The police were over here constantly, at least three times a week. I think they were drug dealers. No one really knows for sure what they were up to. All I know is that she—Barbara McKinney—was always in some kind of trouble."

Well, that would explain why they'd wanted to get out of here so fast, Julie thought.

"Oh, isn't this adorable? Is this one of your kids as a baby?" Lynn was holding the picture of Samuel, nestled sweetly in Tom's arms.

"That's Samuel," Julie softly replied, "our oldest son. He was stillborn thirteen years ago." She always the hated the awkwardness it created when she would tell people that he had died. They never knew what to say, so usually they'd put the picture down and immediately change the subject.

Not Lynn.

"I know how that feels," she said as she gently placed the picture back where she found it. "That happened to us. Twice. Rick Jr. and Gregory." She was silent for a minute, almost in another world, before she started talking again. She shook her head. "That was devastating. Although it was eight years ago, sometimes it feels like it was just yesterday."

"I know exactly what you mean." Julie marveled at the fact that after all these years she'd found someone who knew and understood that kind of pain.

For years she'd tried to explain to friends and family how badly she hurt, how desolate she felt. She'd asked God to send someone to her that wouldn't think she was crazy when she told them her arms felt so empty they ached. Mama and Aunt Cathy had looked at her like she had lost her mind when she confessed that she'd woken up several nights in a row, swearing she'd heard a baby crying.

Lynn nodded in understanding. "I have been through all of that. I don't know about you, but their birthdays are the worst. I am almost non-functional on those days." She was silent for a moment. 'Anyway! Moving right along. I didn't mean to put a damper on things."

"Oh no! Please don't apologize," replied Julie. 'Are you kidding? Believe it or not, you're the first person I've ever met that's been through this. I can talk about Samuel and you understand. No one ever wants to talk about him, and sometimes I need to."

"Well, I know you have another little boy because I see him playing with Jamie. His family lives across the street from me," said Lynn.

"Yes, that's my Will. He's six, almost seven, and Olivia is seventeen, almost eighteen—their birthdays are in a few weeks, right before school starts. Now you know why my kids are eleven years apart." Julie and Tom were used to the friendly teasing about the difference in their kids' ages.

"What about you? Do you have any more children?" Julie asked.

"Yes." Lynn's sudden smile radiated pride. She loved talking about her kids. "Curtis is fourteen, and Hannah is nine. As a matter of fact, I see Hannah through the window jumping on her trampoline. She's quite the little gymnast."

"Wow, you're right. She is quite the gymnast."

There was a high fence around the yard, and every half second Hannah Hennessy flew through the air doing toe touches and backflips, her long, blonde hair suspended in the air, moving in opposite rhythm of her tiny form. Her proud mother was giving Julie all the details on the awards and gymnastic medals Hannah had won. The list was quite impressive.

The doorbell rang.

"That's probably Anne, "Julie said, walking through the living room to the foyer. "We're trying to coordinate a time to meet at the pool this afternoon."

Just as she predicted, there stood a smiling Anne at the front door with her pretty blonde-haired daughter, Kayla, by her side.

"Hey, girls. Come on in." Julie smiled and stepped aside to allow the two in. "Look who's here! Your sweet neighbor from across the street just stopped by to introduce herself."

"Hello, stranger!" Lynn said to Anne while she reached over and affectionately pinched Kayla, on the cheek. "What's this I hear about you guys going to the pool today?"

"Why don't you suit up and go with us?" Anne asked. "We've been going to the one off Dale Boulevard across from the ball field. I'm bringing drinks, and Julie is packing the snacks. All you have to do is show up and work on your tan."

"That'd be fun," said Julie. "Lynn, you have to come!"

"Okay." She laughed. "You twisted my arm. What time do I show up?"

Anne looked at her watch. "Hmm, let's say an hour, give or take a few minutes."

"I'll see you ladies then." Lynn smiled. "I'll let myself out."

She walked to edge of the lawn, stopped, and turned to look back at the front of the house.

Olivia watched the woman from her bedroom window. With a pivot, Lynn strutted up the sidewalk, around the corner, and out of sight.

Olivia didn't know which was stranger: the fact that the woman was her mom's age and dressed like a hooker or the smug, almost creepy smile she had on her face while staring at their house.

CHAPTER 4

The pool was empty when Anne, Kayla, and Jamie arrived at one o'clock. Jamie ran ahead to grab space where they could all sit together, dragging three chaise lounge chairs together and placing them side by side.

As Julie was unloading towels and a cooler, Lynn pulled up in her white Mustang convertible with the top down, music blaring. Hannah tumbled out of the car, running to meet up with Kayla. The two girls immediately started whispering and giggling as they wandered off to the diving board. A teenage boy with a brooding expression grabbed a towel and an MP3 player out of the backseat of the car.

This must be Curtis, Julie thought as he walked past her, adjusting his earphones. He had curly brown hair that covered his ears and just skimmed the bottom of his eyebrows. *Cute kid.* She smiled at him, but he brushed past her without any kind of acknowledgement, reminding Julie of her first few encounters with his mother.

Typical teenage attitude, she thought as she turned around in time to see Lynn's seductive emergence from her car. She slowly slipped one leg out and then the other, revealing four-inch black espadrilles that laced halfway up her toned calves. Julie was pretty sure Lynn was aware she had an entranced audience in three teenage boys standing by the snack bar, gaping as she slowly removed her t-shirt, revealing a black string bikini, which left almost nothing to the imagination. She had the flattest stomach Julie had ever seen and not an ounce of fat anywhere. Her dark hair was pinned up on top of her head, and she wore a pair of black Chanel sunglasses.

Julie suddenly felt old and dumpy in last season's one piece with Tom's t-shirt thrown over it. Maybe being friends with Lynn would inspire her to get back into shape.

Within the three short months that Julie had moved into the neighborhood, the three became inseparable. Besides the daily trips to the pool, they shopped, tried new restaurants, and took their morning walks together. Many nights after their families were fed they'd sit in Julie's sunroom or on Lynn's deck and sip iced tea. They laughed over silly jokes, cried at sad movies, and spent countless hours talking about everything and nothing, sometimes past midnight into the wee hours of the morning.

Still, it was Lynn that Julie felt the strongest connection to. She thanked God for finally sending her a friend who would listen patiently, without judgment, when she wanted to talk about the baby.

Julie, on the other hand, always listened attentively when Lynn needed to talk about her babies. Understandably, losing baby Rick had been devastating on its own, but the death of her second baby, Gregory so soon after the first loss had understandably traumatized her. She told Julie that his loss had caused her so much pain and guilt that she'd suffered a nervous breakdown and spent almost a month in the hospital.

Apparently, the baby had spent the last few months of her pregnancy performing all sorts of acrobatics. One day, she felt his movements becoming less and less obvious until he stopped moving altogether. Thinking he was cramped and probably tired, she saw no reason to become alarmed and actually decided to take advantage of his quiet spell to rest that afternoon. Later that evening after dinner, her water broke, and after several hours of intense and grueling labor, little Gregory was born with the umbilical cord wrapped around his neck.

"I should have known that something was wrong" Lynn cried that day as she replayed every painful detail. "Especially after Rick. I should have been more aware. I should have *known* something was different; something was *wrong!*'

"Oh, sweetheart, there is no way you could have possibly known what was happening."

"I spent the first six months of that pregnancy so paranoid that what happened with little Rick might happen again that I think I drove my doctor crazy. I mean, I called him for every little thing—I guess I just didn't want to overreact."

There was nothing to say to that. She could reassure Lynn till the cows came home that she wasn't to blame for what happened, but she knew it would be futile. Maybe Lynn should have gone to the emergency room or at least given her doctor a call. But Julie understood all too well. She too had taken many unnecessary trips to the doctor or the emergency room when pregnant with Will only to be told to relax, that all was well, something she just couldn't bring herself to believe until she held that sweet bundle of joy in her arms.

Julie smiled to herself, thinking back to that conversation. It was funny how things worked out sometimes. It had taken her moving halfway across the country to find the solace she needed to finally lay Samuel to rest.

As she lay down that night, she'd felt a peace she hadn't felt in quite some time. It felt good. She loved her new surroundings, her new home, and had gained two wonderful new friends. Before she drifted off to sleep, she thought that maybe, just maybe, it was possible to be as happy here in Virginia as she had been in Mississippi.

CHAPTER 5

It was a given that since Julie, Lynn, and Anne were so close that their husbands also would become friends. Saturdays the guys usually played golf and then met up with the ladies for a barbecue or a night out. This particular sultry Sunday evening, they'd decided to have the weekly cookout at Rick and Lynn's. It had been another pleasant evening of food and fun, but when she couldn't stop yawning, Julie thought it a perfect time to wrap up the evening. While everyone was listening intently to Bob and Tom argue over who had the better golf game, Julie slipped off to the kitchen to start cleaning and packing her dishes to take home. Before she closed the door to go inside, Rick slipped up behind her and followed her.

"I've been trying to catch you alone all night, so I could talk to you," Rick told her, his voice almost a whisper, as he closed the door behind them. Julie began rinsing out her dishes she had used to carry her famous Southern potato salad and baked beans in. "I am so glad that you guys moved here. Not only are you and Tom such a great asset to this community with fixing up your house and all, but you've been such a great friend to Lynn, and I really appreciate that."

'Are you kidding?" She grabbed a hand towel from the sink. "She and Anne both have made this move so much easier for me. I am a Mississippi girl, born and bred, and never knew that after living somewhere else for a few short months I could be this happy."

Rick leaned in closer and lowered his voice. "She hasn't had it very easy, and sometimes it's very difficult for her to make friends."

"No worries. I completely understand. When you've been through what she's been through—what you've *both* been through—well, sometimes it's hard to open up," Julie said, stacking the dishes. "We lost one baby and that was hard enough. I can't even imagine what it must have been like for you all to go through that twice."

Julie didn't catch the puzzled look on Rick's face. She was too busy talking about how good it felt to be able to confide in Lynn about her loss and how she felt that Lynn too had benefited by being able to talk so openly about babies Rick and Gregory.

She was still rattling on when finally Rick put his hand to his temple and said, "Whoa, back up. I'm not following you."

Julie stammered, "Lynn told me about the loss of your babies and—"

Rick shook his head. "No, that wasn't us, must've been someone else. We just have Curtis and Hannah."

Her face turned red. "Rick Jr. and Gregory?" she asked timidly.

At the mention of Gregory's name, he snapped his fingers as if a lightbulb had come on. "No, that was my brother and his wife."

Julie just looked at him. She was completely and utterly speechless.

"Such a tragedy."

She was only half listening as he kept talking.

"He died of SIDS..."

Her head was spinning.

"Only three months old..."

Julie was the only one who didn't hear the glass break as both bowls slid from her hands to the hard kitchen floor.

"Because it sounds like she's a liar, plain and simple," Tom remarked dryly as he stood behind his wife and massaged her tense shoulders. It seemed to be the only answer he could think of to the age-old question of why.

"But this makes no sense! None at all!" Julie cried as she got up from the chair and walked to the window. She watched from the sunroom as the lights went out one by one at the Hennessy house. "I *finally* find someone who knows exactly what I went through, what I felt, everything, and now...now it was all a *lie*?"

She felt like she'd been stabbed in the heart with a dull knife. Why would Lynn do this? Why? Good grief, the woman had even cried, shed real tears, over these babies. She'd even described being in the hospital with a nervous breakdown, for goodness' sake!

Tom pulled her away from the window, gathered her to him, and kissed her on the forehead. "Sweetheart, no offense, but sometimes what I love most about you can also be your biggest fault. You always want to think the best of people, and because of that, you think with your heart instead of your head."

"And I think you use your head too much and your heart not near enough," Julie snapped. She had always accused him of thinking that everyone was guilty until proven innocent instead of the other way around, which probably explained why he was hardly ever hurt or disappointed in others. If you didn't expect anything in the first place, then you couldn't be hurt.

"Why don't you come upstairs, and I'll show you what I'm thinking with right now," he said with a wink, hoping to cheer her up and hoping she'd take him up on the offer.

Saying no to him in that regard was something she never did. But there was no way any romance was taking place tonight. Not after this.

Later that night when the house was quiet, she lay awake in the dark, remembering every heart-to-heart talk, every emotion. She thought back to every hug, every tear, every heartfelt moment they had shared all because of a common bond, a bond that never existed. *But why?*

Julie wasn't so naive to think that people didn't exaggerate, even lie, for various reasons, whether it was trying to stay out of trouble to wanting to impress others. But *this?* What could possibly be the value in it? She was beyond hurt. It was as if she were losing Samuel all over again.

She could hear the gentle sounds of Tom breathing as she stared at the reflection of the moonlight bouncing off the ceiling.

As she tossed to the right, she saw the lace curtains gently move in the breeze. Feeling a sudden chill, she pulled the sheet over her shoulders. *What do I do? Do I ask her about it?*

And what would she say?

"By the way, now that I know your two dead babies are a figment of your imagination, is there anything else you've been lying about?"

She tossed and turned relentlessly, rehearsing various dialogues in her mind. Nothing came out right. She wanted answers. But she knew she wouldn't get them. Regardless of how many times she'd practice what she wanted to ask Lynn, she knew she never would.

Because there was one thing Julie hated more than liars: confrontation.

CHAPTER 6

Julie didn't sleep well at all that night and waking up to loud sounds of construction the next morning did nothing to improve her mood.

Looking out the window, she watched a backhoe digging up the Hennessey's' backyard. If she hadn't been so distracted, she might have been curious to know what workers were doing there so early in the morning. However, when she glanced at the clock on the microwave, she was surprised to see it wasn't as early as she'd thought. It was nine thirty. Yikes! She never slept that late. She'd better get started on her errands and chores if she and William were going to head to the pool.

"Pick a chair," Julie said a few hours later, motioning Anne over. "By chance, do you have a Diet Coke or Diet Pepsi in there you can spare? All I have is a twenty, and I hate to break it. Once you do, it goes fast, you know."

"Oh yes, I know it," Anne agreed as she opened the cooler and tossed her friend a Diet Sprite instead. "Sorry. You'll have to settle for this."

"Hey, beggars can't be choosers. Thanks," said Julie as she popped open the top.

Anne removed a hot pink beach towel from her bag and smoothed it over the chair. She rubbed tanning lotion over her slender arms and legs and then sat back to relax.

"So what's up?" asked Julie between sips. She had decided to keep quiet about last night's revelation. There was no use getting Anne caught up in the middle.

"I'm just busy getting those two ready for school," Anne replied as she nodded in the direction of Jamie, who had just jumped into the water with Will, and Kayla, who was now fussing at the little boys for getting her hair wet.

"You'll have to tell me where the bus stop is in the neighborhood," stated Julie, keeping a protective eye on the kids.

"Sorry, can't help you. My kids go to Catholic school across town, which means I have to get up an hour earlier than the rest of the world, drive them ten miles across town through rush hour traffic, and then turn around and fight afternoon rush hour to pick them up. Every day. Five days a week. It's exhausting."

"Yeah, wears me out just hearing about it." Julie set the Sprite can aside and picked up a bottle of sunscreen. "I'll check with Lynn about the bus stop. Speak of the devil. Hello!' She hoped her voice sounded enthusiastic. Right now, even looking at this woman felt wrong.

"Hi, ladies!" Lynn called and waved. It was just her and Hannah with Curtis nowhere in sight. She was wearing a daring one piece cut down to *there* with legs cut out above her hip bone. *How many suits does this woman own?* Julie wondered. This was at least the fourth one she'd seen her in.

"Sorry I'm late. I had to stop by the hospital, and it took longer than I expected," she whispered when she got close.

"Hospital?" Anne and Julie said in unison. Lynn put her finger to her lips. "Shh. I don't want to talk about it in front of Hannah."

Julie lowered her voice. "Did something happen to Rick or Curtis?" Maybe that's why her son wasn't with them today.

"No, no," said Lynn, suddenly flippant. "Just a routine visit." That was all the information she offered, so Julie didn't push the issue.

Anne and Julie made small talk for the next half hour, but Lynn was quieter than usual. Julie couldn't help but wonder if Rick had blown the whistle on her and maybe Lynn was feeling chagrined for being caught in a lie. Maybe when the two were alone she'd broach the subject and ask why she lied. When Anne got up to make a trip to the ladies' room, Julie used that alone time to press Lynn further.

"Is everything okay, Lynn? You're just not yourself today." There, Julie thought, I've opened up the conversation, so she can explain why she felt the need to lie to me.

Lynn said nonchalantly, "There is so much going on right now. I have to check in at the hospital at least once a week because I have a brain tumor and—"

"Oh, Lynn!" Julie gasped, sitting straight up in her chair. 'A brain tumor?"

"It's not as bad as it sounds. It's stopped growing, and my doctors monitor it on a routine basis. I just had to have blood work done today, that's all."

Julie pushed her feelings aside as she took Lynn's hand in her own and squeezed it. "Are you going to be okay?"

"I'll be fine. Don't worry. My doctors are confident that it will keep shrinking with continued radiation."

"Thank God." Julie sighed, leaning back in her chair. "I'll keep you in my prayers. Please keep me posted, okay?"

"Of course I will." Lynn smiled. "But really, I'll be fine." She lay back in the chaise lounge and closed her eyes, soaking in the warm rays of the afternoon sun.

Julie stared at Lynn's face, glistening with suntan lotion and slight smile on her lips. She remembered a news story she worked on when she was an anchorwoman in Jackson. A prominent man in the community had been arrested after taking a sudden, uncharacteristic interest in preteen girls. Upon completion of a medical and psychiatric evaluation, it was discovered that he had a brain tumor. When the doctors removed the tumor, the deviant inclinations disappeared, and he was back to his old self. Could that be what was going on with Lynn? Was the tumor causing her to lie? Maybe she believed the stories.

"So what's everyone's plan for the week?" Lynn asked several hours later as they were packing their things to go home. "We're going out of town for Hannah's gymnastic meet. We're taking the dog to the kennel, but I need someone to feed the cats for a few days. Any volunteers?"

"I can do it." Julie raised her hand. "Just let me know how much food to give and how many times a day they need to be fed. When are you leaving?"

"Tomorrow morning. I'd also appreciate both of you just keeping an eye on the house in general. Last night, Rick saw three strange men loitering in front of the house looking in car windows. He took Killer outside with him and told the men that all of the houses on this street had security cameras."

Referring to the Hennessy's 150-pound Rottweiler, Anne said, "I don't think you have anything to worry about at your house with that beast!"

"And none of the houses really have security cameras that I know of, but they didn't know that. Figured it would squelch any ideas they might have of coming back and stealing something," said Lynn.

"Quick thinker, that man of yours," said Julie. Anne nodded in agreement.

"Anyway," Lynn continued, "I'd rather not have the cats outside either. We've started construction on our pool today, and I don't want them to accidentally fall into the big hole in the backyard if it rains. You know; cats and water, not a good thing. By the way" she turned to Julie and asked almost a little too sweetly "when are you starting on your pool?"

"We've put those plans on the back burner for now," Julie answered, not quite catching the syrupy sweet, sarcastic tone in Lynn's voice. "I'm trying to get my Virginia real-estate license and really don't need any distractions—or expenses—while I'm starting a new business."

"You know, I have *always* wanted to be a realtor," Lynn said, removing the sunglasses from her head, and tossing her thick, dark mane. "I think I'll get my license too after the kids start back to school."

Julie left the pool a few minutes ahead of Anne and Lynn. She didn't notice, nor did she know, that the white Mercedes-Benz parked a few spaces down that matched her white Mercedes to a tee was Lynn's brand-new car.

CHAPTER 7

Anne waved at Julie as she was locking the front door of the Hennessy's house. Both cats had been fed and now had a fresh litter box.

"I'm walking down to get Jamie; he's playing hockey with Will and Robbie and some of the older kids. Wanna come?"

"Sure. I need to call Will in too, so he can have a bath and eat dinner. I'm meeting Tom at the Capitol for an event tonight. I want to make sure he's taken care of so Olivia won't have to fight him to get in the tub. I swear, we almost have to hogtie that child to get him to take a bath or shower."

Anne smiled and nodded in agreement. "What is it about boys and soap?"

Julie laughed. "I've got one that one won't go in the bathroom and one that won't come out," she said, referring to the effort teenage Olivia put forth to leave the house looking and smelling clean and the effort that was nonexistent with six-year-old Will.

When they reached the opposite end of the cul-de-sac, Julie smiled and gave a warm hello to Shelley

Johannes, Robbie's mother, and another woman that she hadn't yet met.

"Julie," asked Shelley, "have you met Clara? Clara, this is Julie Patterson, Will's mom."

"Oh yes," replied Clara, a very elegant, well-dressed woman with a silver, chin-length bob. She was an older woman, and it didn't take long for Julie to realize the drink she was holding in her hand was a cocktail, not iced tea. "You're the family that just bought the McKinney house, aren't you? The work you did on that place is nothing short of amazing."

"Well, thank you," said Julie. "It was a lot of hard work, but fun too."

Loud roaring of at least half a dozen motorcycles riding into the neighborhood broke up the conversation. Julie's sudden change of expression wasn't lost on Clara. She gently touched her hand to Julie's arm and reassured her, "Honey, *they're* not the ones around here you have to worry about."

She pointed to the brick, two-story house across the street. One by one, each of the bikers parked their Harleys in the drive. "That's where Johnny Browder and his wife, Marty, live. You'll see police cars parked in front of their house all hours of the day and night, but it's just because Johnny is friends with a lot of them; he does their bike repairs."

Julie was relieved. "That makes me feel better then if he brings the police around. Lynn Hennessy said that her husband saw a couple of men hanging around a few nights ago, and they were looking in people's car windows."

"Honey, you cannot believe a word that comes out of that woman's mouth. She is a pathological liar!" Clara said matter-of-factly as she took a swig of the red liquid concoction she'd been nursing.

It was obvious that Clara didn't care much for Lynn, or maybe it was just the cocktail talking.

"She's told some real whoppers," Clara continued unabashedly. "Not just one, but many. The worst one was last year when a child that used to live in this neighborhood had leukemia. Everyone in the community came together to help this family and just support them in whatever way they could. Lynn couldn't stand that all the attention was on someone else other than her. So she got up during one of the fundraisers for this little girl and announced that Hannah, her daughter, was also sick and in desperate need of a heart transplant. Well, that is just ludicrous because at the time Hannah was ranked number two in the state for gymnastics. There was even talk about her training for the Olympics. Now, I ask you, how could she compete on such a strenuous level if she had a bad heart? No way!

"To top it off when someone asked Rick about it, he just gave them the funniest look and said they must have Hannah mixed up with someone else because she was perfectly healthy, thank you very much, and then he practically shut the door in her face."

Julie stood there silently, taking in what she'd just heard. She almost told them about Lynn's madeup babies and then thought better of it.

"I'm sorry. I shouldn't have thrown all of that at you, but frankly, Lynn Hennessy is a very sore subject with me. I'm sure you'll make your own decision, but I'm just warning you to be very careful," Clara concluded as she swished the drink around in her glass.

Shelley threw in her two cents' worth. "I don't understand that woman at all; she'd rather lie when the truth would be easier."

At that moment, a hot, sweaty Will ran up behind Julie and grabbed her by the hand. "Mom, I'm starving! What's for dinner?"

"Spaghetti," said Julie, tousling his hair, thankful for the distraction. "Let's get you home because I'm going to have to go meet Daddy in a little bit. Ladies, I'm going to have to cut this short; I have somewhere to be in an hour. Shelley, it was good to see you again, and Clara, it was so nice meeting you."

Julie slipped her arm around Will as they turned for home. Jamie caught up with them, and the boys scrambled ahead, leaving her alone in her thoughts. She tried not to be one of those people who let her opinions be influenced by gossip, but it was hard not to be after the shocking revelations about Lynn's babies. Now after what she'd just heard from Clara and Shelley, she wasn't sure what to think.

She stopped and waited for Anne to catch up to her.

"I probably won't go to the pool tomorrow," Anne said. "Kayla has a birthday party to go to, so Jamie and I are going to meet Bob in the city for lunch."

"I have plenty of things to do around the house." Julie shrugged. "So I'll just stay home myself and get caught up."

Julie hesitated for a moment before asking, "Do you remember the night at Lynn and Rick's when I dropped the glass bowls and they broke into a million tiny little pieces? Well, let me tell you what happened."

"No way!" Anne exclaimed after Julie told her that Lynn's babies had never existed. "That can't be." She was silent for a few minutes, then she said, "I heard her tell you everything about those babies— what color their hair was, how much they weighed! She even cried. And they weren't even real? That is so messed up!"

"Yeah, my sentiments exactly," Julie said softly. "I am so devastated by this, Anne. Number one, I thought I had found someone who understood what it's like to lose a child. I mean, that bond you have with someone when you think she's been through something like that only to find out there wasn't a speck of truth to any of it. I feel so hurt. Then I feel guilty feeling that way when I know she has a brain tumor, and maybe that's why—"

"You mean ovarian cancer," Anne corrected her.

"No, brain tumor," Julie said. "She told me yesterday at the pool."

Anne didn't have to say anything else. Her expression said it all.

"She told *me* she had a brain tumor," Julie said. "But let me guess; she told *you* she has ovarian cancer?"

"She talks about it all the time. From the first week I met her, it was one of the first things she told me about herself, from the details of her chemotherapy to how many times she has to see the doctor."

They both stared at each other in disbelief, not knowing what to say, both feeling like gullible fools.

After a few seconds, Anne shrugged. "I'm not a psychiatrist, of course, but maybe she's just insecure and thinks she can only make friends if people feel sorry for her. Or maybe she's just trying to relate to the person she's with at the moment, something to bond her with that person, or maybe she lies to make herself more interesting."

"Maybe so," Julie said, still not totally convinced.

Late that night, on the way home from Tom's office event in the District, Julie filled him in all the things she'd heard that day. He listened intently, shaking his head, advising Julie that she'd best steer clear of Lynn.

"Anyone who will lie *to* you. will lie *about* you," he'd advised for all it was worth. As much as he loved his wife, it irritated him to no end that she always took on people as projects, usually scumbags that didn't deserve it and never failed to let her down. But he knew she wouldn't listen to him. She'd have to learn for herself. Again.

"I know what you're thinking," said Julie, which was another thing that drove Tom crazy. She always presumed to know what he was thinking. "You're thinking that she has a problem with the truth—"

"Ya think?"

"And that she'll hurt me," Julie continued, ignoring his sarcastic tone. "But honestly, Tom, I don't think Lynn has a mean bone in her body. I think, and so does Anne, by the way, that she just lies to get attention. As long as she doesn't lie to hurt anyone, I think I should still be her friend. I happen to think that I can be a positive, Christian influence on her."

For the most part, Julie felt satisfied at the conclusion she'd come to. But for one split second before she drifted off to sleep that night, red warning flags were popping up everywhere, flying at full mast. And she chose to ignore every one of them.

CHAPTER 8

It was the first day of school with lots of hustle, bustle, and excitement in the Patterson house. It was a new school and important to Julie that everyone make a good first impression. Mama had been a teacher, and Julie knew the gossip that went on in the teachers' lounge. The children that were not well dressed and unkempt were considered unloved and neglected by their parents. Julie had thought that ridiculous but at the same time could not stand the thought of someone, *anyone*, thinking for a moment that Olivia and Will were anything less than adored.

Olivia, at this age, was no concern. Will, on the other hand, was a bit more difficult. He didn't understand why it was a problem to wear the sweat-soaked shirt he had worn outside the night before when he'd been playing soccer. And why did he have to take a shower and brush his teeth every morning? He was positive that no one else's mom made them do that.

Once the children had breakfast and were all dressed and spit-shined, they posed for the traditional first day of school photo that their mother insisted on each year. They stood in the same exact pose as the year before, so Julie could fuss over how much they had grown or changed.

Olivia wore a cute, slightly above the knee Lilly Pulitzer dress they had bought a few weeks before at Sherman Pickey in Georgetown. Her long, brunette hair was pulled back in a ponytail, held tight by a pink and green Lilly print ribbon that matched her dress. She looked so pretty, but Julie knew her daughter was nervous and sad about starting her senior year at a new school in a new city.

Will, on the other hand, could barely contain his excitement. New city new school, new friends—it was all an adventure to him.

Tom drove Olivia to school while Will pleaded with his mom to let him ride the bus.

"Go ahead and let him ride," Tom intervened. "Be happy that at least one of our children is excited about the first day in a new school."

Tom definitely had a point, so she compromised. William could ride the bus, but she would drive to the school and meet him there. Julie wouldn't be able to relax until she'd had a chance to check out the classroom, the teacher, and the general feel of the school.

The bus stop was half a block from the house. The children all stood in single file in their brand-new school clothes and backpacks filled to the brim with fresh school supplies. William fit right in, as if he'd lived there his whole life.

"Is this Will by any chance?" asked a heavy-set brunette woman. She was so tall that she towered over Julie and the other moms. Her hair was pushed back with a thin navy headband. There wasn't a line or blemish on her face, and her smile revealed perfectly straight, white teeth. She had a friendly smile and a lilt to her voice that made Julie like her immediately.

"Yes." She smiled and extended her hand to the woman. "I'm Julie Patterson."

"I'm Donna White. Will is in Molly's class. We saw his name on the list last week, and someone told us that you all had just moved into the McKinney house."

Molly had already introduced herself to William, and they were chatting. Actually, Molly was doing the chatting. William couldn't have gotten a word in if he'd wanted to.

When Julie got to the school, she checked in at the main office, wrote her name neatly on the name tag given to her, and stuck it on her right breast pocket. The school secretary then pointed her in the direction of Mrs. Randolph's first grade class.

"Don't you look great?" Julie heard Lynn's familiar voice behind her. "You are all dressed up this morning. Where are we off to?"

Julie didn't think she was all that dressed up. She wore a plain, white shift dress that she had picked up at Sherman Pickey the day she took Olivia shopping for school clothes. A white, light-weight cardigan was draped across her shoulders, mainly because she thought she was a little too chubby for bare arms. She had on minimal jewelry just a simple pearl necklace with matching earrings. She was dressed very conservatively, nothing special. Lynn, on the other hand, was wearing her pajama bottoms, fuzzy house slippers, and a light-weight, low-cut, tight t-shirt. No bra.

"I'm just headed over to Falls Church to take my real estate exam," Julie answered, suddenly self-conscious, wondering if maybe she wasn't a little too overdressed after all. "I want to hurry and get in this morning, so I can be home by the time the kids get home."

"Well, good luck on your test," Lynn said, turning to walk out the door. She seemed oblivious to the stir she was creating as some of the students slapped their hands over their mouths to stifle their giggles. Julie saw one mother elbow her husband in the gut as he turned to watch Lynn from behind as she strolled down the hallway.

Poor Hannah. How embarrassing it must be for the poor child to have her mother come up to the school with half of her breasts exposed.

Julie heard Mrs. Randolph before she saw her. As she entered the classroom, she saw that the big voice came from a tall, blonde, tan woman wearing a denim jumper with a schoolhouse appliqued on one pocket and an apple on the other. The children were already busy unpacking their book bags and putting their supplies in their assigned desks.

The teacher spotted Julie and smiled. "Hi, I'm Susie Randolph. Whose mom are you?"

"I'm pleased to meet you, Mrs. Randolph. I'm Julie Patterson, William's mother. We just moved here from Jackson, Mississippi, a few months ago, so this is a new school for us."

"Well, welcome to the area. Now, let me see. Which one is William? And does he go by Will or William?"

"He's the little blonde at the second desk from the front, right there in the middle. And I'm about the only one that calls him William, but either one is fine."

William didn't notice his mother in the room. He was organizing his pencils, notebook, and other supplies and listening to Molly, who was still chatting away.

"I just wanted to make sure he did okay with this being a new school and all. But I see he's doing just fine," Julie said.

"You know, I could use some help about one day a week if you're interested. I have a few other moms volunteering, and if you were able to help out, then I'd have my week covered. Unfortunately, school budget doesn't allow for teachers' aides this year, so I have to rely on the parents."

"I'd love to. Do you need me for any particular day?"

"I'm thinking Thursdays but let me look at my workbook. I'll send a note home today with Will and let you know."

"Sounds great," said Julie, shaking Mrs. Randolph's hand before she left.

The first week of school, she cried with Olivia when she came home at two thirty and laughed with Will when he got home at four.

Olivia missed her friends from Mississippi, and none of the girls at Hylton had made an effort to greet her or include her. She encouraged Olivia to make the first move, but Liv was shy until she got to know someone. Still, Julie was hopeful that once the semester got underway and her daughter could see the various activities the school had to offer, she'd fit right in.

Will was the complete opposite. He couldn't wait to get home and tell his mom and sister about the excitement of his day. If he missed his old school, his old friends, he never mentioned it.

September in Washington meant back to the hustle and bustle of politics. It also meant galas, benefits, and other social events that wives were expected to attend. Tom had promised her that here she could attend only what she chose, with the exception of White House events. And he always required her presence at those.

Another great perk of Tom's new position was the use of a car and driver. Julie had felt it pretentious to have Tom's driver, Dale, drive the thirty miles to Woodbridge when she could just as easily get in the car and drive herself. It made no sense to have the man drive his black sedan all that way and then have to turn around and take them home again a few hours later.

Her attitude about that changed when at the last event it took her forty-five minutes to find a parking spot and then another ten dollars for the cab ride when she couldn't find anything less than eight blocks away. She'd decided the next time she'd be relying on Dale after all.

It was six when her chariot pulled up. Three weeks had gone by since she had taken and passed her real estate exam. Tom had simply been too busy at work to take her to celebrate, so instead he sent Dale to pick her up to attend the March of Dimes gala with him.

A few years after Samuel's death, the Mississippi March of Dimes had asked her to be their spokesperson. Her exposure as an anchorwoman on the local ABC affiliate, as well as a former Miss Mississippi, would benefit the organization, and she felt it would help her make Samuel's existence more meaningful. Now that she was so close to Washington DC, she was happy to continue that relationship with the organization on the national level.

She wore a long, red sleeveless sheath that just skimmed to the top of her toes in front and had a slight flowing train in back. She wore a simple strand of pearls and carried a black beaded clutch just big enough for a cell phone if the kids needed to get hold of her.

"You look great, Mom," Olivia said as her lips brushed her mom's cheek. "Don't worry about us; I'll just make some hot dogs and mac and cheese."

"Nope," said Julie. "I left money on the kitchen counter for Pizza Hut delivery. I left enough for breadsticks and a two-liter bottle of Sprite too. You should be set for the evening."

"Have fun. What time do you think you'll be home?"

"Mmm, not late, I wouldn't think. Your dad still has to get up early, and I'm volunteering at Will's school tomorrow. I'm sure it'll probably be about ten-thirty or eleven."

Before walking out the door, she called to Will in the next room. "You be good for your sister now, ya hear?" He agreed and came running to the door to give his mom a big bear hug.

It was ten-fifteen when Tom and Julie arrived home. Tom tipped Dale before he drove off; then he and Julie paused, hand-in-hand, on the sidewalk at the edge of their lawn, both still giddy from the night's music and dancing.

Tom looked up at the stars and commented on what a beautiful night it was.

"How are you?" he asked her, looking into her eyes. "I'm sorry. I know I've had some really late nights, but starting in the next few weeks I shouldn't be so late every night."

"I feel bad that you've had to spend so much time away from home, but you did warn me that would happen."

"Are you happy here?" He bent down to look into her eyes.

Her smile and voice were sincere. "Very! Honestly, I can't even believe how happy I am! I love our home. I've made some wonderful friends. I even think Olivia will start to adjust as the year progresses. I'm happy that we're here."

He cupped her face in his hands and gently kissed her on the lips before drawing her into his arms.

"Okay, you two! Get a room!" Startled, the couple looked around and saw Lynn taking Killer for his nightly spin around the neighborhood.

"You two clean up pretty good. And with the chauffeured car, I take it you didn't go down the street to McDonald's for dinner."

Tom told her where they'd been. The three chatted for a few minutes, but the mosquitoes were out in full force and about to eat Tom alive, so they begged off for the night. Lynn wished them a good evening and went on her way.

William was tucked away in bed, and Olivia was sitting on the sofa in the formal living room when they went inside.

Tom kissed his daughter and then snuck into the kitchen to help himself to leftover pepperoni pizza.

"Did you have fun?" Olivia asked her mother.

"It was a very nice evening," Julie answered. "The event was held in the lobby of one of the Smithsonian museums—I don't remember which, but the atmosphere was beautiful, and the food was good, too. How was your night? Did you get your homework done?"

"I didn't have any tonight, believe it or not." Julie believed it because Olivia had always been very studious and conscientious of her grades. "Will was good—he even took a bath without arguing."

"Maybe he's sick," Tom said, grabbing a slice of pizza. "I'll go upstairs and check on him."

"Okay, Mom," Olivia said when it was just the two of them. "I have to tell you. I think Mrs. Hennessy is just downright *weird*."

"Why do you say that?"

"Because *all* she did is stand on her deck and stare at us. All night."

"Is she doing that again? I thought she'd given up on that." Julie plopped down in the recliner, removed her high heels, and began rubbing her sore feet.

"Well, at first I thought maybe she was looking at something on the ground over in their yard. We were sitting here on this couch right by the sunroom, and I didn't think she could really see in that far. After about twenty minutes, she started to creep William out, so I waved at her just to prove to him that she wasn't looking at us. Well, she waved back! Then she stayed there for the rest of the night. We moved to this seat over here so she couldn't see us," she continued, pointing to the floral loveseat against the wall.

"When Will got interested in *SpongeBob SquarePants*, I snuck upstairs to look outside from the spare bedroom window, and she was *still* there. It's dark in that room, so I left the lights off because I knew she wouldn't be able to see me. I just watched her, and she stayed there the whole time you two were gone, just staring down into the house. She just now went in the house when she saw your car pull up."

"No," answered Julie. "She didn't exactly go inside. She got the dog and took him for a walk. We just talked to her."

"Okay, so don't you think that's creepy that she watched this house the whole time, and then she picked the time you came home to walk the dog?"

"I agree that sounds a little strange. But the fact is she doesn't have any friends in this neighborhood, and now that she has friends in Anne and me, she just might be acting a little overzealous."

"Mom, you don't get it, do you? We were building a pool, so now her family has to have one. You have a white Mercedes; she went out and bought one exactly like it. You mention you're getting your real estate license; now she says she getting hers? This is just too creepy."

"Don't you worry about me, little missy." Julie brushed her off, trying to hide the fact she too found the whole situation creepy. "I'm the mom, and I'm the only one allowed to do any worrying in this family."

"Well, you always tell me to listen to that inner voice, Mom. And my inner voice is telling me that that lady is crazy."

CHAPTER 9

"I don't want to wear the green shirt, Mom! Olivia always wears green; that's a girl color!"

"Your dad wears green all the time," argued Julie, although she couldn't remember anything he had that was green. Actually, he wore white every day—white shirts with black suits, just like every other man in Washington DC. That fact wasn't lost on William.

"White won't show up in your pictures though." Julie tried to reason with him.

"Look, Mom. Here's the picture form. It says right here that you can pick whichever color you want behind you, and I'm gonna pick blue."

"Okay." She gave in. "Wear whatever you want"—Will started to cheer—"but it must be clean, and it must match your pants!"

Sure enough, he bounced down the stairs a few minutes later in a white polo shirt with plaid preppy shorts and his favorite tennis shoes.

"I'm helping Mrs. Randolph today. Do you want to ride with me?" Julie asked, hoping he'd say yes.

"No, I wanna ride the bus with my friends."

So Julie drove to school by herself. It was crazy trying to find a parking spot. Many parents had decided to be at school for picture day, and they were all trying to find the closest parking space to the school.

Forget this, Julie thought as she parked on a side street in a residential area. *I need the exercise anyway!*

Mrs. Randolph looked so relieved to see her that Julie thought the teacher was going to hug her.

"Oh, thank goodness you're here!" the woman exclaimed. "I have four upset kids; three are at their desks crying because they forgot to bring the envelope with their picture money! I was able to get hold of Sazar's mother, but she doesn't speak English. Can you just help me get them settled while I get the rest of the class ready and figure out what to do?"

Julie smiled. "I can do better than that. It's only ten dollars for an eight-by-ten. Every parent should have his or her child's school picture." She reached for her purse and got out the checkbook. "I'll just go ahead and cover it. But there is one condition." Julie looked the teacher in the eye, and Mrs. Randolph looked back at her suspiciously. Usually when people put conditions on things they wanted something in return. But she was surprised when Julie told her, "You can't tell anyone that I'm doing this. It's not a big deal; it's only forty dollars. I just don't want parents to feel like they need to pay me back or feel like they owe me. So please promise me that you won't tell *anyone*."

"Cross my heart," promised Mrs. Randolph, going through the familiar motion. Julie gave the teacher the check. She thanked Julie and put the check in her pocket to give to the photographer.

After pictures, the class settled down. Mrs. Randolph had Julie go to the craft room to make copies of an assignment she was going to hand out later. There wasn't much else to help out with that day, so she left right as the children were going to the cafeteria for lunch.

She had no sooner put her car in gear when her cell phone rang. It was Lynn.

"Hey, wondering if you wanted to have lunch today," she asked.

Julie hesitated. She didn't really want to, but on the other hand, she didn't want to go home to an empty house. She decided lunch with Lynn was the lesser of two evils. "Where do you want to meet?"

"Why don't you just come to my house and we'll decide?"

Julie agreed and started to say goodbye, but Lynn kept on chatting.

"I have been *so* busy today" she continued, not even stopping for a breath. "I was getting groceries this morning, and I saw this woman with three little kids, and I bought groceries for her. I must have spent over a hundred dollars."

"That's wonderful, Lynn. I am sure that lady appreciated your help!" *See*, Julie thought, *I knew I was right. Lynn is a good-hearted person.*

In Julie's book, being good-hearted always canceled out any other character flaw a person might have even if that flaw was being a liar.

"Yep, we got to talking, and she told me how bad she had it, and so I just said, 'This one's on me.' I spent way over a hundred dollars. Then I gave her a ride home. Oh my goodness, it's just awful, that house. So I told her that I'd take her shopping for clothes for the kids anytime she wanted. Yes, I did, anytime she wanted."

Now the conversation was starting to make Julie feel funny. Weird. But why? She thought it was great that Lynn had seen someone in need and reached out to them. If more people would do that, the world would be a much better place.

She was finally able to get Lynn off the phone about the time she pulled up to her house. Lynn already had her keys in hand, so they jumped in her Mercedes and drove to Joe's Place, an Italian diner on Jefferson Davis Highway.

"We love this place." Lynn kept chatting away. "Almost every time Rick and I take the kids out to eat, we come here."

Standing in the buffet line, Lynn still didn't shut up. Her voice was loud, and people started to stare as she retold the story of buying groceries for the woman she'd met earlier. Only this time she'd spent over *two* hundred dollars. Julie was sorry she had agreed to the lunch.

"I am so glad I was able to help that poor woman. I tell you, she was so happy she just cried. Do you know one time I saw a homeless woman over by Potomac Mills and I took her inside right then and there and bought her a brand-new coat? A brand-new one. I told her to pick out whatever she wanted. Money was no option."

All during lunch Lynn droned on and on about all the random good deeds she had ever done, everything from giving her lunch away when she was in kindergarten to funding a stranger's college education to...

A lightbulb came on for Julie! She knows what I did today. She knows that I paid for those children's pictures, and she wants me to admit it. Why? And how could she know? No, she can't possibly; the teacher promised she wouldn't tell anyone. Good grief. It just happened less than forty minutes ago; there is no way she could know. Could she?

"One time, I gave away some of our furniture. Have you met the Willises that live next door to Anne?" Julie had her mouth full so she shook her head no, so Lynn filled her in. "Well, last year, Joyce had cancer and they'd just moved in. All of their money was going to her doctor bills, so I gave her our sofa and loveseat. She couldn't believe someone would do something like that."

I am not telling her that I paid for those kids' pictures today. Somehow, she knows, and for some odd reason she wants me to brag about it.

The more Lynn realized that Julie was not going to confess, the more she pressed the issue.

"Rick did put his foot down at me giving away the car though," Lynn bragged. "I called him at work to ask if I could give the car away, and all the ladies he works with said to him, 'Is Lynn at it again? Why, that girl just can't help herself. She's always trying to help someone.'"

Julie couldn't get out of the car quickly enough when they returned to the house.

"Do you want to come in for a cold drink?" Lynn offered.

"No, thank you. I've got to get some things done before the kids come home from school. Thank you so much for lunch."

Julie waved good-bye, and as she walked away, Lynn stood with arms folded across her chest, watching her until she was completely out of sight.

"I think it's probably just a coincidence," Tom said very logically when Julie told him about it later. "But it is weird nonetheless."

Olivia disagreed. "I don't think it's a coincidence. She was either there when the teacher gave the check to the photographer or Mrs. Randolph ratted you out."

"No," said Julie. "Mrs. Randolph promised she wouldn't tell. I think you're right in the fact that Lynn must have been there when she handed it over to the photographer."

She pushed it to the back of her mind and didn't think about it anymore—until another strange incident occurred.

About a week later, Tom and Will left to spend some quality father-son time at the batting cage. Olivia was sitting at the computer working on a social studies assignment. Julie was hunkered down on the couch with her feet tucked up underneath her, in the beginning stages of a brand-new novel she picked up at Barnes and Noble a few days before.

Just as she was turning the fourteenth page, the doorbell rang. She pulled back the curtain and saw sweet Molly White and her mom, Donna, on the doorstep.

"Well hello, ladies!" said Julie. "This is a nice surprise. Would you like to come in?"

"Oh no," said Donna. "Molly was just wondering if Will could come to her birthday party this weekend.

We're having it on Saturday, and it's just going to be at the house."

Julie thought for a minute. "I don't see any reason why not. I don't think we have anything planned. What time does he need to be there?" Julie asked, stepping inside the door to grab her date book, flipping over to view Saturday's schedule.

"It starts at noon and should be over around two thirty" Donna answered. "Nothing fancy, just pizza and some games."

"Oh, he'll like that." Julie winked at Molly as she penciled it into her date book. "I'll make sure he's there."

She had just gotten settled and comfortable again, her hand reaching for the book, when the doorbell rang again. Now who?

She glanced out the window. It was Lynn, wearing a pink twin sweater set, pearl necklace, and navy slacks—an exact replica of the outfit Julie was wearing last week when Lynn had taken her to lunch, except Julie's sweater set was red.

"Hey, Lynn. How are you?" Julie tried to sound upbeat, but inside she was hoping this wouldn't take long. After a month of reading nothing but real estate study guides, she really, really wanted nothing more than to just enjoy a good novel.

"I just need someone to talk to. Do you care if I just sit and vent for a while?" Lynn asked.

It was a warm night but still cool enough that they didn't need to run the air conditioner. The windows were open, and there was a slight breeze.

"Why don't we just sit here on the front porch," offered Julie, patting the concrete next to where she sat. "The mosquitoes aren't biting tonight, and I like being able to sit out here before the cool fall nights set in. Is that okay with you?"

"Sure."

Julie went inside for a quick minute to fix them both a glass of iced tea and brought it back out. Lynn reached for the glass, and when she did, Julie caught a glimpse of tears in her eyes.

"I don't know what to do." Lynn sighed. "Since Rick retired from the army he hasn't been able to find a job anywhere. His army pension doesn't start for another few months, and even then it won't be enough to pay the mortgage and pay the bills."

"Has he been going on any interviews?" Julie asked just to be polite. She didn't want to pry.

"No. He's not even looking," Lynn snapped. "And we're already behind two months on our mortgage. I barely have enough to buy groceries, let alone pay for Hannah's gymnastics and Curtis's guitar lessons."

Is this the same woman who claimed just a few days ago that she supplied a stranger with over one hundred dollars, no, two-hundred dollars' worth of groceries, not to mention the brand-new Mercedes sitting in her garage?

"You know, we've declared bankruptcy five times!" declared Lynn.

Julie didn't know much about the law; but she didn't think it was possible for someone to legally declare bankruptcy five times, was it? And who would willingly admit to that if it *were* possible? There are some things better left private.

But she didn't say anything. She just nodded her head in what she hoped Lynn would interpret as being understanding. Spending time with this woman was becoming increasingly uncomfortable.

"You are so lucky, Julie. Your husband has a great job, and you don't have to worry about anything like this. And I can see that you and Tom love each other."

"And anyone with eyes can tell that Rick loves you," answered Julie truthfully. "Look, Lynn, I know this must be hard for you, but I'm confident that he'll find a job."

"I hope he finds one *before* we lose our house," Lynn said, her voice dripping with sarcasm. "Every morning I look outside to see if the repo man has come to take the car. And every morning I circle jobs in the newspaper that fit his qualifications. He just looks at me and then grabs the remote and watches TV, or he naps all day."

Julie didn't know what to say to her. Part of her was wondering if Lynn was revealing something to her in exchange for information. As if she were saying, "Okay, I've told you my deepest, darkest secret, now yours." The other part of her was wondering if she was telling the truth at all, or was this just another lie?

Why did being around Lynn always give her these conflicted, confused feelings?

Finally, Julie spoke from her heart. "I don't know what your beliefs are, but when I'm really down or stressed or worried about a situation I'm in, I just give it over to God. I let Him deal with it. That doesn't mean it always works out the way I want it to, but I always know He will take care of me and do what's best for me. There is just a peace in knowing that."

"Then will you pray for us?"

"Of course I will, sweetie."

Satisfied, Lynn got up, hugged Julie, and went back home.

When she was out of hearing range, Olivia stuck her head to the screen and told her mom, "I would never have revealed anything so personal about my family like that. I don't like her, Mom. Oh, and don't tell me you didn't notice her hair was fixed exactly like yours."

Julie had noticed. She sat silently on the porch for a few more minutes. Lynn was the most emotionally draining woman that Julie had ever been around. Determined not to let a beautiful evening and the chance to enjoy her daughter go to waste, she slapped her knee and jumped up.

"You know what I could use, my dear? A Slurpee from 7-Eleven. How 'bout it?"

"Are you buying?"

"Nope, your dad is! I found this five-dollar bill in his pants pocket when I did the laundry!" They both put on their flip-flops and walked up Frostman Court, making their way up the hill to the 7-Eleven on Minnieville Road. Olivia grabbed the largest cup size they had and filled it to the top with a cherry Slurpee. Julie settled on the smallest size, knowing this late she'd be up all night if she didn't.

She wasn't paying attention to what she was doing, and when she turned around she bumped into a man wearing a black pinstripe suit. Well, now a black and *red* pinstripe suit.

"Oh my goodness!" Julie exclaimed in embarrassment, horrified at what she'd just done. She was grabbing napkins and trying to blot the drink off of his suit, but she was only making it worse.

"Don't worry about it!" The man laughed. Julie knew that laugh! It was Rick Hennessy. "I'm going suit shopping this weekend After twenty years in the army, I haven't had much use for civilian clothes. Don't tell anyone, but I've already worn this suit to work twice this week."

"To work? You're working?" Julie gasped. "I mean, *you're working!* That's great!"

"Yeah." He smiled proudly. "My first civilian job. I got a call back from Raytheon about a month and half ago."

"You've been working for a month and a half?" Less than twenty minutes ago she'd been led to believe that the man standing before her was a lazy louse who was willing to let his family be homeless before he'd lift a finger to find a job.

"Yep!" he said proudly as he slipped off his Slurpee-drenched jacket and held it gingerly over his arm, trying not to stain the rest of his clothes.

"Well, congratulations! I knew you'd find something," was all Julie could think to say. She purposely avoided eye contact with Olivia, who was making the "crazy" circular motion with her finger next to her head.

"Can you believe that?" Julie said as she and Olivia made the short trek back to the house.

"Um, have I mentioned to you that I think that lady is crazy?" Olivia's tone was sarcastic but playful.

"Yes, several times, thank you very much."

"I'm waiting." Olivia stopped walking.

"For what?"

"For you to say, 'Yes, honey, you're right. Lynn Hennessy *is* crazier than a bed bug.'"

"Okay, you're right."

"About what?" Olivia was loving this.

"Yes, you're right!" Julie snapped. "That woman is a nut case. Satisified?"

"Perfectly."

CHAPTER 10

When Janine McLellan overheard the ladies at church congratulating Julie on passing her real estate exam, she approached her about working for McClellan Real Estate. Janine's father, Phillip, had started the company thirty-five years before, and she had grown up in the business, working as her father's assistant until she was seventeen. She skipped college after high school, instead opting to attend real estate school. She had her broker's license by the time she was twenty-five and was a full partner in the company by the time she was twenty-nine.

Five years ago on Christmas Day, Phillip McLellan handed his daughter a small silver box with a beautiful, shiny, red ribbon. Inside the pretty box were the master keys to the office. He announced that he and his wife, Ruth, were calling it a day and in a few weeks would pack up and move to their condo in Florida. McLellan Real Estate was now hers.

Under Janine's management, McClellan Real Estate grew from a small mom-and-pop operation to a company with eighty-two active agents and multi-millions in sales.

Janine had liked Julie the first time they met. She appreciated that Julie never seemed to know a stranger and just had a special way with people. Her assessment had been right on the money. Julie sold five houses within the first four months. It was December, and Julie had been so busy that she really hadn't had much time to volunteer for Mrs. Randolph each week or see most of the ladies in the neighborhood unless it was before or after school. She did manage to have lunch with Anne a few days a week, and of course she saw Donna and Shelley at the school bus stop every day.

Every afternoon, promptly at three forty-five, she'd stop whatever she was doing to meet Will when he got home. Usually he chattered a mile a minute, or he'd run off and play with friends. However, one particular afternoon, a week before Christmas when most of the children, including William, were wound tight as a drum in anticipation of the holidays, he was very quiet. When Julie asked him if something was wrong, he told her that Molly's mom, Donna, had fainted in the lunchroom at school.

"Oh my goodness." Julie stopped walking as her hand flew to her chest, a gesture she always made when she was surprised or upset. "Is she all right?"

"She came to eat lunch with Molly. They were sitting there talking and laughing, and all of a sudden, Miss Donna just fell back on the floor. The ambulance came and took her away, and Molly started to cry until her grandma came to get her."

Oh, that poor child. She must have been terrified. "I'll go check on her first thing in the morning."

"Are you receiving visitors today?" Julie asked when a pale, pajama-clad Donna answered the door the next day.

Donna invited her in. "I guess news travels fast around here, huh?"

"Will was so worried. We all were, and still are! Are you going to be all right?"

Donna's eyes started to mist. "I've had heart problems since I was in my early twenties. Actually, it tends to just stop every once in a while, so I wear a defibrillator. That way, when it does stop, the defibrillator will jump-start it. Well, that's what happened yesterday."

"Okay, so this has happened before and the doctors know what they're doing."

"Yes, but the worst thing is that I can't do *anything* for six months. I can't cook. I can't clean. I'm not supposed to do anything around the house, nothing strenuous at all. Driving is completely out of the question." Donna cried. "How am I going to take care of my family if I can't even do anything? And Christmas is next week!"

Julie hugged her. "Oh, honey, this Christmas your family is going to consider having you around as their best gift. Trust me! You know I'm right around the corner. And I know the other ladies would be happy to help out too. You've got James's mother. You know how grandparents are, any excuse to be around the kids. You are not alone in this, Donna. You have lots of love and support from a lot of people. You, young lady, just need to concentrate on getting better."

Later that evening, Julie made some phone calls to Shelley and a few other women in the neighborhood who were either friends with Donna or had kids the same age. Within ten minutes they had all organized enough meals to be delivered to the Whites to feed them for an entire week, up until Christmas Eve.

Christmas was quiet at the Patterson's. They'd opened gifts on Christmas Eve and had the traditional turkey dinner on Christmas Day and then phoned both sets of parents back in Mississippi to wish them a merry Christmas.

New Year's Eve, the couple decided to go ahead with their yearly bash they had thrown since their first year of marriage and invite all their new friends. It was all very simple. Nothing fancy, just potluck, everyone bringing his or her favorite dish or dessert.

Julie left the festive lights and Christmas decorations up throughout the house. The formal living room had a very fancy, ornate Victorian-themed tree with lots of clear lights. Other rooms followed suit, but all had smaller, more casual trees. The sunroom was a different story. A humongous, live tree stood in the middle of the room. William and Olivia spent two hours decorating the tree, standing on ladders to reach the top half and climbing underneath to make sure each branch had an ornament. The room resembled a starlit night as clear, twinkling lights hung from not only the tree but all across the glass wall.

The guests started to arrive at seven forty-five. Lynn and Rick were the first to show up. Julie really didn't want to invite them, but it was rude not to when the whole neighborhood had been.

The kids gathered around the tree while the men congregated in the kitchen near the food, talking jobs and cars. The women settled into the formal living room.

A few of the ladies were even newer to the neighborhood than Julie. She had hoped that everyone could chat and get to know one another better. But no, Lynn made it her night. She dominated every conversation, and no one else could get a word in edgewise.

She talked about their poverty although she did at least finally give Rick credit for having a job. Then in the next breath she would completely contradict herself and talk about how she had bought winter clothes for half the kids in school, and they'd recently bought Rick's parents a new house.

Julie bristled as Lynn revealed in great detail about the babies she had lost. (Now their names were Rick and *Christopher* rather than Rick and *Gregory*). Anne quickly looked at Julie, who'd tried unsuccessfully to steer the conversation on to something or someone else.

A few ladies, during a short break between stories, took the opportunity to hightail it into the other room. Blanche Burns, whom Julie had wanted to get to know a little better, left the party entirely because Lynn's boring me-me-me dialogue was getting on her last nerve.

Anne tried to rescue Ming Brooks, a beautiful, young Asian woman who was married to a marine deployed to Iraq. But it was too late. Lynn was telling her about her experience in the Gulf War during the early nineties.

"You must go back to the states immediately, on the next flight!" her commander told her. "We just got your blood work back, and you're pregnant."

Supposedly she got on the very next flight back. About an hour later, while she was safe and sound on the plane, somewhere over the ocean, her whole platoon, including the commander, were all attacked by a bomb and killed. *She* was the only survivor.

Anne almost choked on her eggnog, Julie bit her tongue, and Ming dabbed at her eyes, obviously touched by Lynn's story and probably more than a little scared for her husband fighting overseas.

Saving the day without realizing it, Hannah ran to Lynn's side from the other room. "Mom, it's eleven thirty. Let's go home so we can watch the ball drop on 'New Year's Rocking Eve."

Yes, Julie thought. *Finally, she is going to leave!*

"I need to get to bed anyway," Lynn sighed. "I have been so tired lately from the chemotherapy, and I really shouldn't have stayed up so late."

"Chemotherapy?" Donna gasped.

Wonderful! Here comes the brain tumor story!

"Yes, I have breast cancer," Lynn said.

Breast cancer?

Julie was furious. How dare she! So many women were either fighting gallantly or had succumbed to the cancers that Lynn so nonchalantly claimed to have. These women had been bedridden, bald, and knocked to their knees by the treatments it had taken for them to fight and still didn't always survive these cruel diseases. And here she sat with a long, thick, full head of hair. She jogged every morning and worked out at the gym every night. This woman was leading a full, healthy, active life, *claiming* to be sick when she knew people who would give their right arm to do *half* the things Lynn did every day.

And Donna, who because of her own health issues had to have assistance with everyday domestic duties, was falling for it. Hook, line, and sinker. Just like Julie herself had done.

At that precise moment, Julie made a decision.

She would speak or acknowledge Lynn in passing, but there would no more socializing. No more shopping trips, no more lunch dates, no more dinners out. If she came to the house, Julie would come up with excuses to not let her in.

Starting tomorrow Julie was doing something that was extremely hard for her to do with anyone she had a relationship with. She was letting go.

CHAPTER 11

Donna felt good and was getting stronger every day. After three weeks of being waited on and being cooped up, she was getting a bit of cabin fever. Today was the kids' first day back to school after the holidays, so she bundled up and accompanied them to the bus stop.

"I feel so bad for Lynn," she told Julie. "I called her yesterday to check up on her, and she was so sick she stayed in bed all day. She said she thought the party the night before had worn her out."

What? In bed all day? Julie had seen her walking Killer twice with full makeup and hair styled! Later that afternoon, she had invited the Pattersons and the Mumforts over for coffee and dessert. She didn't know if Bob and Anne had made it over there or not, but the Pattersons respectfully declined, much to Tom's relief and, surprisingly enough, to Will's.

"She gives me a funny feeling, Mom," he had told her after he'd heard Julie telling Lynn that they wouldn't be over; they wanted to relax and spend the day as a family before returning to work and school. "I don't like her."

Why hadn't he told her this before? Surely she would have listened, wouldn't she?

"Anyway," continued Donna, "I'm going to make dinner for them tonight and take it over."

This woman is not even supposed to cook for her own family, and here she is putting her own health in jeopardy for the likes of Lynn, who can't make up her mind what kind of cancer she has. Oh, Donna, you are such a dear, sweet person. But I cannot let you do this.

"Uh, I don't think that would be a good idea," Julie stammered, wondering what excuse she was going to give to back that statement up.

"Really? I don't want to intrude if they are private people."

Julie jumped on that one. "Uh-huh. As a matter of fact, I'm *surprised* that she told you she had breast cancer."

Very surprised indeed! She resisted the urge to warn Donna about Lynn. She was a big girl and could make her own decisions. Besides, she remembered how she felt when Clara and Shelley had tried to warn her.

Julie used the rest of the day to get the house in order from the holidays. She took down the trees and placed the ornaments in their proper boxes to store away for next year. She saved Will's room for last because it always took the longest to put back in order. She loved that boy, but he sure did know how to trash a room, that's for sure.

She picked up the last box from his room to carry to the attic when she tripped over a shoe.

"Rats!"

Bending over to pick up the contents, she suddenly felt a strange sensation. Like someone was watching her. The hair on the back of her neck stood up, and a slight cold chill ran down her back. She pulled her cardigan tighter around her.

Glancing out the window, she saw Lynn standing on the edge of her deck watching her. Julie waved to be polite, but Lynn didn't return the gesture. She just kept staring. Julie stepped away from the window.

She has to have been watching the house for a while to know what room I'm in. It isn't like the sunroom where the whole side of the house is glass.

Julie was right. Lynn *was* watching the house. She'd watched all morning just like she'd been watching every morning since Julie moved in—watching, waiting for some sign of activity hoping to see where Julie was going, what she was wearing or doing.

"She thinks she's better than everyone," Lynn snarled, "with her perfect house, perfect family, perfect life."

Cardinal Estates was *her* neighborhood. She and Rick had been the first ones to build in that subdivision. She'd worked hard to make sure they had the nicest house, the flashiest cars, the best of everything. She had crowned herself queen bee of this place, and she wasn't about to relinquish her title to anyone—especially not that newcomer bitch.

She'd been afraid when the Pattersons moved in and started making that trash pit of a house look like a show property. She'd become downright panicked when it looked like they were building a pool. She'd demanded that Rick have one built in their yard as soon as possible. She'd had to use her feminine wiles, as she always did, but it was worth it to beat the Pattersons to the punch.

She would teach Julie Patterson that she was no competition for Lynn Hennessy. Neighbors would see that outsider for what she truly was: a desperate, pathetic wannabe.

However, when it wasn't working out quite like she'd hoped, she'd had to adopt a different strategy.

So she traded in the sports car for a Mercedes just like Julie's, started to wear her hair like Julie's, and had even started to dress just like her. That one had hurt because as much as Lynn liked to show off what God gave her, Julie insisted on covering it all up.

None of that mattered though. Regardless of how hard Lynn tried to upstage her, Julie was still everybody's little darling. Lynn didn't get it. That woman couldn't hold a candle to her in the looks department. She stood in front of the full length mirror and admired what she saw. There wasn't a line on that face. Her bottom was firm. Her large breasts stood at attention, not saggy like most women her age. Like Julie. Chubby, pathetic Julie.

It had almost sent her over the edge the day she'd heard Mrs. Randolph bragging to the faculty about Julie paying for those snot-nose little brat's school pictures. It was only forty fucking bucks. But no, to hear them tell it, you'd have thought she'd spent her whole life savings.

An evil smiled crossed Lynn's lips.

She'd had to teach a lesson to the last lady that lived in that house. It looked like she was going to have to teach this one a lesson as well.

CHAPTER 12

Julie was not a crybaby, far from it. When things got tough, she got tougher. She would roll up her sleeves and hit whatever crisis or challenge life dealt her head on. She had always had a deep, abiding faith, knowing there was nothing she couldn't handle with God's help.

Even when she found out that Samuel would not be born alive, she didn't lose control. It was months before she even really allowed herself to cry.

So why was she losing it now? Why did she feel like she had this dark cloud hanging over her? Like some sort of impending doom? She didn't believe in the supernatural, ESP, psychic visions, or any of that mumbo-jumbo. She convinced herself that it must be some kind of depression. That made sense. She had been so busy helping her family get settled in their routine when they had moved from Mississippi to here, so naturally she had neglected her own needs. All she needed was some time for herself.

Janine had suggested that Julie cut back on her work schedule. It was May, the real estate market in northern Virginia was booming, and Julie had been working nonstop. With help from her boss, she disbursed several of her clients to her colleagues so she could at least have every weekend off.

The next few Saturdays, the family spent time visiting interesting places of Washington DC and the surrounding area. Tom and Olivia enjoyed the Museum of Natural History while Will favored the Air and Space Museum. Julie's passion was Mount Vernon, the estate of George and Martha Washington.

The rest and time with her family must have been what the doctor ordered. For the first time in a while, Julie felt *good*. Janine had been right. All she needed was to ease up on herself a bit.

Unfortunately, that peace was short-lived.

"I need to talk to you," Donna whispered to her at the bus stop. She had fully recovered from her heart attack and was able to drive and go back to her normal routine. "Mrs. Randolph says she needs to talk to you as soon as possible. She's been getting complaints about you at the school!"

"What do you mean, complaints?" Julie asked, puzzled.

"Someone has been calling *and* coming up to the school telling her that William is always home by himself."

Julie almost laughed. "Oh, Donna, that's silly and explainable. Sometimes I'm not here when he comes home from school, but Olivia always is. Just because there's not a car in the drive doesn't mean—"

"That's not it, Julie." Donna continued in a hushed tone even though no one was around. "They say that William is being neglected, abused. He's home all night, and he's hungry and—"

"Who's "they"?" Julie demanded to know. This wasn't the least bit funny.

"Mrs. Randolph wouldn't tell me," said Donna. "She just said she wanted to talk to you as soon as possible. Julie, she was asking me all kinds of questions."

"What kind of questions?" Julie asked, her voice getting louder, panic starting to set in. Who would say such ridiculous, hurtful things?

"Wondering if I ever see you go out at night. Has Will ever come to our house wanting to eat? Do I think he's getting enough to eat? Is he—"

"Are you kidding me?" The severity of the accusations started to sink in.

"I think she believes it," said Donna.

How dare that teacher, or anyone, for that matter, think she would ever, *ever* leave William alone even for a few minutes! Or that he wasn't being fed or properly cared for! They had gone to hell and back to have that child, and he was very loved. How dare *anyone* think or say anything less.

Without another word, Julie ran. She grabbed her purse and her car keys and told Olivia to go to the bus stop to wait for her brother. Though Julie tried to stay calm to not alert Olivia that there was a problem, Olivia knew her mother well enough to know there was something going on.

"I'll explain later, Liv," she called as she went out the door, slamming it behind her. "I've got to catch Will's teacher before she goes home."

But she was too late. Mrs. Randolph was gone for the afternoon. She ran into her neighbor Shelley Johannes picking up her daughter, Whitney, from band practice.

Shelley was startled when she bumped into Julie almost running around the corner in the hallway. It wasn't the friendly, smiling Julie she was used to either. It was a Julie she'd never seen, an eerily quiet, steely, reserved Julie. Shelley was a pretty tough cookie; she'd been banged up a time or two in her life and had the scars to prove it, but there was a hardness in Julie's voice that frightened her, a hardness that she didn't know someone like Julie was capable of.

Right now, everyone was suspect to Julie. She knew what these allegations meant. Someone was trying to take her son from her, and she didn't know who. With Whitney right there, she didn't want to make a scene, so she got as close to Shelley as she could.

"Shelley, please tell me that you don't believe for one second that I would ever—not even for a minute—leave my son home alone." Even though they were about to bump heads, Julie's voice was so quiet that Shelley had to strain to hear her.

"No," answered Shelley. "Why would you ask?" Julie didn't have time to answer.

Mrs. Randolph's phone number was listed, thank God. Julie dialed and prayed that she'd answer.

"Mrs. Randolph, this is Julie Patterson," she said when the teacher picked up the phone. She didn't even give the woman enough time to say hello. "Donna White told me everything, and I want to know who told you these lies!"

"I can't tell you who told me. Just go talk to your neighbors," said Mrs. Randolph. "Get it figured out and then come talk to me."

"Was it one of my neighbors?"

"Yes, I can tell you it was one of your neighbors. Just go question them." She wasn't putting Julie off. It was against school policy to reveal the source, especially when authorities hadn't been called. She had even put herself out on a limb by talking to Donna White, but she'd wanted to give Mrs. Patterson a heads-up before it all hit the fan. And it would hit the fan because the person doing the talking was persistent in her accusations and showed no signs of letting up.

"Then if it's one of my neighbors, it's just a misunderstanding. My schedule has been so hectic. I put William on the bus in the morning. His sister just turned eighteen, and she is there with him when he gets off. I can understand why someone would think he's alone because there are no cars in the drive...so I know it appears...I'm sure if you would just explain—"

Mrs. Randolph cut her off. "It's more serious than that. This person is accusing you of leaving him alone all hours of the day and night. They watch him come home to an empty house. At dinnertime, he's so hungry that he goes up and down the street asking for food because there's no food in the house and no one at home to take care of him. And when you are home, this person says you abuse him."

"These are all lies! You can't possibly believe any of this!"

"There's more," replied the teacher.

More? How could there be more?

"I'll put it to you this way, Mrs. Patterson. This person has given me enough information that by law I am supposed to call the authorities, but I'm giving you the opportunity to do your own investigation. Once you've talked with your neighbors and you've figured out who this is, come in and talk to me." The teacher was doing her best to give Julie the benefit of the doubt. She couldn't just come out and give the person's name that was doing this. She'd lose her job. She took a deep breath. "I will tell you this person told me that they had to buy his shoes and winter coat this year"

Julie was horrified. Mama had been a teacher for thirty-five years, and she had seen authorities come in and take a child from his home for less information than this. Yes, more times than not the calls to social services had been necessary, but not always. She had seen her share of overzealous social workers trying to carve out their career on situations just like this.

"What else did this person tell you?" Julie felt like she was going to throw up.

"I can't say anymore tonight. Come in first thing in the morning and we'll talk. In the meantime, go question your neighbors."

"Oh, you bet I will," Julie said as she slammed the phone down.

"Mom, what is going on?" Olivia had heard parts of the conversation.

Julie explained what was going on as she frantically put on her shoes to go interrogate the neighbors.

"Mom!" she cried. "You have got to call Dad!"

Julie had tried desperately several times to do just that. But each time there was no signal. Tom was spending a few days in Denver for a meeting. He then rented a car and was on his way to Kansas City with several stops in between to meet with clients. She had left more than one message to call as soon as possible.

"This has Lynn Hennessy's name all over it," Olivia stated emphatically.

"Yes," Julie agreed as she tied her shoes. She grabbed her sweater. "I know it's her. I've heard her brag more than once about buying someone's, winter coat, shoes, heck, even a house! But we have to be able to prove it."

If this had happened back home, back in Mississippi, this would not be an issue. Everyone who knew Tom and Julie knew they lived for their children. Anyone who knew Olivia and Will knew they were the happiest children alive. She had been a model citizen, an anchorwoman, Miss Mississippi, for God's sake! How could anyone believe this about her?

But they'd only lived in Woodbridge for nine months, not long enough for anyone to really know them. And that's what scared Julie the most.

CHAPTER 13

It had been seven years since Julie left WPAT Channel 16 in Jackson, Mississippi, as an investigative reporter. After seven years, her interviewing skills were probably a little rusty, but she still remembered the basics. Yes, as far as she was concerned, she had a foolproof plan. She was sure of it.

She would ask a few questions but just leave out one important element. She wouldn't reveal the line about this person buying William's clothes or winter coat. If it was indeed Lynn, and she knew as sure as she breathed that it was, then her inflated ego would fuel her need to feel important, to be the hero. She wouldn't have just told the teacher about buying these things. She would have felt the need to brag about it to others as well. Now Julie just had to know who else she had told.

She started with Shelley since she felt like she owed her an explanation for the way she'd behaved earlier. That would kill two birds with one stone. Let the interrogations begin.

"You're sure you haven't heard anything?" she asked Shelley.

"No, not a thing," answered Shelley truthfully. "But if I do, I'll let you know as soon as possible."

"This sounds like a Lynn Hennessy stunt if you ask me," Clara piped up. She was perched on a stool in Shelley's kitchen smoking a cigarette, blowing perfect smoke rings into the air.

"The teacher refuses to tell me point blank who is doing this," answered Julie. "She just told me to question my neighbors. So that's what I'm doing."

Clara continued, "Didn't anyone ever tell you about the people you bought your house from? The McKinneys? Lynn Hennessy drove that family crazy."

No, Julie hadn't heard the story. Clara was only too happy to clue her in. "Bill and Barbara McKinney's daughter was the one I was telling you about who had leukemia when Lynn decided to upstage her at the fundraiser and tell everyone that Hannah needed a heart transplant. It drove Lynn absolutely mad that this family was getting so much attention over that poor little girl being sick. That family was going through so much, and you never met a sweeter woman than Barb, just a beautiful person. Everyone in this neighborhood loved her, and Lynn couldn't stand it. She did everything she could to make that woman's life a living hell. It got to the point that Barb wouldn't even leave the house. She wouldn't even go out to the mailbox. But that didn't matter. Lynn would call the police and make up something about Barb harassing her or some other crazy story. As if they didn't have enough stress already with their child being ill, then they had to deal with the police. Even though everyone knew that Lynn was the culprit, they could never prove it."

"How awful."

"It gets worse. When Barb's husband, John, would be outside doing something, Lynn would drop by in a pair of cutoff shorts and bikini top and be all over him. When he resisted her advances, she went home and told Rick that he'd been hitting on her. Rick came over and punched him out. He tried to explain to Rick what had really happened, but of course Rick believed Lynn's version. After that, she'd receive flowers and gifts that everyone was sure she was sending to herself and say they were from John. She even called his boss and complained that he was calling and harassing her from work. His boss didn't believe it for a second, but of course after that, and the fact that Lynn called the police on them for bogus incidents, it just got to be too much. On top of having a sick child, those dear people had literally been driven out of their own home. She simply drove Barb crazy. She refused to step outside the house. One night, they just up and left. No one has heard from them since."

So that's why the McKinneys had left the house in such a mess, abandoning most of their belongings. It was incomprehensible to her what those people must have gone through, but if it was anything like she was feeling right now, no wonder they fled in the middle of the night and didn't even take their things.

That wasn't all. The more people Julie questioned, the more she learned about the trouble and chaos Lynn always seemed to leave in her wake.

She was raising the Lopez kids because all Lisa cared about was working out at the gym. She was never home when the kids got off the school bus, so Lynn would have to take them in and feed them an afternoon snack and sometimes dinner if Lisa decided to stay and work out longer. But Lisa swore that her children had never set foot in the Hennessy home.

Brooke Williams told of the time that Lynn had called the police on their youngest daughter, Jenny, for jumping on the trampoline without permission—topless, with a beer in hand, no less. When the police came the next day to question Jenny, they found out that she had been out of town for two weeks visiting her grandparents in New Jersey. Lynn retracted the story when Brooke marched up to Lynn's house with Jenny's bus ticket in hand.

Still, none of this provided Julie with the concrete proof she needed. Glancing at her watch, she realized it was almost getting to the point that it was too late to knock on doors. Still, she had one card yet to play: Anne.

"I got a call from Will's teacher today." Julie wept; anger, fear, and exhaustion finally taking its toll. "Someone's been calling her and telling her that we've been leaving William home alone. I thought everyone knew that Olivia was home with him. Who would do this? Who would make this up? If you know, please tell me! The teacher says this person has told her so much garbage that by law she's required to call social services."

Anne's face turned white as a ghost, and Julie knew that Anne knew *something*. "Since February Lynn has been telling me weird stories about William being all alone, like from the time school is out until two or three in the morning. Then she'd go for a while without saying anything. A few weeks later, she'd tell me that he'd come and knock on her door late at night because he was scared or he was hungry. She'd go over to your house and there wouldn't be anything in the house to eat, and nobody would be home. And then just last week she told me that she'd had to buy his winter wardrobe and winter coat."

Bingo! The "winter wardrobe and coat" story. *Those* were the exact words she had waited all night to hear. Anne's kids didn't go to Enterprise. Mrs. Randolph and Anne didn't know the other existed. The only way Anne would have heard about someone buying Will new winter clothes and a coat would have been if the guilty party had told her. Lynn Hennessy was guilty as sin.

Julie didn't realize how long she had been out until she walked in the door and saw the old grandfather clock—the small hand on the eleven, the big hand on the three. William had been in bed for hours. Olivia fell asleep on the couch waiting for her mother, her English literature book still in her hands.

She stood at the sunroom windows and stared out into the darkness. Every light was on at the Hennessy house, and she could see Lynn inside moving around from room to room, busy as a bee. Julie had to fight the urge to not march over to that house and give Lynn a tongue-lashing she'd remember for the rest of her life, but her anger was so strong she didn't trust herself to stand face-to-face with the woman.

Instead she walked to the phone, picked it up, and started to dial. Her hands started trembling. She slammed the phone down. Now was not the time. Lynn would deny it anyway. No, she would wait until tomorrow after she met with Mrs. Randolph. The teacher had told her there was more. She needed to be armed with all the facts and details before a confrontation.

Julie walked slowly into the sunroom and stood at the palladium window with her arms crossed, deep in thought. She saw something moving, and it took a few minutes for her eyes to adjust past the glare of the window to see that it was Lynn bustling about on the deck. She smiled and waved, but Julie didn't move. Lynn bent at the waist, thinking that Julie couldn't see her, and waved again. Still, Julie didn't budge. Lynn's demeanor took on a sudden change as she stood up straight in an erect, defiant manner, meeting Julie's stare eyeball to eyeball, as if she were daring her to be the first to break away.

It seemed like an eternity before Lynn finally retreated inside with Julie still watching as she drew the shades and turned out the lights. Julie suddenly exhaled, gasping for air as if she had been underwater, waiting until almost losing consciousness before coming up for air. Feeling lightheaded, she stumbled to the sofa.

"Mom, are you okay? What happened?" Olivia asked, still half asleep. "What did you find out?"

"It's Lynn," Julie answered, her hand to her chest in an effort to calm her labored breathing.

"Social services aren't coming, are they?"

"Honestly, sweetie, I don't know. I hope not. I'll figure all this out tomorrow. Just say your prayers for Jesus to watch over us and to protect that woman," she muttered under breath.

"Okay Mom, I know you've always told me to pray for my enemies, but why does *she* need protecting?" Olivia was confused.

Julie replied, "Because she'll need Jesus to protect her if I ever get a hold of her."

CHAPTER 14

Julie spent that night alone in the formal living room sitting beside the phone waiting for Tom's call. It was 7:00 a.m. the next day when the call came, and she was still wide awake.

At first there was dead silence when she told him. Then a loud, angry "what?" came through the receiver with such force that she had to hold the phone at arm's length while he went on a tirade. "I'm canceling all my appointments and coming back on the next plane. Don't go anywhere near that woman until I get home."

Worry, combined with exhaustion, quickly turned into relief knowing that Tom would soon be home. He'd know what to do. There was no time for rest anyway. She wanted to get to the school early and allow ample time to meet with the teacher before the students started arriving at eight forty-five.

She stepped into the shower. The hot water started at the top of her head and trickled down her body, refreshing her senses and giving her a renewed energy.

She was careful about what she wore. Whether she liked it or not, she was being judged, judged on her ability to care for her children, her ability to be a good mother. Period. She pulled out a turquoise St. John's suit with gold trim around the lapel and the button-holes, matching skirt skimming the top of her knees. She wore cream-colored shoes, the same color as her double strand of pearls and matching earrings. Her blonde hair was pulled back in a tight chignon.

This definitely does not look like a woman who is so poor she can't feed or clothe her children, she thought as she looked at the woman staring back at her in the full-length mirror. Julie was dressed to kill, and she knew it.

Now for William. She laid out a light blue Ralph Lauren polo shirt and khaki pants with white, flat-soled sneakers. She knew he'd throw a fit about wearing this to school. Normally these were Sunday school clothes. But under these circumstances, he would just have to grin and bear it. Easier said than done, of course.

"Look, baby, I do not have time to argue with you today. I know the other kids don't dress up like this for school. But I need you to do this for the next few days." Julie tried to reason with Will.

"I look like a geek!" He started to cry.

"You do not look like a geek." Julie tried to comfort him, but it was no use. She dropped to her knees to meet him at eye level. "I need to tell you something." She didn't want to worry him, but he would know soon enough, and she'd rather he hear it from her.

Then a terrifying thought came to her. What if social services showed up and they insisted on taking him, even if there was no merit to the accusation? No! She couldn't think like that. *Stay calm, stay focused.*

"Someone has gone to Mrs. Randolph and told her terrible lies," Julie began. "She thinks we leave you at home by yourself and don't take care of you."

Will didn't see the problem in this. "Well, what's wrong with that? I don't know why I can't stay home by myself. I'm big now."

"Yes, you're big," his mother said as she caressed his cheek. "But you're not big enough to stay home by yourself yet."

"But why do I have to look stupid just because somebody thinks I stay home by myself?"

"Well, it's not fair, but sometimes people will judge you by your appearance. And right now it's important to look nice." Julie hoped that would satisfy him for now. But why would it? She was an adult and even she thought it was a ridiculous concept.

After Will had his breakfast and reluctantly put on the clothes his mother had chosen for him to wear that day, she dropped him off at Donna's so he could catch the bus with Molly.

Julie got to the school at the same time Mrs. Randolph was opening her classroom. She flipped on the lights and invited Julie to take a seat.

Julie's exterior was the epitome of cool grace. Her legs were crossed at the ankles and her manicured hands folded softly in her lap. She may have looked the quintessential Southern lady, but inside she was a boiling pot ready to blow its lid. Her toes were curled into tight balls, like surrogate fists. She struggled to keep her voice steady and self-assured.

"I took your advice and talked to my neighbors, and they confirmed what I already knew. So please start from the beginning and tell me exactly what Lynn Hennessy has been telling you."

"Mrs. Hennessy has come to me several times over the past few weeks," said Mrs. Randolph, getting down to business. "She says that she watches William go through the garage, and she can see him when he goes in the house. No one is home. At first, she thought it was just for a few hours, and then she realized it's until two or three in the morning. She says the back of your house is glass, and she can watch him all night.

"Several times, according to Mrs. Hennessy, Will has shown up at her house crying because he is literally starving. Apparently when she brought food to your home your electricity had been cut off and he was living in filthy conditions. She also told me that your family is having financial difficulty and that she's bought all his winter clothes. She also bought his winter coat, and she paid to have your heat and electricity turned back on."

"That is absolutely preposterous!" Julie said, her voice going up an octave as she leaned forward in her seat. "Everything she has told you is a complete fabrication! There's not even a fraction of truth to any of this!"

"But why would someone just make this up?" the teacher asked.

"Why did she tell me she had two stillborn babies when she didn't have any at all? Why would she tell me that she had a brain tumor, but yet she told two other people that she had other forms of cancer? I don't know why! I don't know what makes someone do something like this!" Julie's voice was now shaky and high pitched.

Mrs. Randolph sighed and shook her head. "She has called me at home crying because she's watching him go hungry, and she feels so bad for him. She didn't know if she should call the police or go over and get him herself and take care of him. Mrs. Patterson, there is no shame if your family is having difficulty—"

"Do you know who my husband is, Mrs. Randolph?" Julie stood up, putting her hands on the desk and moving in closer to the teacher. "My husband is Thomas Patterson IV. He is on a first-name basis with the president of the United States and prime ministers of two other countries. He is an expert in his career field and is one of the top-paid professionals in this town. Do you think I need Lynn

Hennessy, or anyone else, for that matter, to take care of my family? I don't think so."

Mrs. Randolph didn't respond.

"If I'm such a bad mother and she's witnessing all these terrible things happening to William, why hasn't she called social services?" asked Julie.

"Because she wants *me* to" answered Mrs. Randolph. "She says she's afraid of being caught in the middle because she's so close to the situation, but she's also afraid for him if someone doesn't step in. She's also called Mrs. Breckin, the other first grade teacher."

"She wants *you* to do her dirty work for her because she's afraid she'll get caught filing a false report," Julie argued. "No one loves and cares for her children more than I do. *No one.*"

Neither said anything for a moment, and then Julie asked, "So now what? Are you going to call the authorities?"

"Not at this time. Although I have to admit, Mrs. Patterson, I still wonder why someone would conjure up these stories if there wasn't a grain of truth. The fact is, I don't see any signs that Will is being abused or neglected. But I will be watching."

"Oh, so will I. As well as my attorney." As Julie walked away, she turned and looked at the teacher one last time. "Let me know if she calls you about anything else."

"Absolutely," replied the teacher. She could hear Julie's shoes as they click-clicked down the hallway.

She sighed, sat back in the swivel chair, and rubbed her neck. Every fiber in her being told her that this child was not being mistreated in any way. Exactly the opposite. She'd never met Will's father, but she knew his mother and sister doted on him. Still, as a teacher, she was obligated to report these things.

But on the other hand, why was Mrs. Hennessy insistent that the boy was being neglected? Even abused? She was so convincing; she *cried*, for goodness sake. She either believed it herself or she was a good actress.

Her good friend Mrs. Breckin stuck her head around the corner.

"Hmmm," she said. "I just saw Mrs. Patterson high-tailing it down the hallway. That's not good, I'm sure."

"No." Mrs. Randolph sighed. "She's very upset. I'd hate to be Lynn Hennessy right about now."

"Actually, I'd hate to be *her* right now," said Mrs. Breckin, pointing in the direction of Julie.

"Now what?" asked Mrs. Randolph, not really wanting to know.

"Last night, we were getting ready for lights out at our house when the phone rings. It's Lynn Hennessy. Bob told her I was in bed, but she insisted I come to the phone. It seems Will's older sister works at a dance studio with Lynn Hennessy's sister. Well, last Saturday Will's sister shows up at work in tears. Apparently, Will's sister and his mom had a big fight over the fact that there was no food and no money.

Will starts to cry because he's hungry, and his mother starts hitting him and telling him to shut up—"

"Good grief Sherry!" Mrs. Randolph called Mrs. Breckin by her first name. "I am so confused. You've seen this lady. She volunteered for me for five months. Will gives no indication that he's abused; you've never seen a happier kid! And did you notice the suit she was wearing? The jewelry alone would pay for my family to eat for a whole week."

"But why would someone just make something up unless there wasn't some truth to it?" Mrs. Breckin stated.

"That's the way I feel, or felt, anyway," said Mrs. Randolph, rubbing her head. She felt an awful headache coming on.

"Either way, you know we have to go to Mr. Brown with this," Mrs. Breckin said.

Unfortunately, Mrs. Randolph knew her friend was right. She glanced down at her wristwatch. Eight twenty. She'd have to hurry if she was going to file her complaint to the principal before the students arrived.

CHAPTER 15

When Olivia got home from school that afternoon, she found her mom sitting at the dining room table, her head in her hands, softly crying.

She tossed her book bag on the floor and went to her. "Mom, what's wrong? What happened?"

"Your dad just called, and he can't get an earlier flight. He won't be home until late Sunday night, and I really need him here. I got a call from Mr. Brown, Will's principal, and he wants to see me first thing tomorrow morning. And he wants you to be there, too."

"Me?" Olivia asked nervously, although the more she thought about it, the more she thought it was a good idea. She looked forward to having the opportunity to tell everyone how crazy all this was. No one was more involved in her children's life than Julie Patterson—even more than Olivia wanted her to be sometimes.

"He didn't say why. He just said he'd like to have the whole family there except for Will." Julie blew her nose into a tissue.

Olivia knew what her mom needed right now. She went to the cupboard and got a long-stemmed glass and filled it with ice from the automatic ice maker. Then she popped the top off a can of Diet Coke and poured it over the ice.

"Come on, Mom." She motioned to Julie. "Let's go sit out on the deck and have a drink." She handed Julie the glass and then got a cold can of Sprite from the refrigerator for herself.

The warm, humid air was thick, but the tall trees provided shade from the hot sun. There was a nice breeze blowing from the west, and for a while the two sat in silence, both lost in their own thoughts.

"Hi, Julie. Hi, Olivia!" came Lynn's light, cheery voice across the fence. Disgusted, Olivia got up and stomped inside. Julie followed right behind her.

Julie and Olivia arrived fifteen minutes early for their eight o'clock meeting with the principal and William's teacher.

Mr. Brown was a tall, young, handsome African American man with a strong resemblance, Julie thought, to Tiger Woods. Although he was dressed very professionally with a navy jacket over tobacco-colored, pleated, pressed trousers, Julie thought he looked more like a college freshman than a school principal.

He shook hands and introduced himself to Olivia and Julie before closing the door to his office. Julie noticed various family pictures standing upright in frames on a tall, oak bookshelf behind his desk. There was a photo of what Julie assumed was his wife with two small children, a boy and girl, the girl resembling the woman in the picture, the little boy identical to Mr. Brown. Judging by the children's ages, he was obviously older than he looked.

Just as Mr. Brown sat down behind his desk, there came a knock on the door.

"Yes, come in." Mrs. Randolph entered the room, nodded a good morning to everyone, and took a seat at the side of the desk between the principal and Julie and Olivia.

With everyone present, Mr. Brown got straight to the point. "It's been brought to my attention by Mrs. Randolph, as well as Mrs. Breckin, that some allegations have been made against you concerning your son, William."

"There is absolutely no truth whatsoever to any of this garbage," Julie stated firmly.

"I told you that if I heard anything else I'd let you know," said Mrs. Randolph. "I heard more yesterday, which is why we're here talking with Mr. Brown."

"Now what?" asked Julie as Olivia reached over and grabbed her mother's hand and held it tight.

"Is it true that your daughter works at a dance studio with Mrs. Hennessy's sister?" asked Mrs. Randolph.

"Yes, but what does that have to do with this?" Julie looked at Olivia and then at the principal and the teacher.

Mrs. Randolph looked straight at Olivia to gauge her reaction. "Did you and your mother get into a fight last weekend about coming home and finding out your little brother had been home alone for wo nights without anything to eat?"

Olivia was struggling to keep her composure. "No! First of all, I haven't worked for the past two Saturdays because I have had speech and debate tournaments, so that conversation never happened. Second of all, my brother has never been home alone. Ever. Third, you people are making my mother out to be a terrible mother! That's just not true. My mom is always there for us. *Always!* I wasn't allowed to stay home by myself, even after school, until I was fourteen."

"Has your mother ever hit you or your brother?" the teacher interrogated.

"Absolutely not!"

Julie stepped in. "This is so wrong, and you know it! You know that William does not fit the profile of a child who is being neglected and abused. Look, I have no idea why Mrs. Hennessy is doing this, but I—"

"I want you to both relax," Mr. Brown spoke to both mother and daughter. "Mrs. Randolph had no choice but to come to me. That's her job. It's the law. The minute she hears accusations like this, she has an obligation to report it. She put it off longer than she should have, and I'll deal with that later, but she's told me she has no cause to believe that Will is being abused or neglected. But we have to let you know that the accusations are still being made. And we have to ask these questions."

"How long has this been going on?" Julie wanted to know.

Mrs. Randolph said, "She's been coming to the school as well as calling me at home for the past two or three weeks."

"She wants William taken away from me, doesn't she?" Julie started to shake. Mrs. Randolph and Mr. Brown made brief eye contact, but no one said anything.

"Doesn't she?" Julie repeated. "She wants you to call social services because she wants them to remove William from our home. Am I right?"

"Yes," Mr. Brown said. "She's been very adamant about that."

Julie was a boiling pot of emotions. Fear, hurt, and anger churned inside her until she was ready to burst.

"We're not going to call social services," Mr. Brown said, his voice very quiet. He didn't believe for one minute that Mrs. Patterson was anything less than a doting mother. He'd seen Will enough times this past school year to know that he was a happy, well-adjusted child.

"What if she, Mrs. Hennessy, calls them herself since you refuse to do it?" Julie asked.

Julie turned to Mrs. Randolph. "You believed this at first! How could you? I've been to this school countless times, spent hours next to you, volunteering. How could you possibly for one second believe any of this?"

"I didn't want to believe it," the teacher said. "But my first thought was why would someone make something like this up? It's just beyond my comprehension that someone would be that cruel."

Mr. Brown assured Julie that they would no longer be accepting Lynn's calls in regards to anything with William or their family.

"If we stop taking her calls and feeding in to this, then I believe that she will give up," Mr. Brown reasoned. He was sadly mistaken.

CHAPTER 16

It had been three days since the abuse allegations had surfaced. For three days Julie kept vigil by the window, knowing, fearing that social services would come. Every unfamiliar vehicle that drove by sent a streak of panic through her.

In the house, she didn't allow as much as a dirty spoon to linger in the sink or a speck of dust to settle on the furniture in anticipation of an investigation. She almost drove poor William crazy by chasing him down with a damp washcloth every time he had a smudge of dirt on his cheeks. If social services did show up, they'd find not only an immaculate home and happy children but a mother that put June Cleaver to shame. She wore heels and pearls to do every household chore. Whether it was cooking dinner or scrubbing the bathtub, Julie always looked like she'd stepped out of the pages of *Good Housekeeping*.

The mere sight of Lynn Hennessy was enough to ruin Julie for an entire day. It didn't help that suddenly the woman would show up every place that Julie went: 7-Eleven, Safeway, the gas station. Even her yard wasn't safe. Every time she stepped outside, Lynn was there, in her space. If she tried to talk to a neighbor, Lynn would come out and immediately take the conversation. If Julie was gardening, Lynn would walk the dog back and forth in front of Julie's house.

Lynn was waiting, wanting, *daring* Julie to say something to her, to ask her if she had done this. Of course she'd deny it. But she couldn't even get Julie to look at her, to even acknowledge her existence.

Finally, Lynn couldn't take it anymore. She picked up the phone.

"Julie, this is Lynn. Have I done something to offend you?" Her sugary sweet voice even made *her* want to gag. She'd have that fat girl eating out of her hand in no time flat.

But Julie's voice was cold as ice.

"I sent a certified letter to you yesterday. You should get it tomorrow." Click.

When the mail arrived that day, Lynn signed for the letter and ripped it open as fast as she could. She felt a rush, an excitement! She couldn't wait to read it.

*I have been made aware by the principal and teacher at Enterprise Elementary School of the false allegations of child abuse. You have specifically been named as the culprit of these lies. If you try to approach this family or step on our property I will call the police.
-Julie Patterson*

Tom was furious with Julie.

"Didn't I tell you we'd handle this when I got back?" He looked rough. He hadn't changed clothes in two days, nor had he shaved in that length of time.

"I couldn't wait for you! I have been scared out of my mind that the authorities are going to show up!" she cried.

"So let them come! We have nothing to hide!"

"She is trying to take Will away from us!" Why didn't he get it?

"Nobody is going to believe what she is saying! So let her call!"

"They did believe her at first, Tom! The teachers believed her! I've been up there two or three times already, not to mention that I've talked to them on the phone. Yesterday, they called me *and* Olivia in for a conference."

What was wrong with him? Why couldn't he see that Lynn was waging a campaign to take their little boy from them? He didn't seem to be the least bit afraid, and that made Julie fighting mad.

They went to bed that night without speaking. When she woke up the next morning, Tom had already left for work.

It was 7:00 a.m., and Julie was stepping in the shower when the phone rang.

The caller ID said, "Prince William County Schools."

Great. Now what?

It was Mrs. Randolph.

"I just wanted to let you know that yesterday when school was out, Mrs. Hennessy called me again. I had bus duty, so I couldn't come to the phone. I told the school secretary to tell her not to call me anymore. Then she sent the secretary back out to get me; it was an emergency. I still didn't take her call."

Julie started to cry. "Thank you for letting me know. And thank you for not taking her call. Maybe she'll stop now."

"She doesn't give up so easily. She called me at home last night," continued Mrs. Randolph. "I didn't even let her finish. I just told her to not call me anymore."

Julie didn't speak, but Mrs. Randolph could hear her softly crying through the phone.

"Are you going to be all right?" she asked.

"Do you remember the day that I was at the school during picture day and I wrote a check to the photographer because some of the kids had forgotten their money? Did you tell anyone at all that I had done that?"

"Yes, I told a few people."

"Why? I made you promise me that you wouldn't tell."

"Because I just thought it was so nice," explained Mrs. Randolph. "No one ever does anything like that around here. I was just in awe! I know you told me not to tell, but I didn't see any harm in—"

"The harm is that Lynn knew, and she couldn't wait to see me that day and tell me all the good deeds she had ever done, from buying groceries and food for people to buying their furniture. And apparently Will isn't the only person she's bought a winter coat for," Julie said sarcastically. "She also bought one for a homeless lady and then tried to give away her car to some other poor, needy soul! For some reason she wanted me to admit that I had donated the money for the pictures. I wouldn't, and it almost drove her crazy."

"Well," the teacher replied, "she definitely has some kind of weird fixation with you because when I refused to take her call, she sent a note to school with Hannah to give to me."

"A note?" exclaimed Julie. "Do you still have it? I want to read it!"

"I don't have it anymore. I sent it back to her with a note saying that we don't want to get involved," Mrs. Randolph said.

The only time Julie stepped out of the house that day was to get the mail. Anne pulled up beside her and came to a halt.

"I heard about your phone call today."

"Which one?" Julie asked, slamming the mailbox door, and tucking the mail under her arm.

"Me and the kids were getting in the van, and Lynn comes running up our driveway wanting to know if I had any idea why you aren't speaking to her. Call me a coward, but I just played dumb. She said you called her this morning and—"

"She told you I called *her*?"

"Yes, she said you called her first thing this morning and just started babbling something about a letter," Anne continued.

"*She* called *me*. I can prove that from caller ID. Anyway, I told her that I'd sent her a certified letter that I didn't want her near my kids or on my property or I would call the police."

"This is just so creepy. What on earth possesses a person to do something like this?" Anne asked.

"I wish I had a dollar for every time I've asked myself that same question." Julie squeezed Anne's hand affectionately. "Look, thanks for everything. Thank you so much for just…for just being here.

"Excuse me, young man. Is that where that goes?" Julie chided as Will plopped his book bag on the wooden island in the middle of the kitchen.

"Oops, I forgot," said Will. "I'll take it to my room. Oh, Mom?"

"Yes, my love?"

"Mrs. Randolph gave me a note to give to you." He dug deep to the bottom of the book bag through all the old papers, broken crayons, and various pencils. He pulled out his faded blue notebook with the frayed edges from the wear and tear of the school year. He gave his mom a folded-up note that was sticking up from the edge.

"Thank you, darlin," Julie said and patted his bottom as he ran off to do his homework.

Julie opened the note.

Mrs. P,
I sent the letter back to Mrs. H and told her not to contact the school about this anymore. I told her that the school does not wish to be involved.
Sincerely,
Mrs. R

Julie folded the paper back and sighed with relief. She gently tucked it in her top drawer under her scarf box for safekeeping. She heard Tom come through the front door calling her name. It was only four. Why was he home so early?

He handed her a business card. "Ron Moorehouse, Attorney at Law." She gave him a puzzled look and asked, "Who's this?"

"He was a referral from one of the guys on the Hill. He has a reputation for being one of the best and toughest lawyers in Prince William County. I think it might be a good idea for us to see him. I made an appointment for nine tomorrow morning. I think we need some professional counsel on this."

Excellent idea, Julie thought. They would be one step ahead should Lynn decide to call social services.

At eight thirty that evening, Lynn called the house. It was Wednesday night, and the Pattersons were at their weekly Bible study at church. Lynn didn't leave a message. Instead she called Tom's cell phone and left her message there.

"Tom, this is Lynn Hennessy. I just wanted to tell you that I heard about what's been going on at the school, and I am just appalled someone would do such a terrible thing. I know she thinks I did it; I want to tell her that I'd never do such a thing, but she won't even talk to me.

"Honestly, I think she might just be embarrassed because I brought over some bags of clothes for William when you guys were having financial problems. Anyway, I'm sorry she's hurt. Let me know if I can do anything to help. Bye."

"Save that message!" a furious Julie ordered Tom. "I want our attorney to hear it! That statement about the bag of clothes when we were having money problems is just what she told the school! She wouldn't do anything to hurt me, my ass."

"Julie! You're getting way out of control," Tom chastised her for her language.

"You think I'm getting out of control?" Julie cried. "But you think this is no big deal—"

"Yes, I think it's a big deal, okay? I made an appointment with an attorney, didn't I? I just think you need to keep your emotions in check," he explained. "You're a Christian, and you are allowing this to make you do and say things you normally wouldn't. Just be careful. People, *especially* our kids, are watching how you handle this."

He was right, and Julie knew it.

"But I don't have to like it," she muttered to herself as she stomped up the stairs to bed.

CHAPTER 17

Julie was up bright and early the next morning banging and clanging pots and pans under the ruse of cooking breakfast. The noise had the desired effect, as Tom slowly made his way downstairs. Even in his wrinkly plaid robe, his tousled hair, and the morning paper stuck under his arm, she thought he was the most handsome man she'd ever seen. However, at this particular moment she wasn't about to tell him that. Instead she slammed the refrigerator door and threw the half-opened bacon package on the counter.

"Please don't be quiet on my account," said Tom dryly. "I was ready to get up anyway."

With that, he sat down and snapped open *The Washington Post*. She silently poured his morning coffee, and before long the aroma of bacon and eggs wafted through the house, summoning Olivia first and then Will a few minutes later. Tom had decided to take the day off since they had the appointment with the lawyer, so he handed Olivia his car keys. She was more than happy to drive to school and not have to take the bus, especially since it was her dad's BMW. She loved driving that car.

An hour later, Julie walked Will to the bus and kissed his cheek before he got on. She knew it wouldn't be much longer before he'd put a stop to any public display of affection from his mother, at least in front of his friends.

All the kids were on the bus, ready to drive away when the driver caught sight of Hannah Hennessy running down the sidewalk. The driver came to a halt and waited for the girl to enter. She then watched in the big overhead mirror until she was satisfied everyone was seated, put the big yellow vehicle in gear, and drove away.

Julie turned quickly to walk the half block back to her house and collided with Rick. She didn't even bother to say excuse me. She didn't want to mess with him today. Number one, she was still too angry to talk about it, and second of all, she was in a hurry to keep her appointment with the attorney.

"Julie, Lynn did not do those things to you that you are accusing her of." He had to walk at full throttle to catch up with her.

"Oh really?" Julie stopped dead in her tracks, her arms akimbo. "Are two teachers, the principal, and the neighbors all lying?"

Rick continued, "You have to look at this objectively. Most of the women in this neighborhood are just jealous of Lynn. They always have been and-"

"Is the teacher jealous? Is the principal?" Julie snapped. "Listen to me, Rick. Your wife told Anne the same exact things she told the school. Anne's kids don't even go to Enterprise! Anne and the teachers don't even know each other; they've never met!"

"I'm telling you it wasn't her!" he argued. "Besides, no one believes this garbage about you abusing Will! That's ridiculous!"

"No, your wife was pretty convincing. She had them believing it at first!"

By this time they were in front of the house, and Tom was walking to the car. He left the driver side door open, walking to the sidewalk to see what was going on between Julie and Rick.

"You're not listening, Rick! Mrs. Randolph, Mrs. Breckin, and Mr. Brown *told* me it was Lynn! She not only went up to the school, but she called both teachers at home—not just once but many, many times. She lied and told them that she bought his clothes, and he wouldn't have had a winter coat if it hadn't been for her. She comes to our house and brings him to yours in the middle of the night when we're not here. She called Tom's cell phone and told him I was just upset and embarrassed because she gave us clothes when we were having financial difficulty; we've never had financial difficulties! And she hasn't given us clothes!"

Rick shook his head and smiled. "This is crazy! No one, especially our family, thinks anything like that. I'm telling you—"

Tom stepped in. "Here. Have a listen."

He flipped the phone on and replayed the message with the speaker on. Rick winced as Lynn's voice resonated loud and clear. As soon as the message was over, Tom flipped the phone closed and shoved it into his pants pocket.

"When the teachers finally refused to take your wife's phone calls, she then started a letter writing campaign. We have a note from the teacher that states they sent the letter back to her and told her not to contact them again. If you also don't believe she did that either, I can go upstairs and bring you the proof."

Rick looked down at his feet and then looked from Tom to Julie without saying a word.

"Do you remember the night I told you that I didn't know how you had gotten through losing two babies when it devastated us to lose one? Lynn told me that Rick and Gregory were your stillborn babies."

He stared at the ground, refusing to make eye contact with her or Tom.

Still agitated, Julie continued, "Was she ever in the Gulf War?"

His expression was blank.

"Was she in the Gulf War?" Julie repeated the question.

"No."

"Does she have a brain tumor?"

"No."

"Breast cancer? Ovarian cancer? Any kind of cancer at all?"

"No!"

And Julie *knew* that Rick believed her. He knew that every word she said was true.

"From what I've heard, I'm not the first person to live in this house that she's had a problem with," Julie said.

That touched a nerve.

Rick's voice cracked as he mustered the words, "I'll take care of it."

CHAPTER 18

"That was a huge waste of time and money," Julie huffed as she slammed the car door shut.

They had just spent the last hour and a half rehashing the events of the past few days with the new attorney. Ron Moorehouse was a former roommate of Congressman Kenny Hulshof when both attended the University of Mississippi law school. Kenny had assured Tom that Moorehouse was definitely someone you wanted on your side when you were in trouble.

Tom was pretty sure they weren't in trouble. But he did want to have their bases covered just in case.

For the most part, he thought Lynn Hennessy was harmless. Narcissistic, maybe. But he mostly thought she was just perturbed because some imaginary spotlight had shifted from her to someone else.

The woman certainly craved attention, that's for sure. He'd made that observation the first few times the couples had gotten together. One-upmanship was her specialty. No matter what someone had achieved, where he or she had been or what he or she planned on doing, Lynn had done it, seen it, or was getting ready to do it, only better.

Although Tom had never cared for Lynn and he had expressed this to Julie, it was fruitless. Once Julie decided to take someone under her wing, there was no stopping her. It didn't help that the bond was solidified when she thought she had found another woman that understood her pain of losing a baby. Julie had been so hurt when she found out that Lynn's babies weren't real, just a cruel fabrication.

"Tom!" Julie's voice brought him back to the present.

"What?"

"I was asking you now what do we do?"

Tom sighed. "I don't think we need to do anything. Honestly, I don't think Lynn is going to bother us anymore. She came too close to getting caught." He took her hand in his and brought it to his lips.

Tom continued, "Besides, I agree with Ron. Since social services weren't called and the school has dropped it, we really don't have a case."

"What about false accusations?"

"Why pursue it when no charges were filed? Besides, Rick told us he'd take care of this. Let's give him a chance."

Julie looked at him and gave him a weak smile. Maybe he was right. Lynn wasn't able to accomplish what she'd set out to do. Maybe she would give up and leave them alone.

She did her best to sound confident. "I think you're probably right. It's over, so I just need to move on."

Tom smiled. "That's my girl." He kissed her hand again.

That afternoon she left Tom at home in his study checking his e-mails from work and punching away on his Blackberry.

She mouthed the words "I'm going to the office" and dangled the keys in the air. He winked at her and waved as she grabbed her briefcase and headed out the door.

"Where are you off to?" sounded a voice behind her, startling her so badly she dropped the car keys.

"Sorry, I didn't mean to scare you," it was Anne. "I just wanted to check on you. I haven't seen you for a few days."

"I've been AWOL from my office, so I thought I'd better go in. How 'bout you?"

"I'm fine. I've been worried about you though. Are you all right?"

Julie was quiet for a minute. Then she smiled and said, "Yeah, I'm okay. Or I will be once this situation dies down."

She asked Anne if she'd heard anything else through the neighborhood grapevine.

"Only what I hear from Lynn herself," said Anne. "Actually, she's been at the house every day since this whole thing started. She keeps telling me over and over that she didn't do this and that the teachers are angry at you for accusing her. She is really trying to cover her tracks."

"Has she forgotten that she told you the same story she told the teachers?" Julie asked.

"She says the school set up a meeting between you and her, but you declined to show up," Anne said. "That's not true, is it?"

"There is nothing I'd like more than to meet with her in front of the teacher," Julie answered dryly. "You know if there had been a meeting scheduled wild horses couldn't have kept me away."

Anne nodded. "That's what I thought. I'll let you go then."

Julie told her goodbye, put the car in reverse, and backed out of the driveway. In the rearview mirror, she saw Lynn's car come barreling around the corner. There was plenty of room for her to drive around Julie and go on her merry way. Instead she paused, waited for Julie to put her car in drive, and followed behind her.

The real estate office was exactly two miles away from Cardinal Estates. At the last minute, Julie pulled into the drive-thru to grab a quick bite. Lynn pulled in right behind her.

Julie rolled her window down, pulled up to the speaker to place her order, and drove around to the side to pay for her meal. Still, Lynn was on her bumper.

The pretty young Asian girl at the window handed her a sack and a medium Diet Coke. Julie quickly dropped the change in her purse, placed the drink in the cup holder, and drove away. If she hurried, she could get away before Lynn could catch up.

She pulled into the parking lot of McLellan Real Estate, driving past the parking space reserved for the agent of the month. She'd had the privilege of parking in that spot for four months in a row, skipping the last one because she'd been so preoccupied with the latest drama. Now she was ready to buckle down and get back to work and reclaim that spot.

Grabbing her briefcase, food, and drink, she shoved her hip against the car door to close it.

One of her coworkers was exiting, and he held the office door for her as she walked in.

"Thank you!" she said with a big smile.

As the door closed behind her, she didn't notice the white Mercedes, identical to hers, parked along the side street, the woman behind the wheel scrutinizing her every move.

CHAPTER 19

"Hark! Who goes there?" Janine sauntered up to Julie and gave her a warm embrace. "How are you, stranger?"

Julie replied enthusiastically, "I am pumped up and ready to get back to work!"

"I am glad you said that because I have a young couple in the conference room that needs a house. And guess what? They don't have a realtor!"

Julie frowned. "Who has desk duty?"

It was always the rule that the agent on that day's phone duty got first crack at walk-ins, provided they didn't already have an agent.

"It's supposed to be Rodney Walker, but the day care called and told him to pick up his little boy. Chicken pox. Anyway, everyone else is already assisting other clients. So you're it. Knock yourself out."

"Don't mind if I do," she said enthusiastically. After all, if that agent of the month parking spot was going to be hers again, she needed to buckle up and get moving.

She took just a few minutes to organize her papers and take a drink or two of her Diet Coke. She left the cheeseburger untouched on her desk. She could hear her mama's voice. "There are hungry children in Africa that would love to have just one bite of that, young lady."

Maybe I'll package it up and send it to them, she thought and then immediately felt guilty for finding humor in starving people in third-world countries. But then again, after the past couple of weeks, she was happy she had any humor left at all.

She grabbed a large manila folder containing a sales packet and another one with an agent agreement inside. She pushed the down button on the elevator, stood back, and took a deep breath. It felt so good to be back at work.

———————

It was 6:00 p.m. when Julie got home. She had worked with three separate clients that day and had driven over one hundred miles. The kids had already eaten; Olivia had made sure of that. Tom wouldn't be home until late.

She poured two tall, cold glasses of sweet iced tea just like she'd grown up with in the South, grabbed her cell phone, and went out to the front porch. She missed those early days when Anne used to come over and they'd mull over their tea for hours. Yes, Lynn had been a part of that too, but that was in the past. Time to move forward.

"Meet me on my front porch and I'll have a big old glass of Southern sweet tea waiting for you," Julie said when Anne picked up the phone.

"All I heard was sweet tea, and I couldn't get over here fast enough!" Anne laughed as she plopped down on a chair beside Julie. She took the glass that was offered her and brought it to her lips.

"I'm glad you called. I wanted to see you before we take off to Florida for a week. My parents have a summer home there, and we're going to meet them. How about you and Tom? Any plans for the summer?"

"Nope, summer is the busiest time of year for a realtor, I'm afraid. We might take a day trip to Williamsburg or maybe go to King's Dominion."

King's Dominion was a large amusement park just north of Richmond on Interstate 95.

"Hmmm, are you able to stomach the rides, or do you puke your guts out like I do?" Anne wanted to know.

Julie feigned shock. "I am no sissy, I'll have you know! Why, I can ride—'

"Oh, Anne, *there* you are!' Lynn was standing just to the edge of the grass on the sidewalk, careful not to step onto the Patterson's property.

"I hate to bother you, but I really need to borrow your mixer. My old thing finally gave out, and I am right in the middle of baking a cake."

The next thing Julie knew, she was sitting on the front porch alone, holding two half-full glasses of iced tea.

Lynn's mode of operation was so obvious to Anne. Lynn no more wanted that electric mixer than the man in the moon. She just wanted to invade Julie's space. It was her way of gaining power and being in control.

She knew she should have gone to Julie as soon as Lynn had started talking trash. Lynn was a liar, but good grief, falsely accusing someone of child abuse and neglect? Who does that? Anne hadn't believed for one minute that Julie was guilty. And honestly, she thought Lynn was just spouting off. She never dreamed that she would actually go the school!

Anne also noticed on more than one occasion Lynn following Julie. It wasn't just her imagination either. Her husband, Bob, saw it too but told Anne to mind her own business.

"This whole thing will die down," he'd said. "Lynn will give up and forget about it or go on to someone else."

Anne wasn't so sure about that. Every time Julie came over to her house or they'd stand on the sidewalk to talk, Lynn would get between the two and take over the conversation. No matter that Julie might be in midsentence, Lynn would butt in and completely cut her off.

Julie never came unglued, never spoke, looked, or acknowledged Lynn in any way, shape, or form. Anne suspected that probably drove Lynn crazy.

Julie's silence didn't fool Lynn for one minute. She knew that Julie was mad enough to spit blood. Her reputation as Supermom had almost been tarnished. *Almost.*

Okay, so she's won this round, Lynn thought bitterly. She had been this close, *this close,* to convincing Will's teacher to call social services. She'd had fantasies of Julie crying for mercy while the authorities ripped the little boy from her arms, her friends and neighbors standing by, watching while she crumpled to the ground in despair and humiliation. What would they think of their sweet, precious Julie when she'd been charged with child abuse?

Lynn was *not* used to failing. Julie was tougher than she'd given her credit for. *No problem,* she thought. It was time to step it up to the next level.

"Will you please take this seriously?" Julie cried to Tom. "I am not being paranoid!"

"I never said you were being paranoid!" Tom shot back. "I am saying that you're blowing this out of proportion."

"Everywhere I am, she is there. That woman is stalking me, and I'm afraid of her!"

Tom was getting frustrated. "We live in the same neighborhood. You're going to have to get over the fact that you're just going to see her from time to time."

"Don't you think I know that?" Julie was angry. Why wouldn't he support her on this? Why couldn't he see what this crazy woman was doing? "I can handle 'time to time'. But this is *all the time!* I am trying to tell you that she is everywhere. I can't even stand in my own yard and have a conversation without her coming over and butting in!"

"All she wants from you, Julie, is a reaction. That's all. Eventually she'll give up."

"You are totally wrong, Dad," said Olivia. She was leaning on the threshold of the kitchen door in a pair of cutoffs and t-shirt, hair up in a ponytail. She grabbed an apple out of the fruit basket and tossed it in the air and caught it. "She is taunting you, Mom. She's letting you know that she got away with it, and there's not a darn thing you can do about it."

Unlike her dad, Olivia believed her mother had every reason to be afraid. Anyone who would come out of the starting gate with such serious accusations needed to be feared. Lynn had been brave enough, or crazy enough, depending on how you looked at it, to kick this show off with a big bang. Her plan hadn't worked, but she had gotten away with it, which would only fuel her future endeavors.

Something told Olivia that Lynn Hennessy was nowhere near finished with her mother.

CHAPTER 20

Julie was up bright and early to meet her colleague Ron Willis at the office to finalize a sales contract.

"My clients are over the moon," he said as he pulled out a chair for her. "Great job!"

Julie smiled. "Oh, I'm so happy. This is such a sweet young couple, and they're expecting a baby in a few months, so we were kind of in a hurry to find them something."

"Can you all be ready to go to settlement in thirty days or so?" Ron asked.

"I don't see why not," Julie answered as she signed the final paperwork. "They've secured their loan through Commonwealth Bank. Provided the home inspection and the title work go through okay, I don't see anything holding us up."

"Good enough." He smiled, confident that Julie had covered all her bases. He was impressed with her knowledge of the business, considering the fact that she was fairly new to the industry.

Julie couldn't wait to phone her clients, the Cunninghams, to tell them the good news. When Riley

Cunningham answered the phone, Julie cheerfully told her the contract had been ratified and to call the moving company. The young woman's shrieking in the background was all the indication Julie needed to know she was pleased.

Thank goodness someone is happy. Heck, I'd settle for normal. She was sick to death of living in a constant state of tension. Every week was something new.

Lynn would tell people the Pattersons were near bankruptcy, so the Hennessys were paying their mortgage. They were strapped for cash, so Lynn had bought their groceries. Julie didn't think anyone believed the lies, but it was still embarrassing nonetheless.

It didn't help that all she and Tom did these days was argue. His workload kept him away from home most nights and at least three out of four weekends, which added to the stress. She didn't feel safe when he was away. He thought she was overreacting. She thought he was underreacting.

"I know exactly what I need today," Julie said to herself after finalizing the settlement date with Riley. "A little retail therapy."

The thought of shopping greatly improved her overall mood. Her purse slung over her shoulder and keys in hand, she marched out to the car like a woman on a mission. Slipping the key in the ignition, she tried to decide where she would go.

Potomac Mills in Woodbridge was the world's largest indoor outlet shopping mall. But honestly, she didn't feel like running into someone she might know. She decided to go somewhere where the chances of that were slim. It would give her some much-needed time alone.

That left several other options. Springfield Mall. No, still too close. There was Landmark Mall in Alexandria. Pentagon City was a nice shopping center, but she really didn't want to pay for parking. Mazza Gallerie was one of the most elegant shopping centers in the District, but she didn't feel like fighting the Saturday Georgetown traffic.

That left Tyson's Corner. She had lunch at the Neiman Marcus cafe and then stopped at the Lancôme counter on her way to the shoe department. Nothing like throwing down a couple hundred to make a girl feel like a million.

Several carefree hours later, with purchases in hand, she clicked the button on her keychain to unlock the back door of the Mercedes and placed her new purchases on the hook behind her seat. The three pairs of shoes (one pair of silver strappy ones and two pairs of pumps, one black and one navy for work and church) were gently laid side by side in the floor of the backseat.

She imagined Tom fussing and wagging his index finger at her for spending too much money, but she didn't care. She had made her fair share of the money over the past several months, and today's treat was just what the doctor ordered.

Her lighthearted mood came to a screeching halt as she pulled into the drive. What was that on the front of the house? Large, random spots of paint? A huge yellow spot stuck to the siding just to the right of Olivia's bedroom window. Another two, a deep red color, covered the garage door. Another yellow splatter spread completely over the top of the front door, and a deep blue-purplish glob was stuck to the windowpane. The force of what seemed to be a small paintball had been so hard that it had cracked the window. The thick, sticky substance was seeping its way into the house and onto her beige carpet.

"Oh my word!" It was Salena, Julie's neighbor across the street. "What on earth happened?"

Julie shook her head. "I don't have a clue. I just got home and found this!" She swallowed hard and then cleared her throat to keep her voice steady. "Did you see anything, Salena? Did anyone drive by? Did you *hear* anything?"

"Honey, I can't even hear myself think. Wendell is so deaf that he has to have that blasted television as loud as it can go."

Forcing a smile, she thanked Salena, excused herself, and then ran around the back of the house to avoid getting paint on her hands from the front door. Tom was lying on the couch watching a golf game on television when he heard her high heels clicking across the deck, beating out a cadence that let him know before he even saw her that something was up.

"Come out here quick!" Julie cried. "Someone shot the house with a paint gun, and it's completely covered with paint!"

Tom slipped on his house shoes and tried to keep up with Julie as she ran out the back door. How women could maneuver so fast in high heels was a lifelong mystery to him.

The house was every bit as bad as she described. To make it worse, the paint had been there for a while too. He saw where the paintballs had hit and exploded on impact. The drip marks were streaking downward and had dried before hitting the ground.

"Did you hear anything?" Julie asked him. "This had to have made quite an impact."

Tom answered her grimly, "Yeah, actually, I did hear something. I heard a couple of thumps, but it wasn't that loud. It made me sit up, but then when I didn't hear anything else, I went back to watching TV."

Julie rolled her eyes. If he heard something, then why didn't he get up to check it out? Maybe he could have seen whoever it was that decided to use their house as target practice.

"I'll call the police," Tom said, running back into the house.

One of the Lopez twins saw Julie bent over looking at something on the ground. The girl rode up on her red Razor, bent over, picked up a green paintball, and held it at eye level.

"I know who did this!" Kendra exclaimed as she gently rolled the paintball between her thumb and forefinger, careful not to let it burst. "There are hundreds of these over in the Hennessy's driveway. And I just saw Curtis Hennessy get in the car with three other boys, and they each had a paintball gun."

"The police are on their way," called Tom as he came around the backside of the house.

"Oh, wait till you hear this." Julie repeated what Kendra had just told her.

Tom went to take a look for himself. There weren't hundreds, as Kendra had described, but within fifteen feet of the Hennessy's house, spread throughout the lawn, he could see at least thirty to forty paintballs.

By the time he'd made it back around to his house, a policeman was already there. He was taking pictures of the front of the house and scribbling notes on a small notepad.

"Do you have any idea who might have done this and why?" asked Officer Burton, a big, burly man who Julie assumed had seen his share of crime. He probably thought something this minor was a waste of his time. If he did feel that way, he sure didn't let on.

"Well, yes," answered Julie. The policeman looked at her with his pencil cocked, ready to take notes on the small, blue, spiral notepad. As she continued to explain, she pointed straight at Lynn's house.

"The woman that lives in that house right there."

Officer Burton turned to get a look and then focused his attention back to Julie. He didn't say anything but with a nod encouraged her to continue.

He patiently listened to Tom and then Julie before he spoke. "Okay, so she would definitely be our main suspect, although I agree with you that the son probably did it. I still need more proof. Let me go over and have a chat with them."

Julie was sitting on the front step when Officer Burton came back around about twenty minutes later. Tom had drug out the power washer and was preparing to clean off the dried, cakey mess.

Officer Burton shook his head. "Well, I'm certain the Hennessy kid or one of his friends did this, but unless someone actually saw them do it, I can't charge them with anything. And of course his dad's not talking."

"But what about the fact that Kendra saw these boys get in the car with paint guns?" Julie asked.

"It's still not enough," the officer replied. He promised to go ahead and file a report even though no charges would be filed.

"What I would do if I were you," Officer Burton advised, "is get in touch with your homeowners' association and tell them your suspicions. A lot of times they work closely with your neighborhood watch, and they might be able to find someone who actually witnessed something."

Julie agreed to follow up with the homeowners' association the first of the week and then thanked the officer for his assistance. She watched Tom as he prepared for the tedious job of cleaning the outside of the house. He was unwinding the water hose and running warm, sudsy water from the power washer before the paint became permanent.

"Officer," Julie asked before Burton got in the squad car, "where do I go to get a restraining order?" She pointed to the house. "This whole situation is escalating and getting way out of hand."

Burton answered, "Unfortunately, Virginia doesn't issue restraining orders unless it's against a family member. Until someone actually witnesses her doing something to harm you, there's little recourse you can take."

Julie thanked him. Taking another long look at the damage, she wondered what would have to occur before somebody—anybody—could see what was happening and help her.

Two weeks after the paintball incident, Tom was still seething. Especially when he got the bill to replace both the carpet and the broken window.

Without telling Julie, he arranged to meet Rick one evening after work. He was the first to arrive and on his second drink when Rick got to Glory Days in Smoketown Plaza.

Rick insisted that he'd grilled Lynn and that she'd had nothing to do with the child abuse accusations. "I even talked to the principal, and he confirmed Lynn was in no way involved."

"You're lying, Rick," Tom replied. "The principal specifically told us that it was Lynn who instigated the whole thing. She wouldn't let it rest until they finally told her to back off,"

"That's strictly he said/she said." Rick smirked before he brought the bottle to his lips.

"Actually, it's not," Tom said. "You see, when the school started refusing to take your wife's visits and calls, she decided to start writing letters. Although we weren't allowed to read them, we do have our own little note from Mrs. Randolph saying that she sent the letters back."

Rick looked down into his drink. Tom flicked his wrist to check the time. Four-fifteen. The principal was still probably in his office.

"Why don't we drive over to the school? We can discuss this with Mr. Brown face-to-face."

Rick clenched his jaw but didn't move.

Tom smiled. "Ah, I see you're not willing to do that."

He paused for a moment to give Rick a chance to explain or to defend Lynn at the very least. Instead he sat silently, nervously tapping his fingers on the side of his Bud Light.

"Look, Rick, all we want is to live in peace."

"Then tell your wife to stop stalking and harassing mine." Rick slammed his bottle on the table with enough force to startle patrons at the surrounding tables. Suddenly aware of the unwanted attention, he lowered his voice. "Every single day there is a laundry list of things that Lynn tells me—"

"I've known Julie since we were six years old," Tom said, standing up. "She doesn't have a history of doing anything remotely close to what you're accusing her of. She has always gotten along with people and never had any problems. Bet you can't say the same for Lynn, can you?"

Rick didn't answer.

"Drinks are on me, buddy," Tom said as he flipped a twenty-dollar bill on the table, leaving Rick alone at the bar, stewing in his thoughts.

CHAPTER 21

"Hello?" Julie answered, cradling her cell phone between her head and neck. *Ouch, that's uncomfortable. I definitely need to invest in a headset.*

"Where are you?" It was Tom. She looked at her watch. Three-fifteen. He never called in the middle of the day.

"I'm on my way home from the office. Why?"

Tom's voice sounded chipper. "I have a surprise for you."

"A surprise? What is it? Tell me! I can't wait that long!"

Tom laughed. "I have to stop and pick it up on the way home. I'm leaving the District right now; and if traffic cooperates, I should be home about five or six."

Julie was excited. She loved surprises. When was the last time someone had actually been able to pull one over on her? She thought hard and then gave up. It didn't matter. What mattered was that Tom was making an effort.

At 5:20 Julie and the kids dropped what they were doing when they heard the familiar hum of the garage door going up. Tom had let Olivia in on the little secret a few days ago, so she claimed her post by the kitchen counter, the best seat in the house to gauge her mom's reaction to the gift.

The car engine cut off followed by the sound of the driver's door closing. After a few moments of silence, the kitchen door cracked open. Expecting Tom to come through the door she was completely caught off guard when a little white fur ball of a puppy walked in, a miniature schnauzer only six weeks old.

"A puppy!" cried Will.

"Oh, how precious!" Julie gasped as the dog licked her face. "Where on earth?"

Her laughter resonated throughout the big house. *When was the last tine they'd heard that joyful sound?* Tom thought. Too long, he decided.

"Mark Rupert, the new attorney in our office? His mother-in-law has a kennel out in Middleburg. She was giving them away."

Julie looked confused. "*Giving* them away?"

Tom shrugged. "Apparently, the American Kennel Club doesn't recognize white as a color for schnauzers. They're supposed to be salt and pepper colored, or they can be black but just not all white; otherwise, they can't be shown."

I don't care what color she is, Julie thought as she held her new baby close to her.

"And," Tom explained further, "I thought it might help to have another little girl around the house since ours is going to college soon."

Olivia scowled. "Oh great. So I'm being replaced by a dog."

"It appears so." Julie winked. "What should I name her?"

"It needs to be something really feminine," Olivia said. She thought for a minute. "How about Colette?"

"Colette?" said Will, obviously not happy with his sister's choice. "What kind of dumb name is that?"

"We're studying the French writer Colette in my literature class. I think that's a pretty name."

Julie agreed. "Then Colette it is."

Olivia's joke about being replaced by a dog was prophetic. Three months later Julie bravely held back her tears, clinging to Colette with one arm and waving goodbye to her daughter with the other as they left the campus of Mississippi State. Safely out of sight, Julie cried into Colette's soft, white coat and held on to her for dear life during the thirteen-hour drive back to Virginia.

The pup got a full day to recover from the trip before she was whisked off to Barkley Square, a posh puppy boutique in Alexandria's tony Del Ray district.

Barkley Square was where all the best-dressed dogs in town shopped. They not only carried the finest line of designer dog clothes, collars, and leashes but also a full line of puppy jewelry.

"Here, try this," said Kristina, the store's owner, as she draped a delicate silver necklace with a dangling heart over Colette's head. William scoffed at putting jewelry on the dog, and Julie suspected his father might have the same reaction.

"The jewelry might be a bit much," Julie said reluctantly. Colette did look rather cute with the little heart pressed against her chest.

"Then how about this?" Kristina asked, holding up a pink and green Lilly Pulitzer argyle sweater, just Colette's size.

"That is adorable," Julie said. "Yes, I'll definitely take that."

"I also have the matching Lilly Pulitzer collar and leash." Kristin handed them to Julie for inspection.

A few hours later, back home, Colette, wearing her new collar, would trot a few steps and then stop and sniff the grass. Then she'd take off and run as fast as her tiny legs would take her. She'd just build up a little speed and her clumsy little feet would become intertwined and she'd fall flat on her face.

Before Julie realized it, they'd ended up all the way at the end of the cul-de-sac. Sam Watkins, who lived at the end of the street, was crouched down rummaging through his toolbox. What was he adding to the top of his fence? Was that barbed wire?

She decided to be nosy and just ask.

"I am sick and tired of people jumping over the fence and cutting through my yard as a shortcut to 7-Eleven," Sam snapped. "This 'no trespassing' sign doesn't do a lick of good. They just think they can stomp on my flowers or leave a path through my grass."

Sam's house sat on the bottom of a slight hill. Behind his house was a wooded lot that was adjacent to another housing development. His fence separated the two properties, but the hill on the other side was so steep that it made it easy to just jump over. Julie noticed a path was starting to form on his lawn, and his precious flowers that he and his wife had so lovingly tended were trampled to pieces.

"I tried to talk to the homeowners' association, but it was no use. The HOA president's wife tried to tell me there was an easement running through my property. She said she was a realtor and she had the papers to prove that people could cut through my yard anytime they wanted. Well, we'll see about that."

"Henry Stottle is married?" Julie asked, surprised. She'd heard he was gay. Besides, as far as she knew, she was the only realtor in the neighborhood.

"Rick Hennessy is the HOA president," Sam corrected.

"What?" Julie could have been knocked over with a feather. "Sam, Lynn Hennessy is not a realtor." The nerve of that woman trying to pass herself off as an agent!

"Her boy is the worst offender. I've come out here several times and run him off. The last time, his mother came down here and really ripped me a new one, saying that he had every right to cut through here if he wanted to."

"If you'll go online and go to the Virginia DOPR site, you can enter her name and see for yourself that she is not a realtor," Julie clarified.

Before Sam turned to get back to work, he said, "Well, I'm warning you about that family. They are bad news. It's not the first run-in I've had with them."

"Trust me, you're preaching to the choir, Sam." She gave him the watered-down version of her own experience.

"Unbelievable." Shaking his head back and forth, he warned her, 'Just watch your back, and I'd advise you to not be outside after dark. She's crazy, and I wouldn't put anything past her."

"Well, I don't have much of a choice. I can't just stay inside all the time." Then pointing to Colette, she said, "Besides, when you gotta go, you gotta go."

Sam chuckled as he bent over to pet the dog. "True, true. But I think you should have gotten a bigger dog! The bigger the dog, the better the protection."

When Julie got back to the house, Anne was waiting on the front step.

"I heard about your new dog, and I wanted to come see for myself!" Anne said.

"Colette, say hi to your Auntie Anne."

"Oh, she is too cute!" Anne picked up the puppy. "This almost makes me want one, you know." Colette licked Anne on the face and neck, her stubby tail wagging back and forth.

Julie laughed. "Then I suggest you invest in a carpet shampooer because potty training is not fun. Believe me."

"Okay, on second thought, I'll just come over and play with you," Anne said playfully to Colette, scratching behind her ears. "Then I can give you back when I'm done."

"Anytime," Julie said. "Hey, I hate to cut our visit short, but I have to go inside and get cleaned up. Tonight's the president's dinner, and my driver will be here in about an hour. I need to get cleaned up."

"Yes, please do. We don't want you greeting the leader of the free world and the first lady smelling like a puppy."

She got up from the step and brushed off the bottom of her shorts with her hand. "Have fun tonight. And tomorrow, I want a full fashion report." Julie promised to take mental notes on what everyone, especially the first lady, was wearing and make a full, detailed report.

Nathan, Janine's son, arrived about fifteen minutes before Dale pulled up in his shiny, black Lincoln Continental. Julie went over the rules about bedtime, snacks, and how often the boys needed to take the dog out for her potty break.

"You boys behave and don't have too much fun." She bent to kiss Will's cheek. Turning her attention to the babysitter, she said, "I won't be able to have my cell phone on, Nathan, so I guess in case of an emergency just call your mom."

"No prob," he said as he picked Will up above his shoulders and swung him around.

Julie walked out the door to the sound of Nathan's growls and William's high-pitched giggles as Nathan playfully tossed him onto the sofa.

Tom was waiting for her on the corner of Fourteenth and Pennsylvania. After September 11, no one was allowed to be dropped off directly in front of the White House due to the steel barricades. They'd have to walk another half a block.

"I've got it, Dale," Tom said as he quickly opened the back door to help Julie out of the back. She took his hand as she gingerly exited the car one leg at a time.

"What time should I come back, sir?" Dale asked as Tom shut the back-passenger side door.

Tom looked at his watch. "Oh, I'd say probably about two hours. We'll just meet you right back at this corner at ten."

As the Pattersons entered the White House, the marine band was playing. Men were dressed in tuxedos. Women were dressed in elegant evening gowns. Laughter filled the atmosphere while couples waltzed to John Phillip Sousa's "Queen of the Ocean."

After dinner, the president stepped to the podium, introduced the first lady, and gave a short speech. Afterward, Tom and Julie made the rounds, chatting and getting caught up with friends and acquaintances and dancing to the music.

It felt wonderful to just let loose, to laugh, to breathe. She couldn't remember when she'd had this much fun, when she had felt so carefree. Julie had forgotten that she had once had a life, a peaceful one at that. Now that she'd been reminded of it, she was bound and determined to get it back.

CHAPTER 22

Lynn was bored out of her mind. If she didn't get out of this house soon, she was going to explode. Rick had been in a foul mood ever since he'd come home from that meeting with Tom Patterson a few nights ago. She didn't know exactly what they'd talked about—Rick refused to divulge—but he'd taken the car keys from her and told her not to step outside of the house for any reason, not even to get the mail. He didn't even tell her why. But then he could be so dramatic sometimes.

She was sick to death of *Days of Our Lives*, *The Young and the Restless*, and all those other daytime dramas. Who believed all that crap happened in everyday life anyway? Clicking the remote, she got up and started to pace. She looked out the window. There was nothing worse than being cooped up on a cloudy, dismal day.

Looking into the glass room of the Patterson's home, she searched for some sort of movement. The house was dark and still. That stupid, yappy, little mutt Julie had been lugging around the last few months was fast asleep on the kitchen floor. She looked over at Killer, himself asleep on the sofa. *Now that's a dog,* she thought. Nobody messed with a Rottweiler or messed with a *person* that had a Rottweiler.

Suddenly, like a bolt of lightning, and barking furiously, Killer made a dash for the west side window. With all her strength Lynn wrestled him away before he left scratch marks on the glass, or worse, broke through.

What had gotten the animal all riled up? Now she knew why. Julie was outside the window in the Lopez yard with Antonio and Lisa, a pen and notepad in hand. She could hear Antonio's voice but couldn't make out the words. Every few minutes, Julie's muffled voice could be heard, and then Antonio or Lisa would speak while Julie jotted something onto the notebook.

"What are they doing?" Lynn asked Killer, as if expecting a response. "Or more importantly, what is *she* doing?" Julie was dressed in an elegant beige suit, writing as fast as Antonio was talking. *She thinks she's so important.*

The Lopez and Hennessy homes were very close in proximity only about twenty feet apart. Julie was so close that if there hadn't have been a wall that separated the two, Lynn could have literally reached out and touched her.

Lynn started to sweat. Her heart beat faster. She felt an incredible rush, an excitement, almost like a heat. She wanted so badly to go outside and pretend to weed the garden or walk around the house, anything to make Julie squirm.

Lynn giggled. This was just too much fun. True, Julie wasn't as easy as some of the others had been. She was definitely a challenge.

Rhonda Wilkins had thrown a fit when Lynn had accused her thirteen-year-old son of trying to molest Hannah, who was six at the time. *My goodness, that woman was crazy mad.* She had come running across the street, pounding on the Hennessy's front door. When Lynn opened it, Rhonda grabbed her by the hair and knocked her to the ground. By the time Rick had pulled Rhonda off, she had two clenched fists full of Lynn's dark hair, still grabbing for more. It was comical as Rick stood between the two women holding them both at arm's length, demanding to know what was going on.

"Oh my goodness." Lynn had feigned innocence. "Rhonda, I have absolutely no idea what you're talking about. Why, you *know* we love Robbie like he was our own and would never, ever accuse him of something so atrocious."

As always, Rick fell for it. Rhonda didn't. Her house was on the market three weeks later. Within forty-five days, she and her family were out of there.

Barbara McKinney had been a cinch. As a matter of fact, she was too easy. Nope. Lynn loved a challenge, lived for it, actually. And that sorry excuse for a woman, with her measly, sick little girl, was absolutely worthless. The woman had no spine. She'd refused to fight back when Lynn wanted to play. Instead she stayed inside that rattrap of a house with the blinds closed. When she'd caught Lynn staring into the glass sunroom, Barbara had resorted to hanging sheets, bedspreads, anything she could get her hands on to put over the windows.

You can run, but you can't hide, sweet pea.

In fact, she'd made life so difficult for the McKinneys that they had fled in the middle of the night, leaving their belongings and everything behind. She'd watched it all from the deck, just like she watched *everything* from the deck.

Like the time she'd witnessed Barbara shake poor, defenseless, little Ava until the child fell out of her chair onto the cold, hard kitchen floor. Of course, no such thing had happened.

Quite the contrary! Barbara doted on that stupid child. Heck! Everyone doted on the little invalid. The whole neighborhood had a prayer vigil for six nights in a row, praying for a miracle to cure the little brat's leukemia. Actually, Lynn had prayed for it too. If the kid died, she couldn't take it to see Barb get even more attention than what she was already receiving.

So one night, Lynn picked up the phone and made a call.

"Nine one one. What's your emergency?"

"Oh my God! Please come quick! I...I'm watching my neighbor beat her little girl."

"Where are you, ma'am? How can you see what's happening? Are you sure she's hitting the child?"

Lynn made her voice quiver for effect. "I can see everything through the glass! She's shaking the child, and ... and now she's hitting her!"

"Okay, ma'am, we're sending someone over right now."

Nothing came of it, but that little visit from the police had been the straw that broke the camel's back. Two days later, the McKinneys were gone.

The high only lasted for a few days, and then, just like always, she'd become bored. She had to be careful though. She didn't want to totally alienate herself from the community. After all, she'd need to have some people on her side if Rick was going to keep his position as HOA president. That was important. But still, she was so, so bored.

About that time, fresh, new blood started moving in. It started with Bob and Anne Mumfort who moved across the street into the Wilkins house, followed by the Pattersons into the McKinney house and Sam and Marylou Watkins at the end of the cul-de-sac. From Lynn's deduction, Marylou was almost antisocial. In the time Marylou had lived here, Lynn had only seen the woman two or three times. Anne was pleasant enough but rather mousy. Then there was Julie. *Julie, Julie, Julie.*

What do people see in her?

It infuriated her that Julie hadn't fought back when she discovered it was Lynn who had reported her for child abuse. That made no sense at all. Lynn could feel, could sense, Julie's anger. But still she said nothing. Not one word. Not even a look. No matter how hard she'd tried to tempt Julie into a confrontation, the woman still wouldn't acknowledge her existence.

Yes, this egg was definitely going to be harder to crack.

CHAPTER 23

Julie sighed, feeling a tinge of sadness as she unhooked the digital camera from its charger and placed the strap around her neck. Sure, she was excited about her new real estate listing and the fact she would also be assisting those same clients in the purchase of their new home. But it came at a cost. The Lopezs were not only good neighbors, they were also good friends, and she hated to see them go.

She'd made a call after their initial meeting, and two hours later the "For Sale" sign was firmly planted in the ground. She tucked the 'Julie Patterson" name rider with her phone number under her arm, so she could clip it onto the sign. She was halfway out the door to shoot the photos of Lisa's house for *Homes Magazine*, when Colette plopped down on her haunches looking at Julie with a please-can-I-go-too look.

"How can I say no that precious face," Julie said as she snapped on the pretty pink leash.

Colette lay quietly in the grass while Julie shot photos of the backside of the Lopez house, which featured a brand-new Trex deck that Antonio himself had built a few summers ago.

She took a few more close-ups of the deck from various angles before going around the front to capture shots of the wraparound porch.

"Hi, Miss Julie!" It was one of the twins, but she wasn't sure which one.

The young girl came bouncing out the front door.

"Whatcha doing?" she asked.

"I'm taking pictures of your house to put on the Internet and in *Homes Magazine*." Julie stepped out into the street to give herself more room to get the wraparound porch and two—car garage in one frame. "Perfect," she said as she closed the shutter and snapped the lid over the lens. "These should do the trick. Now, I'll put these on my website, and a lot more people will see your house and—"

"Get that damn dog off my grass!" Lynn's screeching voice pierced the air.

Her outburst caught Julie so off guard that she froze. She looked down. Colette wasn't within five feet of Lynn's yard, and besides that, the dog was sitting quietly at Julie's feet.

Killer, upset by his owner's sudden outburst, hurled his 150-pound body through the open door and ran at full speed toward Julie. She quickly picked up Colette and held her close to her chest, dropping her camera and name rider on the concrete. Julie tried to grab the little girl with her free arm, but it was too late. The child watched in horror as the huge dog jumped on Julie, growling and barking while he tried to get Colette. Julie was able to keep her balance and didn't budge as the animal stood with his front paws on both of her shoulders. Just as she thought the dog would surely bite her head off, a big, sloppy, giant tongue swiped the whole left side of her face, leaving saliva dripping from her earlobe. So the dog wasn't going to eat her or Colette after all.

With all the calmness she could muster, still grasping on to Colette for dear life, Julie said, "Lynn, you need to get your dog off me if you want to keep him."

Lynn bolted out of the house. Julie wasn't sure if she was running out to gain control of Killer or if she was coming to do the job that Killer had failed at.

"You shut the fuck up! You're nothing but a fucking bitch, and everyone wishes you were dead! I hate you, you bitch. Do you hear me! I wish you were dead!" The tiny woman grabbed the Rottweiler with such force that he yelped when she jerked his collar.

"You better watch your back!" Lynn screamed, still wrestling with the dog.

Her venomous words shook Julie to the core. The hair stood up on the back of her neck, and she could feel the sting of tears. Colette trembled and hid her face in the crook of Julie's arm. Still,—Julie remained quiet and poised. She wasn't getting into a confrontation with a child caught in the middle.

"Are you okay, sweetheart?" she asked the little girl, turning her back to Lynn so she couldn't witness her fighting to keep her composure. She thought she would burst into tears at any moment. As for the child, she was so scared she couldn't speak.

Julie looked from house to house in hopes that one of the neighbors had witnessed the incident. The only person she saw was a young woman, a stranger, looking out Lynn's front window.

So that's what this is. Lynn had manipulated the situation and concocted the nasty scene to create a witness to an event that didn't happen. Undoubtedly, the young woman visiting Lynn had been in another room, and when Lynn saw Julie out the window, she screamed at her to get off her property, causing the other woman to come see what the ruckus was all about. *Very clever.*

"I don't understand why Miss Lynn got so mad at you! The puppy was nowhere near her grass!" the Lopez girl said as she started to cry.

But Julie understood it perfectly. This was Lynn's revenge. *Since she can't take my kid, she'll take my dog.*

"Sounds like you handled it right," Tom said when Julie called him. "If you'd have screamed back at her, it would have played right into her hands. That woman is out of control, and before long, she'll self-destruct."

"If she doesn't kill me first," said Julie, only half joking.

"Okay, I think you're overreacting again." Tom, without waiting for her to respond, called over his shoulder to a colleague, "I'll be with you in a minute,

John. Erica, can you bring me the Canadian file? Look, I've gotta go. I'll be home late tonight. Love you. Bye!"

Julie looked at the receiver in disbelief. Overreacting? If she heard that word again, she'd scream. Child abuse charges, stalking, vandalism, and now the woman just said she wished Julie were dead. If the way she was carrying on were any indication, she just might make it happen.

Thank God for Anne and Donna, because everyone else seemed to think this whole thing was nothing more than two jealous women battling it out, trying to establish turf. A couple of people had the nerve to ask her what she had done to make this woman so angry. Even if Julie had done something to her, which she hadn't, who would be this cruel?

But it was Tom's attitude that hurt the most. Of all people, he should be the one to believe her, to protect her. Why couldn't he see that this woman was crazy, possibly even dangerous?

What exactly would it take for someone, anyone, to take this seriously and come to her rescue? Whatever it took, Julie hoped it would happen soon, and she hoped it wouldn't be too late.

CHAPTER 24

Julie stared at the clock on the bedside table. Since 6:10 she had been awake, watching the minutes go slowly by. It was now 8:59, and she hadn't moved a muscle nor shown even the remotest interest in starting her day.

Not that she didn't have a million and one things to do, starting with the necessary paperwork from the past couple of houses she had just sold to uploading the pictures she took yesterday of the Lopez house.

The clock had just changed to 9:06 when Olivia, who was home from college to attend a friend's wedding, tapped on the bedroom door.

"Mom, are you sick?"

Julie made no effort to move, and with her back to the door, she answered in a low, monotone voice "No, I'm fine."

Unconvinced, Olivia walked around to the other side of the bed so she could see her mother's face. Her eyes were open, but they had such a vacant look to them, and there were mascara stains under her lower lashes. Her mother never went to bed without removing her makeup. But then again, her mother had done several things lately that were uncharacteristic.

"It's really unlike you to sleep this late," she said. "I just thought maybe you weren't feeling well."

Her mother was one of those disgusting people who liked to rise at the crack of dawn and usher in the morning all cheery and bubbly. Every morning since she could remember, Julie would thrust open her bedroom door, fully dressed and groomed, and greet her with a gleeful "Good morning!" It should be against the law for anyone to be that happy first thing in the morning, Olivia had thought many times. But these days Julie had been spending more and more time in bed or alone in her room, and Olivia missed those early morning wake-up calls. Now she was watching painfully as her mother unraveled a little bit at a time, and she had absolutely no clue what to do about it.

"I'm okay," came her mom's groggy reply. The process was slow, but one by one Julie put both feet on the floor. She sat on the edge of the bed, still watching the clock move from single to double digits, before gathering the strength to step into the shower.

"Okay, Julie," she said aloud to herself. Her head was tilted back, facing the shower spout, while the warm water trickled down her forehead onto her face. "Get yourself together, girl."

She wasn't meeting with clients that day, and most of the tasks on her to-do list could be completed by phone or personal computer, so she saw no need to bother with hair or makeup. She threw on a pair of jeans and one of Tom's old Mississippi State sweatshirts. She tied her thick, blonde hair, still damp from the shower, back in a messy ponytail.

She was startled when she caught a glimpse of herself in the hallway mirror. Her blue eyes were void of expression, and her usual peaches-and-cream complexion looked dull and pale. Come to think of it, Tom's baggy shirt didn't do too much for her either. *Too bad*, she thought. *Today, I just don't have the energy to care.*

She sat down at the desk to pay bills while Olivia sat by in silence, sadly wondering when her mother had started to look so old.

Julie knew she had whittled away the biggest part of the day when Herb, the postman, pulled up to the curb in the mail truck. She looked at her watch. *Oh my goodness! Three-fifteen already?*

"Hello, sunshine!" Herb called out to her in the affable, cheerful manner that had endeared him to so many of the residents of the cul-de-sac for the past ten or so years. When he got a closer look at her appearance, he was taken aback by her pale, lifeless face. "Are you sick?"

"No, but thanks for the compliment," Julie answered dryly.

"Hey, you're always beautiful." He tried to backpedal. "But you just don't seem yourself today, that's all."

"Hmm," was all Julie could say. She quickly tried to change the subject with an attempt at humor. "What do you have for me today? Anything from Ed McMahon and Publishers Clearinghouse sweepstakes? Maybe my great-aunt Gertrude died and left me a million dollars."

"Do you have a great-aunt Gertrude?" asked Herb.

"No."

"Okay, I guess you'll have to depend on Ed then. Did you fill out the entry form for the Publishers Clearinghouse?"

"Nope."

"Well, you can't win if you don't play." Herb winked as he handed her a small bundle. "But I do have this for ya, mostly junk though."

Julie gave him a sideways glance. "Do you actually look to see what people get?"

His chagrined look told her the answer.

"Well, I'll bet you could write a book about some of the weird stuff that comes through the mail, huh?"

Herb rubbed his chin and thought for a minute before breaking into a wide-mouth grin.

"No, I've never really delivered anything unusual. Darned Fed-Ex and UPS guys get all the good stuff. But I've sure *seen* enough to write a good book, that's for darn sure. Like the time about fifteen years ago, a Virginia congressman's *much* younger wife, whom I won't name, signed for a special delivery buck-naked.

Not a stitch on, I tell ya. And she was quite a looker too." Herb winked.

"Yeah," said Julie, trying desperately to erase the image of Herb ogling a naked blonde bombshell. "I'm sure you've never had anything that exciting in this neighborhood."

"You might be surprised now, young lady, just what does go on here in your own backyard. Take for instance that Widow Stottle up around the corner." He pointed as he continued, "She's the nosiest dad-blamed woman I've ever seen. Seems to think it's her job to keep tabs on the neighbors. If she gets somebody else's mail, which doesn't happen very often, instead of takin' it to him or at least puttin' it back so I can deliver it myself she decides to open it and take a look for herself.

"Of course, if I say anything to her about it, she tries to tell me it was an accident. Yeah, right. She's just wanting in everyone's business."

What on earth ever possessed her to strike up a conversation with Herb? She knew he could go on forever. What was she thinking?

"But the one you really, and I mean *really*, oughta steer clear of is that Hennessy gal. Bad news, bad news," Herb said in a hush.

"Yes, well you're about one year too late," said Julie in a very curt manner as she turned to walk away. She did not want to talk about Lynn Hennessy. Herb, not picking up on the Julie's stiff body language, kept right on talking.

"Hers was the first house built in this subdivision, ya know. The construction crew just started building the house across the street, and she'd parade around all over the place in her bikini. The first few times, from what I could see, the guys didn't pay too much attention to her. Oh, they might sneak a peek or two. She is a fine-lookin' woman, ya know, but other than that they never bothered her, never talked to her, never made any gestures, nothin' like that. I know their foreman, Phill, and he'd never allow anything like that. No siree, that Phill Fournier runs a tight ship. When he hires someone to work, he expects 'em to work, by golly. No messin' around. That company he works for is one of the biggest builders in Virginia. Yeah, Phill and I've had some good times together." Herb smiled, reminiscing. "We went to high school together."

Puh—lease. There has to be an ending to this story in this century, she thought, hoping that her expression didn't reveal the disgust she felt when that woman's name was mentioned.

"Anyway, 'bout drove her crazy that she was struttin' her stuff and no one was noticin' her, so she finally crossed the street and went over there and started a conversation with 'em. This went on for 'bout a week or so. Well, one day when I came through, I noticed there wasn't a soul in sight on the property. Construction came to a complete standstill there for 'bout four days. Well, I just asked Phill one day what was up. He came through the post office before I left on my route, and I asked him what happened." Herb was mad all over again just thinking about it. "They all got fired, that's what happened. 'Cause of that Hennessy gal!"

"Fired? Why?" What could Lynn have possibly done to get a whole construction crew fired?

"That's the interestin' part. Seems she got what she wanted, them payin' attention to her and all. Then she up and called their boss and told him they were sexually harassin' her. The boss told her that he'd have a talk with all of 'em. Phill was madder than a coon dog, tellin' his boss that no such thing was happenin' and that she'd been the one comin' over and botherin' 'em when they were just tryin' to build houses."

Does this woman just sit around dreaming up crazy things to do to people?

"So after that they never spoke one more word to 'er. Phill said if he caught anybody even lookin' in the direction of her house, he'd fire 'em right there on the spot. A few days later, the boss calls Phill in again. Mrs. Hennessy had called the boss again and was threatenin' to call a lawyer if they didn't quit sexually harassing her every time she walked out the door. She said they were always whistlin' and makin' lewd comments, couldn't even go outside in her own yard without 'em harassin' her. Phill says it never happened; these are guys with families, and they needed their jobs. But she just kept callin' day after day. One day, she called the foreman in tears, and the big guy finally had enough. Fired 'em all right then and there. Even

Phill—and he'd worked there since we got outta high school, which was a long time ago."

Good grief! How does this woman sleep at night?

Herb was right. Most of it was junk mail to be thrown in the trash. She stepped away from the desk, and an envelope fell from her lap onto the floor.

Cardinal Estates HOA Management Office? What's this? she wondered, picking it up.

"This shouldn't be a bill." The HOA dues were only forty dollars a quarter, so she had gone ahead and paid for the whole year. When she opened up the envelope, she was very unhappy to see that it was not only a bill but also showed that they owed over 250 dollars in back dues and late fees.

'What? No way!" She dug through her files until she located the checkbook containing the duplicate check made payable to the management company.

Sure enough, there it was. Check number 3125 for 120 dollars. There was a circle drawn in black ink around the check number, the indication that the check had cleared the bank.

Just to be certain, before she called the company and put them through the third degree, she went online and brought up her Wachovia account. She clicked on "Checks" and entered"3125" for the check in question.

Yes, it had cleared. Two months ago. Julie dialed the customer service number on the bill. A young girl with a French accent answered on the second ring.

"Cardinal Estates HOA Management, Cecile Perton speaking."

"Hi, Cecile. This is Julie Patterson at 1214 Raye. I just received a bill for over 250 dollars, and I've paid our bill already. The check was cashed by you all about eight weeks ago."

"Okay, Mrs. Patterson." Julie could hear her typing in the background. "Let me see what I can find. What is your account number?"

"Mmm, oh, here it is at the top of the page: 459213."

There was silence for a few minutes; then Cecile asked in a puzzled tone, "Did you say 459213?"

"Yes," answered Julie. "That's correct."

"That's not your account number." Cecile was quiet again, but Julie could hear the fast click of computer keys. "I'm showing your account number as 326573. And yes, you're all paid up for the whole year; you don't owe anything."

Julie's jaw dropped open when she looked at the bill closer and saw who it belonged to: Rick and Lynn Hennessy, 2210 Frostman Court, Woodbridge, VA 22193.

What the heck? She frantically shuffled papers around on the desk. Shoot! Where did the envelope go? She rifled through the trash. There it was: Tom and Julie Patterson, 1214 Raye Street, Woodbridge, VA 22193.

"The envelope has our name on it but the Hennessy's bill is inside? How did that happen?" Julie demanded to know.

"Summer intern," was Cecile's embarrassed response.

"Which means someone else got *my* statement."

"I am so sorry Mrs. Patterson. We've just been swamped here, and I thought this would be a job an intern could help me with."

"Cecile, I have a question," said Julie. "Is this bill correct? Are the Hennessys really in arrears for two years straight?"

There was a brief silence, and for a minute Julie thought maybe they had been disconnected when Cecile finally answered, "Umm, well, I'm not supposed to—"

"Look, Cecile, I am in a desperate situation." She went into a detailed account of the child abuse allegations, the vandalism, and the stalking. "I should be able to seek some kind of help from the HOA at least on the property destruction, but I can't because Mr. Hennessy is the president of the association, and it's his wife that is doing all of this! Now it looks like I have the proof that according to the bylaws, he can't be president because he hasn't paid his bill in over two years. Am I correct?"

"Yes," Cecile whispered into the receiver. "It's correct. They haven't paid their dues in over two years."

"Bingo!" shouted Julie triumphantly. Now she was getting somewhere. All she had to do was blow the whistle on Rick and he'd be off the board. Someone new, who wasn't married to a crazy, psychopathic terrorist, could now come in and bring some sense and civility to the neighborhood.

"Look, Cecile, I promise I will never tell anyone it was you who confirmed this information. I am going to keep this bill, though, *and* the envelope as the proof I need. Now, if you could tell me just one more thing. Is Jackie Stottle's son still on the board?"

"Yes, he is," Cecile confirmed. "He's vice president. Bill Frederick is the treasurer."

Julie thanked the girl, and as soon as she hung up, she looked up and noticed Olivia standing in the threshold of the office. She folded up the bill and stuffed it back in the envelope and grabbed a sweater.

"What are you going to do now?" Olivia asked, already knowing the answer.

"I'm going up to have a little chat with Mr. Henry Stottle."

"Not by yourself, you're not," Olivia said as she followed her mother out the door.

Julie was a woman on a mission. She walked so fast that Olivia almost had to run to keep up with her. She turned squarely onto the sidewalk and marched up to the Stottle house. Not taking any chances that the doorbell might not work, she pounded on the front door.

Jackie Stottle, with her long, scraggly gray hair down around her waist, wearing a housecoat that looked like it had coffee or something spilled all down the front, and no dentures, barely had time to open the door before Julie asked, "Is Henry here?"

"He's at work. He won't be home until seven. He works at NASA, you know;" she said smugly as she threw in the last tidbit of information. "What can I help you with?"

"Nothing," answered Julie sharply. "I want to talk to him about HOA issues and some things that have been happening in the neighborhood."

"Henry's not the president," the haggard woman answered. "He's the *vice* president."

Julie snapped, her patience all but gone. "I know who the president is. Although, he's not qualified to be that because he hasn't paid his bill in over two years."

"How do you know that?" Jackie asked doubtfully.

"Because I received his bill, that's how!" Julie held it up so she could see the front of the envelope. "You see, it's addressed to me, but inside the management company messed up and sent *me* the Hennessy's bill, which, ta-da, has not been paid in two years."

"They're always messing those invoices up," Jackie said defiantly. "That doesn't mean a thing."

"Actually, it does," Julie argued. "Because yours truly called the management office, and they confirmed that this bill is indeed correct! They also confirmed that anyone who is delinquent on his bill cannot hold an office *and* will have a lien put on his home."

"What do you want Henry to do about it?"

"I want him and the other guy who is on the board to kick Rick Hennessy off and put someone in whose wife doesn't make my life a living hell and who has a kid that doesn't shoot my house with a paintball gun. *That's* what I want!"

"You have no right to go flapping everyone else's bill around the neighborhood," said Jackie, suddenly copping a self-righteous attitude.

Julie shot right back. "I have every right! It's my house and my family being targeted! The police even told me to go to my HOA, but I can't because all this craziness is coming from the HOA president's house! And to top it off he shouldn't even *be* the president!"

"There was no police report about your house being vandalized. I talked to Officer Wilson, and he knew nothing about it and—"

Julie cut her off again. "He wasn't the one that answered the call. And I happen to have that nonexistent report, thank you very much!"

She took a breath long enough to point in the direction of Lynn's house. "*That* woman has the audacity to lie and tell the school that we don't have the money to take care of our children when she can't even afford to pay forty dollars per quarter for her HOA dues? *This*—all of it—is so white trash!"

As Julie turned to walk away, she heard Jackie call her a bitch before she slammed the door.

CHAPTER 25

The buzz around Cardinal Estates for the next several days was that Julie had called Jackie white trash. Blanche Burns, who'd stopped by the Patterson's house to pick up Kevin, asked if it were true.

"I did not call her white trash," Julie tried to explain. "I said *this* is so white trash—meaning this situation, this as in the things that are going on are white trash. Come on! You have to admit that normal neighborhoods and normal people do not act like this."

Blanche laughed and made light of the situation, which hurt Julie deeply. But Blanche wasn't the only one. Far from it. Friends, neighbors, the police, even Tom had trivialized the pattern of events. Just ignore her and she'll stop, they all told her. Well, that's exactly what she had been doing, and all it did was make matters worse. It was as if Lynn wanted Julie to speak to her, look at her, *acknowledge* her in some way.

Anne and Donna were the ones that Julie turned to when she needed to talk. Maybe that was because they were always around to witness Lynn's theatrics firsthand.

For Anne, it went even deeper than that. She was Lynn's confidant, always giving the woman her undivided attention whenever she dropped in to tell her the latest story she'd made up about Julie. She'd thought about telling Lynn what she thought of her and all of her lies but thought better of it. What was that saying her grandfather always told her? "Hold your friends close but your enemies closer."

"She told me that you went to her mailbox and got out all of her bills and showed them to everyone in the neighborhood," Anne confided, always keeping Julie abreast of the latest from Lynn. "She said she has an appointment with her attorney this afternoon, and they are suing you."

"For what?" Julie asked nonchalantly. She had done nothing wrong. "That HOA bill was addressed to me."

"Hmm," said Anne. "I wonder who got ours; we got the Wisemans' from the end of the cul-de-sac."

"See," said Julie. "That's my point; everyone's got mixed up."

Two days later, there was a scathing letter addressed to Julie from Webster, Hanks, and Sweeten, attorneys at law in Manassas, Virginia.

To Julie Marie Patterson,

This is a letter of warning ordering you to cease and desist in your slanderous speech and fabrications regarding the Hennessy family. You called the police and falsely accused Curtis Hennessy (minor child of Rick and Lynn Hennessy) of vandalizing your home. You need to look elsewhere, as he was out of state that particular day.

You are to stop and desist in your slanderous accusations that Lynn Hennessy has told anyone, including school, teachers, neighbors, or authorities that you are neglecting or abusing your child (children).

This law firm is currently preparing to file suit if you do not immediately return Mr. and Mrs. Hennessy's mail to them. May we remind you that tampering with mail or entering mailboxes other than your own is a federal offense and is punishable by law.

If you do not return the Hennessy's mail to this office within two business days, we will be forced to file suit. Please note that we are prepared to prosecute you to the fullest extent of the law.

Signed,

Joan Mitchell Davis
Attorney

Julie didn't know whether to laugh or to cry, so she allowed herself the opportunity to do both for about a minute. Then she called her attorney.

Tom and Julie hadn't consulted with Ron Moorehouse since the school incident. He was quite amused at all that had happened since they'd last spoken, but he was just like everyone else and didn't take the situation very seriously. Julie was used to that attitude by now but was still irked that her attorney, the man she was paying big money didn't even have the decency to at least pretend to care. On the contrary, he chastised her for opening up someone else's mail.

"Now that scares me," Ron said. "If you opened her mail, we're going to have trouble on our hands, even if it came to your mailbox by mistake."

"I did not open her mail. It was addressed to *me*," a frustrated Julie explained for the umpteenth time. Why didn't anyone listen to her? "I opened up a letter that had *my name, my address* on it. I look at this bill and wonder why I'm being charged an outrageous amount for something I have already paid for. When I look down at the bill, I see Rick and Lynn Hennessy's name on the bill. Everyone got someone else's bill. Everyone! It was a huge mix-up at the management office. Apparently the intern just started stuffing envelopes that had already been addressed with no regard as to matching the correct bill with the correct envelope. Not my problem."

Ron was silent for a minute, and she could hear him scribbling notes through the phone.

"Well, one thing I'll say," he finally said. Julie had faxed the letter she had received to his office for his review. "This Joan Davis hasn't a clue on how to write a professional letter; I'm made to wonder if she didn't have her own intern concoct this mess."

"I think what I'll do is just nip this in the bud. My golf buddy is one of the partners in this firm, and I'm gonna give him a call. I'll just tell him about the letter and that there is no need to make a mountain out of a mole hill, so to speak. I'll tell him that we talked, and you're gonna play nice, and Mrs. Hennessy should do the same."

"*I'm* going to play nice? What exactly does that mean? Can't anyone understand that I am the victim here? She accused me of child abuse. Her son or someone in her family shot a paintball gun at my house. And just a few weeks ago, she screamed obscenities at me while letting her Rottweiler loose on me." Julie paused long enough to thicken her sarcasm. "Oh, by the way, did I mention the fact she follows me everywhere?"

"Why didn't you call the police when she called you names?" her attorney asked.

Julie sighed. "Because I didn't know that was a valid reason to call the police."

"Well," Ron continued, "you could have at least told them about the dog."

"Look," said Julie, frustration welling inside to the point she thought she'd burst, "can't you at least send her a letter like the one her yahoo of an attorney sent to me telling her that she needs to back off and leave us alone?"

"That would be futile. Bull. More worthless than the paper it's written on. Trust me on this. Just let me give her attorney a call and settle this once and for all."

Julie reluctantly agreed and wrapped the conversation up as quickly as possible, knowing that already this was an expensive piece of advice.

She was exhausted. She had begged Tom to move, to allow her to put their house on the market and just move to a different neighborhood. Maybe now they should move in closer to Washington DC so his commute would be shorter, and they could escape from all of the stress and atrocity of the neighborhood. But Tom wouldn't even consider it.

"We're not moving," he said to her coldly. "Maybe if just once in your life you had paid attention to warning signs that were right in front of your face and admitted to yourself that this is a crazy person and then run as fast as you could in the other direction instead of trying to save her, then maybe, just maybe, you wouldn't have put your family in this position in the first place."

Those words were the straw that broke the proverbial camel's back. He couldn't have hurt her more if he'd stabbed her in the heart with a knife. As far as she was concerned, they were finished.

CHAPTER 26

"No! No! You get back here, little missy!" Julie cried as she chased Colette, who decided to run toward the street after digging up newly planted marigolds.

Thank God there weren't any cars coming as Julie tried to coax the little rascal back into the yard. She almost had the puppy in her arms when Colette suddenly veered to the right when she caught sight of Blanche Burns and her Great Dane, Bernie.

Colette ran as fast as her tiny legs would carry her and came to a screeching halt, barking and yapping aggressively at Bernie. Bernie, excited at the prospect of a new playmate, lunged at Colette with all of his strength, stretching his leash to the limit with Blanche on the other end holding him back, her sneakers sliding on the pavement.

Julie was then able to sneak up behind Colette and scoop her up in her arms before Bernie drug Blanche, holding on to the leash for dear life, down Raye Street.

"Colette, all Bernie has to do is sniff and you'd be history," said Julie as she held the squirming, still yapping dog in her arms. Blanche was still desperately but unsuccessfully struggling to gain some type of control over the hyperactive Bernie.

"I'll get out of the street!" Julie hollered over the chaos, knowing that Bernie would follow her and Colette into their yard, making it safer for all involved.

Blanche, finally calming the beast, commanded him to sit once they were in Julie's front yard. No longer intimidated by Bernie's humongous size, Colette squirmed for Julie to let her down, so she could play with her new pal.

"Why don't you put a saddle on him and charge for pony rides?" Julie joked as she watched the two dogs frolic and play.

"No kidding." Blanche was breathing as if she'd just finished a marathon. "He eats like a horse; I'm going to have to take out a second mortgage just to buy dog food every week."

It was sweet to see Bernie, whose heart was as big as he was, get down on all fours so he could play with Colette at eye level. He lay very still as he watched her run circles around him, stopping to gnaw on his ear or bark at him to get up and play.

"Aren't you glad that Colette is the aggressive one and Bernie is so laid back instead of the other way around?" Blanche asked.

"Most definitely."

"Oh, Blaaaaanche!" It was Lynn. "I just saw a big dog over on the next street that is running loose, no collar or leash or anything! I'd be careful if I were you."

"Uh oh." Blanche clipped Bernie's leash back on. "The last thing I need is a dog fight."

Blanche left Julie's yard without so much as a goodbye, pulling Bernie toward home and chatting with Lynn along the way.

Mad that her playmate was leaving, Colette chased after them, nipping at the back of Lynn's ankles. Julie was following after them, trying to catch Colette, who was just out of her reach. Tom was watching the commotion from the front window. Sensing Julie's fear and frustration, he stepped outside and gave a loud, shrill whistle. Colette came to a screeching halt, did a 180-degree turn, and made a beeline for the front door.

Julie ran in right behind her. At the same time, Olivia called from the kitchen, "Mom, you have a phone call!"

It was a gentleman by the name of Reed Kirkpatrick who had driven by the Lopez home and was interested in looking at it.

"What time can you meet us there?" he asked.

"Actually, I live in the house right behind them, so I can show you anytime," Julie replied, catching her breath and happy for the distraction.

"How about now?" Mr. Kirkpatrick asked. "We're parked right in front of the house."

"Sure, but let me call Mrs. Lopez real quick and give her a heads-up. Give me your number and I'll call you right back."

Lisa, anxious to sell, was happy to accommodate even though it was on such short notice. As Julie walked around the corner and up the front stairs, she and the kids were loading up the van to take a quick trip to Dairy Queen to allow Mr. and Mrs. Kirkpatrick some privacy.

The Kirkpatricks, a middle-aged, African American couple, were in the process of relocating from Cincinnati. Mrs. Kirkpatrick had just accepted the job as Prince William County superintendent of schools and was scheduled to start her new job within the next forty days. It was crucial for her to find a home and make sure the family was all settled in before then.

The couple was making their second walk-through of the house, completely engrossed in their own dialogue of where the sofa might go, where Great-Aunt Ruth's china hutch might fit. Experience had taught Julie that when buyers start arranging their furniture in a prospective house, an offer was almost always imminent. She'd only been wrong a few times.

Mr. and Mrs. Kirkpatrick wanted to take one last look at the deck and the overall view of the neighborhood. Then they wanted to discuss an offer.

While they finished looking around, Julie stepped into the foyer to retrieve her stuffed, heavy, leather briefcase. She grabbed the long strap, threw it over her shoulder, and turned to leave the room when she was blinded by a series of flashing white lights.

"What is *that*?" She gently pulled the lace sheet curtain back to get a closer look.

Poised with a camera to her cheek was Lynn snapping picture after picture of the "McLellan Real Estate, For Sale by Julie Patterson" sign.

Why on earth was she taking pictures of a ridiculous sign?

Afraid that Mr. and Mrs. Kirkpatrick might witness this bizarre behavior and change their minds, Julie immediately dropped the curtain and distracted the couple by leading them into the dining room, where she promptly began contract negotiation.

Their timing was perfect. The ink wasn't even dry on the pages yet when Antonio's little red Hyundai pulled up to the garage door. Close behind was Lisa, very frazzled from trying to keep the kids occupied for the past hour and fifteen minutes.

There was no sign of Lynn as Julie shook hands with Mr. and Mrs. Kirkpatrick and promised to get back with them by nine that evening. When they drove away, she let out a sigh of relief and then followed the Lopez family inside.

"We have a contract!" exclaimed Julie, waving the folder in the air. "A full-price one at that! They're not asking for anything, no closing costs or assistance of any kind. The only stipulation is a home inspection to be completed within three days of ratifying the contract. If the home inspection goes well, they'd like to get to settlement and move in within the next thirty days."

"That will work out perfectly," said Antonio. "That could put us in the new house in time for the kids to start their new school."

"Okay then. Let's go over the contract and get the ball rolling."

It was eight and almost dark when Julie bid the happy family a good night. Her own excitement was cut short when she saw the police car parked in front of her house.

CHAPTER 27

Julie's heart sank. Lynn had called the police and told them about Colette getting loose and trying to bite her; she just knew it.

"Hello," Julie said with a hint of uneasiness to her voice, trying to remember where she'd put the dog's rabies and shot records even though she was positive that Colette hadn't bitten anyone. "Can I help you, officer?"

The policeman was tall, and although scrawny, his height and demeanor gave him a very intimidating presence. He looked up from his clipboard.

"Are you Mrs. Patterson? Mrs. Julie Patterson?" he asked in a very gruff, serious tone.

"Yes, sir, I am," Julie answered politely in her soft, Southern drawl. Her stomach was doing flip-flops. Now she remembered! She'd put Colette's rabies tags and vet records in the glove compartment of the car.

"Would you mind telling me why you just assaulted Mrs. Hennessy?" he asked in a tone that implied he'd already found her guilty.

She gave a short laugh and a sigh of relief. This wasn't about her dog at all.

Not amused with her response, he asked, "Are you aware that in Virginia assault carries a two-to five-year prison sentence?"

"I am sorry, officer, but I have no idea what you're talking about. Mrs. Hennessy simply walked by my house a few hours ago. That's all there is to it. She just walked by. You can ask my husband and Blanche Burns, who lives right over there."

He took out a notebook. "I plan to question them as well. Mrs. Hennessy told me they were there when it happened and could back up her story."

Julie was flabbergasted. Which was worse? The fact that Lynn was delusional enough to believe that Tom and Blanche would actually back something up that never happened or the fact that this officer of the law was standing in front of her, treating her like a common criminal? Why, even a blind man could see that she was a proper Southern lady who absolutely did not engage in fist fights, or any other physical altercations, for that matter!

"Tom!" Julie opened the front door and called for him. "Can you please come out here?"

"What's up?" Tom asked the officer, getting straight to the point.

"I just need to ask you a few questions," the officer said, just as curt. "We received a call earlier this evening from a Mrs. Lynn Hennessy. She stated that she was walking by your house when your wife ran down the hill and shoved her to the ground."

"My wife did no such thing. She was in her own yard, minding her own business, talking with another neighbor, Mrs. Burns, who lives at the end of this street. Mrs. Hennessy walked by and interrupted the conversation between Mrs. Burns and my wife. My wife grabbed the dog and came in the house. End of story."

Julie was stunned. "She told you that she just happened to walk by and out of a fit of rage I shoved her to the ground? In my entire life, I have never even *thought* of doing something like that."

Flipping open his metal clipboard and reading over his notes, the policeman said, "According to our report, 'Mrs. Patterson has been harassing and stalking me for the past several months. She believes that I turned her in for child abuse and has had it in for me ever since. Tonight when I walked by her house, she became enraged for no apparent reason and ran down the hill as fast as she could, grabbed me by the shoulders, and shoved me to the ground. Her husband and another neighbor, Blanche Burns, were there when this happened, so they can attest to my story.'"

"She really did turn me in to the school for child abuse. And *she* is stalking *me*. I just try to ignore her, and the more I ignore her, the worse it gets."

He scribbled notes in his report. After a few minutes, he looked at them both and said, "I'm going to follow up with Mrs. Burns, and I'll be back in a few minutes." He flipped the notebook closed, tucked it under his arm, and walked briskly over to Blanche's.

In about ten minutes, the doorbell rang and once again the officer stood solemnly at the door.

He shook his head. "I apologize for the inconvenience, Mrs. Patterson. Mrs. Burns told me the exact same story word for word. There'll be no charges, and I'm going to go over and have a chat with Mrs. Hennessy about the consequences of filing a false report."

Tom asked, "What do we have to do file a restraining order against this woman? Another officer told us that we couldn't, but there has got to be some way to get one issued."

"Unfortunately, no, there isn't. Virginia doesn't have restraining orders, per se. The only way restraining orders are issued is if it's against a family member or if two people have had a live-in relationship. In this case, you just need to stay away from this woman."

"I do stay away from her. I totally ignore her. I pretend that she doesn't exit, and yet she still finds a way to worm herself into every aspect of my life."

"Then just keep doing what you've been doing, and more than likely she'll give up," was the only advice he offered as he tipped his hat, apologized once more for the scare, and left.

The phone rang about fifteen minutes later. It was Blanche, and she was sobbing so hard she could hardly speak.

"Julie, please, please forgive me. You tried to tell me, and I didn't believe you. I just didn't take you seriously. I am so sorry."

Relief washed through Julie's body like a clean spring rain. Lynn had really messed up this time, and finally, *finally* Julie would get the help she needed.

CHAPTER 28

It was a miserably hot, humid day. Julie left the car running and the air-conditioning at full blast as she compared the address on the piece of paper she had torn from the yellow pages to the sign on the front of the brick building.

Yes, this was right the place. CRB, Private Investigators, 4242 Old Bridge Road, Lake Ridge, Virginia. After a quick checkup in the rear mirror, she powdered her nose. Then after sending up a small prayer, she took a deep breath and turned off the engine.

The steel rotating doors to the front of the building reminded Julie of something you'd see in a James Bond movie. Once she stepped inside, the doors slammed tight until a voice came over the loudspeaker asking Julie to state her name and business.

"My name is Julie Patterson, and I have a ten thirty appointment to see Mr. Charles Bishop."

A few more seconds and the steel portion opened with a thud, revealing a thick, bulletproof glass. When the glass door slid back, she was welcomed into the reception area by a young woman with shiny black hair slicked back into a tight ponytail. She was dressed in black from head to toe, reminding Julie of Angelina Jolie in one of her tough-girl roles.

Julie sat down in one of the lobby chairs and took in every detail of the office. She thought that the high-tech, sleek, modern look was cool but very out of place in Lake Ridge, a yuppie suburb with nothing but strip malls, fast food chains, and modest townhouses.

There was a soft buzzing, and the receptionist picked up the phone. She held it to her ear and just as quickly put the receiver back down without uttering a word.

The girl looked at Julie and said, "Mr. Bishop will see you now. Follow me, please."

They went down a long, empty corridor with doors closed on both sides. Julie couldn't help but notice how eerily quiet it was, and when she did see people, it was mostly men in black suits, white shirts, and plain black ties. No one spoke. The whole atmosphere felt very strange, secretive. She expected to see 007 step out at any moment.

Finally, at the end of the hall, the receptionist stopped at the office and gently tapped on the door before opening it. She then turned the knob and held the door open to let Julie enter first.

"Mrs. Patterson, this is Mr. Bishop," she introduced. "May I get you some coffee or something to drink?"

"No, thank you. I'm fine," Julie replied, suddenly feeling very nervous.

A tall, muscular, silver-haired gentleman in his late fifties to early sixties stood up, walked around his desk, and reached for Julie's hand. He pulled a chair and motioned for her to take a seat at a conference table that was in the corner of his office by the window.

Julie smiled demurely. "Thank you for agreeing to see me, Mr. Bishop—"

"Please, call me Chuck," he said, inviting her to take a seat at the table. "Now, what brings you here?"

Julie handed him a detailed written timeline. She described how Lynn's behavior was becoming more bizarre and now escalating to a false assault report resulting in her almost being arrested.

"I was scared to death," said Julie, visibly shaken. "We were all just so shocked that she would go this far—I mean, *nothing* happened—and the next thing I know, this policeman just shows up at my house ready to arrest me."

"Why are you coming to me, Mrs. Patterson?" Chuck asked, tapping a pencil on the table. "What is it that you want me to do or *think* I can do for you?"

"I need help, and I don't know where else to turn. I thought if I ignored her she'd get tired and go on to someone else, but her behavior keeps getting more bizarre, and frankly, I'm scared to death."

The private investigator gave a chuckle as he asked, "What did you do to her to set her off like this?"

Why did everyone always assume she'd done something to start this?

"I have done *nothing*, nothing that I know of, anyway. I have racked my brain trying to think of something I could have possibly done to hurt her feelings or make her angry, but I can't think of anything. But even if I had, what kind of person resorts to these tactics?" Her voice started to quiver, but she willed herself not to cry.

"Please, Mrs. Patterson, forgive me. I didn't mean to make light of the situation. It's just that you're right; it is bizarre, to say the least. I just don't understand why you're here and what you're asking me to do."

"I want you to do a background check on her. As I told you, she's becoming a lot more aggressive. I live in constant fear of what she might do next. I know I can't get a restraining order against her, even though I am not her first victim. I think she's had lots of practice. I know at least two other families left the neighborhood because of her. Maybe, if I had something to take to a judge I could get some kind of protection."

The investigator was silent for a moment.

"I usually don't handle cases like this," he said. "Most of the work we do here is top secret—Homeland Security anti-terrorist issues, things like that."

That explains a lot about this place, Julie thought.

"However," he continued, "this intrigues me. While I cannot do a background check on Mrs. Hennessy without her permission, I can do a background check on you."

Realizing that this concept wasn't registering with Julie, he continued on.

"Doing a background check on you will allow us to ask questions of your neighbors, teachers, even the police. By doing this, we'll possibly be able to gain enough information and have solid proof, hopefully from witnesses, of the fact that she's stalking and harassing you. Maybe I can also track down one of her other victims."

As she put the ink pen to the checkbook, he stopped her. He reached in his pocket, got out a business card, and as he handed it to her, he leaned in closer, looking her straight in the eye to make his point.

"I'll do this," he said, his voice suddenly going cold, his face stern, and his eyes glaring. "But if I find out that you're lying to me in any way, shape, or form, I'll drop you like a hot potato, *and* I'll keep your money."

Julie leaned in to meet his stare. She handed him his check and said, "You're hired."

"There's really only one thing I care about," said Julie, getting down to business. She handed Chuck a list of names on a sheet of tablet paper and pointed to the top three. "These were the individuals she wanted to do her dirty work for her, to report me to social services. To this day, she tells anyone who will listen that she saved my son from my abuse." It still made her blood boil to think about that.

"But then she'll turn around and tell someone else that she didn't make the accusations at all."

Next, she pointed to Anne's name. "This is the neighbor she went to first. She's important because she doesn't know the teachers or the principal, but yet she tells the same exact story. It matches up verbatim. I want a statement from all of these people."

Julie walked to the door, paused, and said one last thing to Chuck before leaving him to get started. "I am embarrassed that I let things get this far. There were warning signs galore that this woman was absolutely crazy. I should have cut her off with the first lie, but I didn't.

"Right now all I want to do is protect my family, and stop living in fear that authorities are coming to take my child away. I shouldn't be afraid to live in my own house."

"I'll get started on this right away," Chuck promised. "I'll call you tomorrow afternoon and give you an update on what I have so far."

On her drive home, she felt that the weight of the world had been lifted from her shoulders.

She wasn't sure what she would do with the private investigator's report once it was completed. But for some reason, after last night's visit from the police, it seemed the right thing, the necessary thing to do. It had even been Tom's suggestion.

Having a policeman show up at your house out of the blue was pretty traumatic, but it had actually turned out to be a blessing in disguise. Tom and Blanche got a chance to see for themselves that all this time Julie hadn't been overreacting, or paranoid, for that matter. This situation was very real.

Fifteen minutes later, as she was pulling in to Cardinal Estates, she noticed a Prince William County police car trailing her. Its overhead lights weren't flashing, so she didn't pull over. Being on her best behavior, she made sure she turned her blinker on in plenty of time before making the left-hand turn onto Tobacco Way. The car stayed right behind her, and she was becoming a little concerned as she signaled left to turn on Raye Street and the car followed her. She pulled into her driveway as the police car did a U-turn and came to a stop alongside the curb in front of her house.

Now what? Julie thought as her stomach turned into knots. She caught a glimpse of Will's face pressed to the upstairs glass of Olivia's room, where he was watching a movie on his sister's television.

"Mrs. Patterson?" the policeman asked politely. Julie looked at his name tag. Officer Burke was much younger than the officer from last night's call.

"That's me," Julie answered, almost wearily, wondering what Lynn had called about now.

Officer Burke pulled out an envelope and handed it to Julie. As she opened it to read it, he explained what it was.

"This is a no trespass issued by the Prince William County Police and magistrate judge for the benefit of Lynn Hennessy. This explains that if you or anyone in your family trespass or step foot on Mrs. Hennessy's property, you will be subject to arrest."

Julie looked at the paper, folded it back, and looked blankly at Officer Burke. "I don't understand what this is all about. I haven't been on her property in almost two years."

"I don't have any knowledge of that, ma'am. I've just been given my orders to deliver this," the young man replied.

"Okay. Thanks, I guess." Julie shrugged as she walked into her house. So much for that peaceful feeling she was experiencing earlier. Welcome back, anxiety.

"Mommy, what did that policeman want?" Will asked before she had the chance to get all the way through the door.

"Can I see that?" Olivia pointed at the envelope. She had been home for a few days for a long weekend and had been packing her suitcase to leave the next morning.

"Sure," answered Julie. "Why not?"

Olivia studied the no trespass order for a few minutes. She handed it back to her mother, her eyes filled with tears.

"This is no big deal to us; we wouldn't go on her property if it were the last place on earth. But what about Will?" she cried. "Mom, he's a baby. What happens if he kicks a ball into her yard and goes to get it? What if he's playing tag with the other kids and he wanders into their yard?"

Julie took Olivia in her arms and pulled her close, stroking her hair. She hated what this was doing to her family.

"Olivia, this will all be over soon. I promise." She held her at arm's length as she told her about hiring the private investigator. "His name is Chuck Bishop. He has promised to get statements from the teachers and principal. Then he's going to interrogate the neighbors. Baby, she has lied to so many people about so many things. By the time Mr. Bishop has the goods on her, we'll have the proof we need to show the authorities."

Olivia wrapped her arms around her mom, holding her tight and wishing she could protect her mother from what she was sure was about to come.

CHAPTER 29

It was straight up noon when Julie finished scheduling the Lopez home inspection and the rest of her paperwork. She had time for a quick lunch, to let the dog outside to do her business, and to take a quick catnap.

Every time she closed her eyes, she thought about the chances of Will accidentally venturing into the Hennessy's yard. He was a child, after all. How many little boys had to worry about being charged with trespassing during a game of soccer or football? He was probably too young to actually be arrested, but the order did include his name, and there was no doubt in Julie's mind that Lynn would push to enforce the order with no regard whatsoever to Will's age or the circumstances. Maybe it wouldn't be Will that ended up in jail, but she didn't want it to be her, Tom, or Olivia either.

Then again, keeping him cooped up in the house was not an option. No, she'd have to set some definite ground rules about when and where he could play, that's for sure. And he'd never be able to play outside without an adult—ever.

Finally admitting to herself that she just couldn't relax, Julie gave up on the nap idea. She freshened her makeup, put on her shoes, and walked downstairs.

"Let's go outside and potty" she said to Colette, clipping the leash onto the dog's collar.

While Colette was walking in circles trying to find the perfect spot, Julie studied the back of the Lopez house, crossing her fingers that the upcoming home inspection wouldn't show any hidden defects. They were such a sweet family. More than anything, she just wanted the transition from this home to their new one to go smoothly. The roof, the siding, everything looked sturdy. But until an inspector got in there and dug around, you never really knew for sure.

She reached in her pocket for a treat for Colette when she glanced across her lawn and saw Lynn standing where the Hennessy/Lopez/Patterson yards met, Killer sitting obediently at her side.

For what seemed like an eternity, they just stared at each other, neither one daring to be the first to break eye contact. For once, Julie's emotions didn't get the best of her. She was calm, cool, and collected. Finally, the timing was perfect to ask Lynn the one question that had burned into her soul for so long.

"Why are you doing all of this?" Julie asked her, being extremely careful to stay as close to her house and as far back from the Hennessy's yard as she could. "Why did you make up lies about William being abused? Did you think the teachers wouldn't tell me that you'd reported me? Did you really think they'd believe you?"

She backed up more and pressed her back against the house. After yesterday's no trespass order, she wanted there to be no question exactly where she was standing.

Suddenly without provocation, Lynn started screaming.

"Help! Help! Oh my God! Somebody please help me! Help me! Keep her away from me!"

What is she doing? Julie thought, confused. This was going nowhere near as planned. Months and months of bottled-up frustration pushed its way up through her gut until it erupted into an angry outburst that even she didn't know she was capable of. "You are crazy! You need to be on medication!"

This was going all wrong. She had a flashback of the day Lynn had screamed obscenities at her, calling her names and wishing she were dead.

"*You're* the bitch!" *There, I've done it*, thought Julie as the words slipped out of her mouth. I have stooped to her level.

A confused construction crew started straggling into Lynn's yard to see why she was screaming, and she played it for all it was worth. "Did you just call me a bitch?"

"Yes, I did!" Julie said, very matter-of-fact, as she picked up Colette and marched into the house.

Finally, after all this time, the opportunity to confront Lynn had been dropped in her lap, and she had jumped at it. She paused for a moment, waiting for that strong sensation of satisfaction to wash through her. It never came.

CHAPTER 30

"Please stay here with me," Julie pleaded with Tom as he stood in front of the large mirror, shaving cream covering his face, the razor suspended in midair, listening while she explained what had just happened. He hadn't been feeling well that morning and decided to go in to the office late that day.

"Why in the world, with the way she has escalated things, would you ever try to approach her without me or someone else with you?" Tom asked in disbelief.

Julie stammered, "I ... I don't know. It was just me and her, and I just thought it'd be the perfect chance to finally ask her why. There was no else around for her to show off to, and so I—"

"Well, that's just great because now that you've actually confronted her you can probably expect another police visit," Tom chastised.

He was right. Fifteen minutes later, the doorbell rang. It was a policeman.

"Please have a seat. I'd like to wait until my husband comes down if you don't mind."

"I'm here," said Tom, coming down the stairs. He took a seat across from the officer. Julie sat on the couch beside Tom with Colette in her lap. The dog was shaking like a leaf which was indicative of exactly how she was feeling.

"I understand that you were served with a no trespass to stay off of Mrs. Hennessy's property" Officer Brown stated.

"That's correct," Julie answered, pointing to herself and then Tom. "Although, we haven't been on her property in well over a year."

"She says this morning you came across her yard and started screaming and calling her names," the policeman said.

"Absolutely not." She hoped he couldn't hear her heart pounding. On the outside, she was calm but adamant. "I absolutely did not go anywhere near her property line. I stayed with my back pressed against my house."

"However, I did call her the *b* word," she admitted sheepishly. "I know I shouldn't have done it; it just slipped out! A few months back, she let her dog loose on me, and she was screaming terrible things. Calling me the *b* word was one of the nicer things she said to me."

Officer Brown listened attentively to the recap of past events.

"So today when I tried to ask her *why*—that's all I wanted to know is why—she started screaming bloody murder and running around. When I realized what she was doing, I just got mad and frustrated!"

"But you didn't go in her yard?" the policeman asked a final time.

"No, sir," Julie replied. "Especially when I know that she is looking for a reason to have me prosecuted; there is no way I'd tempt her."

Officer Brown stood to leave. "Well, she demanded that I arrest you, insisting that you stopped short of attacking her."

Julie sat up straight. "Officer, I am a lady. I do not fight."

He didn't doubt it. He knew she was unnerved right now, scared that he was going to haul her in. He assured her that wasn't going to happen, at least not today.

"But I will warn you," the officer said, "Mrs. Hennessy was furious with me when I told her I wasn't going to arrest you. I told her to feel free to complain to my chief if she wanted, and if she thought I wasn't doing my job, she could always take her complaints to the magistrate judge. She was mad enough that you were going to, and I'm quoting here, 'get away with it again,' that she just might take me up on my suggestion."

Julie spoke through tears. "Now that she knows she can do that, I'm sure she will. I absolutely did not trespass in her yard nor did I even give the slightest impression that I was going to attack her."

"Why didn't you call us when she had her dog attack you and called you names?" the officer asked before he walked out the door.

"I had no clue that I had that option," Julie replied. "I thought you only called the police when someone was trying to break in or had gotten hurt. Besides, the dog didn't do any harm. And I certainly didn't know you could call the police on someone for cursing you out."

He reached in his front pocket and gave her his business card. His personal cell phone was scratched in pencil across the top.

"Carry this with you." He gave one to Tom. "Don't hesitate to call my cell phone if you need to."

"Thank you," said Tom as he gave the officer's hand a firm shake.

Closing the door to the squad car, he said to them through the open window; "I'm going to go over there again, and I'm going to tell her to stay away from you. Now, you do the same; don't try to talk to her or have anything at all to do with her. I'll instruct her to do the same; it's the best I can do."

"Thank you so much," said Julie, ever the optimist, feeling hopeful that once he talked with Lynn she'd back off and let them live in peace.

CHAPTER 31

By 3:00 that afternoon the skies were overcast, and it became a bit chilly, so she changed from a sleeveless, linen blouse to a powder pink sweater set. She gathered her hair behind her neck and clipped it back with a matching pink barrette. Grabbing her briefcase and keys, she closed the door and locked it. She didn't even make it to the car.

A police car pulled up and a young officer got out.

"Are you Mrs. Patterson?" he asked.

Julie felt sick at her stomach. Still, she smiled sweetly and answered, "Yes, I am."

"Oh man!" he said. "You are *not* what I expected!"

Something told her that was supposed to be a compliment, although she couldn't help but wonder just exactly what he was expecting.

"I am so sorry, ma'am, but I have to arrest you." He winced as he said the words.

Julie's heart was beating so fast she was sure it would jump out of her chest. Her hands were trembling. Still, she kept her poise, continued to smile, and led the officer to the front door. "Let's go inside."

The shiny rectangular name tag on his left pocket read, "Murrow."

"Okay, can you please tell me what's going on?" she asked Officer Murrow behind closed doors, trying to keep her composure.

"I have a warrant for your arrest," he said. "It's for trespassing and cursing and abuse."

"I did not trespass; I stayed on my property." She was amazed at how calm her voice was in comparison to how she was feeling.

But I did call her a name, she thought. Oh my goodness, Tom was right. Why didn't I just keep my mouth shut? Haven't I learned by now just how crazy Lynn is?

"I did call her the *b* word," Julie said, ashamed.

"Trust me, I've heard, said, and been called worse than that. In my book, that shouldn't count against you as curse and abuse. Besides, if that were the case, half the population of Virginia would be in jail by now."

"Then why are you here to arrest me?" she asked, confused. "Officer Brown already told Mrs. Hennessy that he wasn't going to."

He flipped open the small notebook he had been carrying and gave her the summons.

Her eyes almost popped out of her head as she read the charges filed with the Prince William County magistrate judge, dated, sworn, and signed by Lynn Hennessy.

> ... in the presence or hearing of another, curse or abuse of Lynn J. Hennessy, or use violent abusive language to such person concerning such person or any of the person's relations, or otherwise use of such language, under circumstances reasonable calculated to provoke a breach of the peace.

Officer Murrow handed her another.

> Without authority, trespass or remain upon the property of Lynn J. Hennessy, after having been forbidden to do so.

She folded the paper and gave it back to him.

Murrow said, "She went to the magistrate and wrote a sworn statement. That overrides our decision. Now I have no choice."

She eyed the handcuffs that were hanging from his belt and asked, "Do you have to cuff me?"

He hated this part of his job. "Yes, ma'am, I'm afraid so."

I cannot believe I am being arrested. Me!

'Am I allowed to take my phone with me?"

"Of course," he answered. "As a matter of fact, is there anyone you'd like to call before we leave?"

"Let me just call my husband real quick." She frantically dialed Tom's direct line.

"Hello," came his familiar voice.

"Tom, the police are here, and I'm being arrested," she said, still trying desperately not to cry.

"What!"

"Lynn went to the magistrate; I'm being arrested for trespass and curse and abuse."

"I'm calling Ron right now. Are they holding you or are they going to let you go?" He was talking so fast and so loud that Officer Murrow could hear him from halfway across the kitchen.

"I don't know," he replied. "It's up to the judge when we get there."

"I'll be right there, sweetheart," Tom said as he slammed the phone down.

"Okay," Julie said, trying to keep a lighthearted tone to her voice. "You take my phone." She held her wrists out for Murrow to put the handcuffs on her. The Tiffany heart bracelet she'd gotten from her family a few years before for her fortieth birthday and the diamond tennis bracelet were a stark contrast from the needle-marked, bruised arms Officer Murrow usually slapped cuffs on. Julie pulled her arms back, removed the jewelry, and offered her arms again.

She had never been so embarrassed and humiliated in her life. Here she was about to be arrested in broad daylight in front of her neighbors and passersby. Who would ever want to do business with her after this? Who would ever believe that she was the one who was the victim, not the criminal?

"I have an idea," Officer Murrow said quickly. "Why don't you walk around the corner like you're going for a walk, and I'll meet you there and then you jump in the back of the car real quick, and I'll cuff you before anyone sees it."

How sweet. How did he know she wasn't just pretending to be some sweet, helpless little Southern belle and then wouldn't take off running like a bat out of Hades when given the chance?

"No, sir," Julie said, straightening her posture, determined to retain her dignity. "You have a job to do, and I am going to make that job very easy for you. The only thing I ask is that you pull the car up just a tiny bit out of sight of Mrs. Hennessy's house. I'd rather not give her the glory of seeing me arrested."

Officer Murrow gave her a slight grin. "Absolutely. You wait here, and I'll pull the car up to where it's out of her sight. Then I'll motion for you to come out, and I'll have the back door open. Right as you get in, I'll have the cuffs ready, and then we'll get out of here hopefully before anyone sees us."

As hard as he tried, it didn't quite work out that way. Yes, he pulled up out of Lynn's window view; and he kept his word by discreetly motioning her to come to the car. But as luck would have it, as she was walking across the yard and as he was putting the handcuffs on her wrist, several of her neighbors drove by, gawking when they spotted the police car. Salena, from across the street, picked that particular time to walk out to the street to retrieve her mail. Stephanie Woods, a neighbor she knew in passing but had never been officially introduced to, strolled by with a 7-Eleven bag in one hand and the leash of her German shepherd in the other. How humiliating.

Murrow gently fastened the handcuffs on her wrist and purposely loosened them so that she could have slipped her hands out if she'd wanted. He still carried her cell phone in his hand and sat it down in the front seat beside him.

"Before I came to arrest you today, she called the station and complained that you were standing on your deck screaming and calling her names. Is that true?" asked Murrow.

"Oh my goodness, no," replied Julie truthfully. "I've been preparing for a home inspection at the house next door and—"

Oh no! Who was going to be there for the home inspector?

As if on cue, her phone rang.

Murrow picked up the phone, looked at caller ID, and asked, "Who is Stud Muffin?"

Julie blushed. "Uh, that's my husband, Tom. Will you please answer it?"

Earlier that week when she'd bought her new cell phone, Tom had decided to program his name into the caller ID list. The next day when she was showing clients around, her phone started ringing, and she'd had to smile at the name he'd assigned himself. Of course, at the time she had never dreamed she'd be riding hand-cuffed in the backseat of a police car when he called.

"Hello, Officer Murrow." Pause. "Yes, sir, I have her in the car now and am transporting her to the station on Route 1."

"Please ask him to call my boss so she can find someone to go to my home inspection." Julie pleaded just loud enough for him to hear her through the receiver.

"It's up to the magistrate once we get there," Murrow told Tom. "But I'll make sure he knows how much she's cooperated, and I'll do my best to persuade him to turn her loose on her own recognizance."

Just like she'd seen on television a million times, the officer took her mug shot and made a copy of her fingerprints. She felt like she was headed for judgment day as she was led down a long, narrow corridor. At the very end, a man sitting in a chair behind a glass wall divider watched her approach. It wasn't every day he saw a woman in heels, pearls, and handcuffs.

At the end of the hallway was a small enclave that was completely out of sight until Murrow and Julie reached the judge's window. Two men, one young and one middle-aged, were handcuffed and shackled to the wall. The young man had a bloody nose and cuts on his face. The older man was talking to himself and reeked of alcohol. Both did a double take when Julie appeared. There was no way Murrow could leave her there with those men.

"Just stand here by me," he ordered while he turned over a file to the judge. They spoke inaudibly with the judge reading the file and then looking over Murrow's shoulder to look at Julie.

The judge shook his head.

Within a few minutes, Murrow turned around and told Julie, "I've talked the judge into taking your case first so you can get out of here."

"Thank you," Julie answered but didn't look at him. She was too busy eyeing the sterile walls and ceiling, the tiles on the cold, hard floor. She shivered. She couldn't wait to get out of this place—she didn't belong here!

The judge was a rail thin, older man with half glasses perched upon the bridge of his long, skinny nose. He looked harsh, but his voice was harsher.

"I understand you've read the charges brought against you," he said. "When your neighbor first came in and filed this against you, I was only going to send the police over as a warning. But then she called back this afternoon and said you were harassing her, standing in your backyard and yelling things, obscenities, at her."

"No, sir," Julie said, sure he didn't believe her. "I would never do that."

"Well, you'll get your day in court, but today I just need you to sign here stating that you're being released and that you promise to show up in court.

"Now, if you can't afford a lawyer, one will be appointed to you," he continued.

Murrow stepped in. "She has a lawyer, sir. Ron Moorehouse."

The judge nudged a form and a pen under the gap of the thick, bulletproof window. Carefully reading each line, she signed her name and kept the carbon copy.

"I did not do this; I did not do these things she's accusing me of," she said softly to no one in particular. Officer Murrow looked at her sympathetically, but the judge wasn't buying it.

"Every criminal insists he's innocent," he snapped as he removed his glasses. "Prisons have no guilty people, you know"

She heard the snickering of the shackled men behind her as she felt her face get hot. She tucked the paper under one arm and held her cell phone and sweater in the other and walked as fast as she could toward the door without running, the sound of her heels echoing through the hall.

"Mrs. Patterson!" Officer Murrow called to her as he caught up with her. He held the door open from the inside as she stepped out. The sidewalks were wet and steam was coming up from the ground, proof that had it had been raining.

"I have an idea that might work," he said. She stopped and gave him her full attention.

"I'm listening."

"We have professional mediators whose sole purpose is to take situations like yours and counsel with both parties and work out a solution that helps everyone live peaceably," he offered. "Would you be willing to do that?"

"Of course I would," said Julie. "I just want this to stop so I can live in peace."

Just then Tom pulled up and came to an abrupt halt. Before she got in the car and drove away, Murrow told her, "I'll set up a time with the mediator and give you a call later tonight."

True to his word, he called at nine that night. Tom took the call, and Murrow told him to be at the police station the following morning at ten. He had talked with the Hennessys, and they too, surprisingly, had agreed to the session.

Julie couldn't wait. Now Lynn would have no choice but to fess up to what she'd done.

CHAPTER 32

Chuck Bishop rang the doorbell at 8:30 the next morning. Julie had called and asked him to meet with her and Tom before they left for the mediation. Even if Lynn were pressured, she knew she'd lie about the abuse accusations. But if Julie had the sworn statements from the two teachers and the principal, she would have exactly what she needed.

"This is absolutely perfect." Julie beamed as she read through his report. Anne's statement was the most significant. Her children didn't go to school at Enterprise. The teachers and school didn't know she existed, so how was it possible that her statement was exactly like theirs if Lynn hadn't fed her the same story?

"Thank you, thank you, thank you!" she cried. She hugged the report to her as if it were a treasured piece of classic literature. "Trust me, today all your hard work is going to pay off! This will all be over, and I will be vindicated."

"I was able to find Rhonda Wilkins and get a statement from her as well. She was hesitant to talk to me at first, but I convinced her that her testimony just might save someone else from going through the hell that she went through, so she agreed. Unfortunately, I had no luck in tracking down Mrs. McKinney."

"I didn't expect you to," Julie replied, only slightly disappointed. "They left absolutely no trail when they left here."

She thanked him again, and Chuck made her promise to stay in touch, to let him know how everything worked out.

When Tom pulled into the police station parking lot, Julie felt elated.

In a few short minutes, Lynn Hennessy, I will sit face-to-face with you and ask you point blank every question I have. And you will have no choice but to answer.

Tom scanned the parking lot to see if he could spot Rick and Lynn's vehicle. Obviously, he and Julie were the first ones there. Julie almost sprinted out of the car.

"Stay calm," he warned her. "You don't want to appear overanxious."

He was right. She slowed down and took a deep breath. Throwing her purse over her shoulder and still holding the private investigators report close to her, she walked through the front door of the police station with Tom right behind her. She looked around the lobby. She didn't see the Hennessys. Either they hadn't arrived yet or they were already in the mediation room.

She spotted Officer Murrow. Tom could tell by the expression on the policeman's face that something wasn't quite right.

"Bad news," Murrow said as they approached. "They aren't coming."

It broke Toms heart as he watched Julie wilt like a fragile flower.

"I thought this was all set up and ready to go," he said. "What changed?"

Murrow shrugged. "I don't know. Mr. Hennessy called me this morning, and all he said was that they changed their minds and they're not coming."

Julie plopped down in one of the lobby chairs. She looked down at the notebook in her lap, the notebook that was to prove her innocence, prove that she was the victim, not the criminal. Now she'd have to go to court to prove it.

Tom wasn't ready to throw in the towel. "Who is the chief of police?"

"Roy Davis," Murrow answered.

"Then get us in to see him," Tom insisted.

Julie's head snapped up. "Yes, please, can we see him? I have a sworn statement from a witness that states that I never left my yard. I'll accept the charge for curse and abuse, but I absolutely did not trespass!"

Murrow agreed. "Follow me."

They went through the security checkpoint, Tom emptying the contents of his pocket and Julie placing her purse on the desk for inspection. Once given the all clear, Murrow keyed in his code to the steel door and led the couple to a reception desk.

Murrow greeted the elderly woman who was typing away on her computer with the phone in the crook of her neck. She gave him the thumbs-up and pointed to Chief Davis's office and nodded her permission for him to go inside.

Murrow disappeared in the chief's office.

"I'm really not interested in looking at your book," Chief Davis said coldly after listening to Julie's pleas for protection. "I think this is nothing more than a neighborhood dispute, and now you're just mad and looking for revenge."

Julie dissolved into tears as she pleaded with the chief. "Please look at this report. It will show you that I have put up with this nightmare for years, and now it's going to a very dangerous level."

But he wouldn't budge. "You have to understand, Mrs. Patterson and Mr. Patterson, that any time someone calls one of my officers on a complaint, he or she has no choice but to respond."

"I understand that," snapped Tom. "But how far does this have to go before I can get some kind of protection for my wife, for my family? What are you going to do to protect *us*?"

"To their defense, sir"—Murrow decided to step in—"Mrs. Hennessy knows how to work the system. I've seen past reports where she's called us and wanted us to arrest Mrs. Patterson. This time when we refused to arrest her after witnesses told us that she didn't go on Mrs. Hennessy's property, Mrs. Hennessy went to the magistrate."

"Then why was she arrested?" Tom asked. "Why does going to the magistrate have precedence over the police?"

"Because if the police feel they don't have the proof they need to make an arrest, the victim can go to the magistrate. The fact that it is a sworn statement of truth by the victim overrides the police decision," Chief Davis explained.

"But *I* am the victim," Julie cried. "Please, please tell me what I have to do, who I have to talk to, to get some kind of protection. I was arrested for a crime I did not commit!"

"And you'll get your day in court," the chief reasoned. 'At that time, you'll be able to tell the judge your side of the story."

"I shouldn't have to do that! I should not have to spend money unnecessarily to prove that I am innocent! The only thing I am guilty of is calling her a bad name, and it took me years of putting up with false accusations, stalking, and vandalism of my property to even get to that point! Out of desperation, I finally hired a private investigator."

"Then you'll have to tell that to the judge when you go to court," the chief answered and rose from his chair to indicate the meeting was being adjourned.

"If you'll just take a look at this, it will show you that I am not the first person she's done this to." Julie wasn't giving up just yet.

Murrow spoke up again. "Chief I had a mediation meeting set up between both parties for this morning. Both parties agreed to be here, but at the last minute, the Hennessys called and canceled. I feel that at least Mrs. Patterson wants to work through this."

Once again, the chief voiced his disinterest in seeing the documents. His county had the biggest immigration problem in the United States. Neighborhood disputes were the least of his concerns.

"You're not interested?" Tom was heated. "We come to you with proof that my wife is being stalked, harassed, and now arrested, and you're not interested? Fine! Come on, let's go." Before walking out the door, he turned, pointed his finger at Chief Davis, and said,

"If anything happens to my wife, I'm holding you personally responsible."

Murrow thought his boss could be handling this a lot better than he was, at least glance at the documents, but he knew better than to argue with the guy, especially in front of civilians. Hopefully, the Pattersons would keep his card and would call if they got in a bind.

"Gee, I guess you ladies just can't get enough of each other, can you?" Ron Moorehouse joked as Tom and Julie took a seat in their attorney's office.

"Just stop," Tom snapped. "Everyone, including me, should have listened to Julie and taken this more seriously from the get-go. If we had, we wouldn't be in this position right now."

"I'm sorry." His client was obviously distraught. "I was just trying to lighten the mood a bit." Her file was on his desk, so he immediately referred to the arrest report that had been faxed to him the day before.

"Your court date is in less than a month, so I need to go over everything that happened, starting at the beginning of the altercation."

"There was no altercation. That's what I'm trying to tell everyone. I stood with my back against my house. I simply tried to have a conversation with her, and she went berserk. End of story. Well, not exactly. I did call her a bitch."

He chuckled. "I hardly think that constitutes curse and abuse. Anyway, do you have any witnesses?"

Julie answered, "Yes. No. Not really." Ron gave her a confused look. "A neighbor across the street was outside. She could see Mrs. Hennessy running around in circles screaming for help, but since I wasn't in the yard she didn't see me. Does that make sense?"

He was furiously writing notes on a tablet. "Have the private investigator take pictures of the area. Take pictures of your yard, her yard. Didn't you say that your yard is adjacent to hers?"

Julie nodded. "Yes, that's correct."

"Also, take pictures of where you were standing, she was standing. Now, according to this arrest report, your court date is set for two and a half weeks from now."

Julie asked quietly, "What is going to happen? I... I've never been to court before, and I have no idea what to expect."

Ron removed his glasses and folded his hands together and laid them on the desk. He looked her square in the eye. "The normal sentence for trespassing is a year, but..."

She sucked in her breath like she'd been kicked in the stomach. A year? She couldn't be away from her family, her little William, for that long!

Tom started to speak, but Ron held his hand up before he could get a word out. "The normal sentence *if you're found guilty* is a year, but since you have no previous record at all, you'd probably get a suspended sentence of six months, maybe less."

"That's for the trespass," Tom said. "What about the curse and abuse charge?"

"That would just be a fine. And, of course, it would be a misdemeanor that would stay on your record." He looked at Julie.

How could this be happening? Julie thought. How could this possibly be happening to her? She'd never been in trouble before. Her whole life she'd been teased for being so squeaky clean. What would everyone back home in Mississippi think if they knew she'd been arrested? What would they think if she went to jail? Worse, what would Mama and Daddy think? And while she might not be guilty of the trespassing charges, she couldn't deny the fact that she was indeed guilty of the curse and abuse.

It was 2:00 a.m. Everyone had been in bed for hours except for Tom, and he was too angry to sleep. Enraged was more like it, not only at Lynn but also at himself, *mostly* at himself.

Julie had tried to tell him what was happening, pleaded with him to take it more seriously. It wasn't that he didn't take the situation seriously. He just thought that this wacko would get bored and give up.

After Julie's arrest, he realized that she'd been right all along. Why hadn't he listened to her? He had been too busy with his career, too busy trying to get ahead, that's why. He didn't think she really needed him. There was nothing she couldn't handle. Or so he'd thought.

He had let her down. Tears spilled over onto his cheeks. Julie didn't know it, but he had heard her talking on the phone with her mother a few nights ago. She thought he was asleep, but he had gotten up to get a drink of water.

"Mama, I'm coming home," she'd said. Her voice was stone cold. Her eyes were dry. That's what had scared him the most, the fact that she wasn't even crying. "No, it's not a visit. I'm leaving Tom." Silence. "No, I'm not going back to Jackson. I was hoping I could move back to Portman, in with you and Daddy. Just for a little while, just until I can get on my feet."

He didn't move a muscle, afraid the floor would creak or that he'd make a noise to alert her that he was listening. She was silent for a long time, and although he couldn't make out the words, he could hear his mother-in-law's voice through the receiver.

"I love you too, Mama," Julie said after a while. Now her voice was starting to crack. "Yes, Mama, I have tried." Silence again. "Yes, Mama, I'll stick it out for a little while longer, just for you, but only because you're asking me to, because honestly, I don't think I love him anymore."

He felt like the wind had just been knocked out of him. He turned and tiptoed back to bed and pretended to be asleep. When she came to bed later, he turned over and wrapped his arms around her, pulling her close, holding on to her for dear life.

He would never forget how she looked when he picked her up at the police station, the terror in her pretty eyes, the cuts on her tiny wrists from where the handcuffs had rubbed them raw, even though she'd sworn they were loose.

How could he have been so selfish? He had always criticized men that cheated on their wives, but he himself had let another woman come between them in ways that neither one of them could ever imagine.

CHAPTER 33

"Your Honor, this is a case about bullying. The defendant is charged with violating Virginia 18.2-416, but, in fact, this case is about bullying."

Julie sat stoically in the seat next to Ron as she listened to the prosecuting attorney begin the opening arguments. This was the first time she'd ever been in a courtroom. She had expected the prosecuting attorney to look like Sam Waterston on Law and Order. Instead he looked like a slick politician you'd see on the cover of a glossy magazine with thick, combed-back hair and an expensive black suit.

"The evidence will show that after Mrs. Patterson saw my client, she went through another neighbor's yard and into Mrs. Hennessy's yard to confront her. On two occasions during this confrontation while she was trespassing, she called Mrs. Hennessy vile and disgusting names. Her demeanor was threatening and angry and lasted well over ten minutes."

Julie cringed. *That's me he's talking about. Me. How embarrassing.*

"This confrontation was a physical threat to my client, Mrs. Hennessy, and was witnessed by at least one other person, a neighbor."

Witness? What witness? She had seen the construction crew at the time of the incident, but they had all given statements to the investigator that they saw or heard nothing from no one other than Lynn.

If Julie hadn't admitted to the curse and abuse, no one would have been the wiser. It would have been her word against Lynn's. But that's not how she operated. If she was nothing else, at least she was honest. Even if it meant she'd have a criminal record.

All she'd wanted to know was why. *Why?* She had every right to know, to ask, and Lynn had twisted it all around. As far as Julie was concerned, Lynn was actually what Julie had called her.

After the prosecutor's statements, Ron stood, buttoned his suit jacket, and calmly began making his case.

"Your Honor, I believe that the evidence will show in this case that the parties were far away from each other, at least thirty-five to forty feet. My client freely admits that she used the *b* word in reference to Mrs. Hennessy. But what we have before us is the age-old battle of what has deemed to be freedom of speech. The evidence will show that my client was attempting to clear the air over a situation that has been ongoing for two years. She basically got disgusted at what she perceived to be an inappropriate response by Mrs. Hennessy, called her the word, broke off the discussion, turned, and walked away."

Julie listened intently while Ron wrapped up the opening statements. She turned and caught a glimpse of Tom sitting six rows behind her. He gave her a quick wink. Before she turned back to face the front, she caught a glimpse of several people from their church, including their minister and his wife, filling up the whole seat behind Tom.

The prosecutor called the first witness, which happened to be Lynn. She was in her element and couldn't wait to get on the stand. This was her moment to shine. Her thick, dark hair was loose around her shoulders, and she was wearing a plain, black pantsuit and three-inch black pumps. On her shoulder she was lugging a large, leather purse. She put her hand on the Bible while she swore to tell the "truth, the whole truth, and nothing but the truth, so help me God."

All eyes were on her as she gently put her purse underneath the witness chair and sat down.

"Mrs. Hennessy," the prosecution began, "can you please tell the court what happened on July 13 of this year?"

"Of course. I was outside with my dog, and all of a sudden Mrs. Patterson came out of nowhere. She was screaming and calling me names, and she just kept coming at me, and I told her to stop! We'd just had the police issue a no trespass against her, and I reminded her that she wasn't supposed to be in our yard. But she just kept coming toward me and screaming."

"And what did she say to you?" asked the attorney. "Could you understand her?"

"Yes, I could. She came at me really fast; I was afraid she was going to hit me, and she started screaming, 'Do you think a no trespass order is going to keep me off your property?' Then she just kept calling me a bitch over and over."

Ron jumped up. "Objection! How many times is over and over? In the police report, the witness states that she was called a bitch twice."

"On to the next question, please," the judge said.

"What was your relationship with Mrs. Patterson like when you first met her?" asked the prosecutor.

"We got along great. We got to be really good friends. We socialized, went shopping together; our husbands were friends."

The prosecutor, slowly pacing with his hands behind his back, asked her to describe what had happened to change that relationship.

"It went sour when she accused me of reporting her to the school for child abuse," Lynn answered.

"And did you?"

"Absolutely not. But no matter what I said or did, I just couldn't convince her that I didn't do this," she said. "She just refused to believe me."

"How did your life change after that?" the prosecutor asked.

"It's been dreadful," said Lynn, her voice cracking as she wiped away tear. "We used to love living in our home and our neighborhood, and now this woman, Mrs. Patterson, has made my life a living hell. I can't step outside my house without her following me everywhere. When I go to the store, walk the dog, or even step out on my lawn, she's always there lurking. I finally had to stop walking my dog because one night she assaulted me—"

"Objection!" cried Ron loudly, startling Julie.

"On what grounds?" asked the annoyed prosecutor. "Mrs. Hennessy is simply stating an event that happened and—"

"To which the police refused to arrest my client because two witnesses at the scene stated in a police report right here"—he reached in his briefcase and produced said report—"that the incident did not happen."

"You'll get your chance to cross-examine the witness, Mr. Moorehouse," replied the judge and then looking back to Lynn said, "Please continue, Mrs. Hennessy."

"It's always something with her. She follows me while I'm driving places; she harasses me. I can't even go in my own yard without her coming outside and screaming embarrassing, vulgar names at me. And this deal with the school; we even called the principal and asked him to set up a meeting for the four of us. He said sure. Well, he set up the meeting, and the next morning when we went, he told us that the Patterson's had declined at the last minute."

We refused? It was all Julie could do to keep from jumping over the witness stand and grabbing Lynn by her hair. How could she keep getting away with lie after lie, especially when she'd just sworn on the Holy Bible to tell the truth?

"The night she hit me, my husband wanted to get a no trespass order against her. But I just couldn't."

She looked directly at Julie, wiped a tear from her eye, and then continued, "We had been such good friends, and I just wasn't ready to take such drastic measures. So instead we called the officer and asked him to set up mediation." She sniffed and wiped her eyes with the tissue again. "Maybe then I could find out why, why she's accusing me of all these things.

"The next morning, we got to the police station, and they told us that the Patterson's had declined. We decided right then and there that we had no choice but to request the no trespass.

"I mean, I'm scared out of my wits; I don't know what she'll do next. I really think she's going through some kind of—"

"Objection! Mrs. Hennessy is not a psychiatrist," Ron said.

"Just stick with the facts, Mrs. Hennessy," the judge admonished her.

"No more questions, Your Honor," the prosecutor concluded.

Ron stood up and approached the railing where Lynn was sitting.

"Are you a truthful person, Mrs. Hennessy?" He asked the question in a nonthreatening way, almost charming.

"Yes," said Lynn, not unconvincingly.

"So you'd call yourself honest. Is that correct?"

"Yes, sir. I'm a very honest person."

"You never lie?"

"Absolutely not."

"Have you ever been convicted of a crime?"

Lynn froze. She looked over at the prosecutor, waiting for him to object. Nothing. He didn't even look up from his notes.

"Maybe you didn't hear me," Ron said as he crossed his arms over his chest. "So I'll repeat the question. Have you ever been convicted of a crime?"

Her voice was testy. "What does that have to do with anything?"

"Just answer the question," the judge said.

"No," she answered, her mouth pursed.

Julie sighed. She was getting restless. Where was he headed with this?

"I need to remind you that you're under oath," Ron continued. "And of course lying under oath is perjury, which is a crime. So, one more time, for the record, have you ever been convicted of a crime?"

"Yes," she finally answered grudgingly.

"Do you care to tell the court what that conviction was for?" Ron said.

"Shoplifting." Her body stiffened as she sat on the edge of the chair, lifting her chin defiantly.

Shoplifting? Julie almost laughed out loud.

"Felony shoplifting," Ron asserted. "Not once, but twice."

"That was a long time ago; I was just a kid," she responded.

Ron walked back to the desk, looking over his shoulder at her while he asked, "Really? You were just a kid?"

He reached in the briefcase and returned to the witness stand with two pieces of paper in his hand.

"I just happened to have a copy of your arrest, which has your birth date recorded right here." He pointed it out. "If my math is correct, you are forty-two years old. Then, as I move down here, it says that at the time of your first arrest you were thirty-six years old and your next arrest you were thirty-eight."

Lynn's face was beet red.

"And you expect the court to believe that you are truthful? I'm finished, Your Honor."

The judge dismissed Lynn. The prosecutor approached the bench and asked to call the next witness, the one who could place Julie in the Hennessy's yard as the charges stated.

How on earth could a witness place me somewhere I wasn't? Julie wondered.

A large woman with a long, gray mullet and wearing polyester pants and flowered smock walked up to the stand. She looked familiar to Julie, but yet she couldn't place her. She watched while the woman was being sworn in, racking her brain trying to remember how she knew her.

"Please state your name for the court," the prosecutor ordered.

"My name is Lois Zimmer." The woman complied. She placed her hand on the Bible and was sworn in.

Now I remember her, Julie thought. She was mixed in with the construction crew that rushed to Lynn's yard to check out the commotion. Why was she here now, testifying for the prosecution?

"Tell me what you witnessed that day in Mrs. Hennessy's yard," the prosecutor said.

Obviously nervous, she leaned her head in too close to the mic and made a loud swooshing noise when she started to speak. A bit embarrassed, she leaned back as she started once again to speak.

"I was in the neighborhood walking with a friend; I live in another neighborhood and came over to walk with her. I saw Lynn, er, I mean Mrs. Hennessy, and I waved to her. She didn't see me, so I started to walk down there. As I got closer, I saw that she was distressed, and she started screaming and calling for help. As I got closer, I saw that Mr. Hennessy was sitting in his car, and I thought maybe they were arguing or something."

Julie whispered in Ron's ear, "That's a lie. Rick had already left for work because I saw him drive off when I walked out the door, and he didn't come back until the police were there."

Ron stared straight ahead, not acknowledging the fact that Julie had just spoken to him, keeping his focus on the witness.

"No more questions, Ms. Zimmer. You may step down." The woman stood up and waddled out of the courtroom while Ron stood up to call another witness to the stand.

"The defense calls Mrs. Blanche Burns to the witness stand, Your Honor."

Blanche answered every question methodically and gave her account of everything that happened that day. She told the court of how she had waved at Rick Hennessy that morning as he drove by in his shiny, black Mustang. She was taking the trash out to the curb and caught a glimpse of Lynn standing by the street. Two seconds later, as she turned to walk to the house, she heard Lynn's shrieking cries of help. Blanche stopped to gawk at the woman's bizarre behavior. She could never figure out who Lynn was afraid of or why she needed help. Blanche had full view of Lynn's yard, and there was absolutely no one there. No one. Period.

"Also, before we finish, Mrs. Burns, wasn't there another incident where Mrs. Hennessy tried to bring charges against Mrs. Patterson? Charges for an assault that never happened?"

"Objection. That's hearsay!" cried the prosecutor.

"Your Honor," argued Ron, "it's not hearsay if Mrs. Burns was actually there when the alleged incident occurred, or *didn't* occur, in this case."

"Proceed, Mr. Moorehouse," said the judge.

Ron turned back to Blanche. "Yes," she said. "She accused Mrs. Patterson of running at her and pushing her to the ground. I was there; she even called me as a witness, Mrs. Hennessy did. Anyway, I was there and that never happened. Mrs. Patterson never approached Mrs. Hennessy; the two never even spoke to each other."

"Is this the same statement you gave to the police?" Ron asked.

"Yes, sir, it is."

"Your witness," Ron said to the prosecutor.

The questioning from the prosecutor was weak at its best. Blanche was a tough cookie and stuck to her guns even when questions were twisted and reworded in hopes of tripping her up.

Finally giving up, he dismissed her. Ron stood once again. "I have one more witness. Mr. Sam Watkins, Your Honor."

Sam Watkins? Why was that name so familiar? The doors to the courtroom opened, and as soon as he walked in, Julie remembered him as the man who was putting up the barbed wire above his fence to keep people from climbing over, one of them being Lynn's son.

"Mr. Watkins, would you please tell the court where you were and what you saw that day in question," Ron asked Sam.

"Yes, sir. It was about 8:15 or 8:20, and I was actually on my way home from walking the dog. I walked by Mrs. Patterson's house first. I saw her standing beside her house, and she was talking to someone. I had no clue who she was talking to; it almost looked like she was talking to herself. All of a sudden, I heard someone, another woman, start screaming like she was in pain or something. I mean, it was a really shrill scream. I saw Mrs. Patterson just kind of throw her arms up in disgust. She told someone—once again I couldn't see who it, was—but she called someone a bitch and then went in the house."

"Did you ever at any time see Mrs. Patterson and Mrs. Hennessy together?" asked Ron.

"No."

"Why couldn't you see both of them at the same time?" Ron asked.

"Because there was a house between them. Both of them were in their respective yards, and they were separated by the Lopez house."

"You never, at any time, saw Mrs. Patterson cross over into Mrs. Hennessy's yard?"

"No, never." Sam was adamant. "And I was there the whole time. Nothing happened. Absolutely nothing."

"What is the reputation of Mrs. Hennessy?"

"Objection! That's hearsay, Your Honor," the prosecutor interjected.

"That's fair," Ron answered. He thought for a moment and regrouped. "Mr. Watkins, what has been your *experience* with Mrs. Hennessy?"

"Everyone and his brother think they can take a shortcut through my yard to walk up to 7-Eleven. I've asked people politely over and over again to please stay off my grass. So many people cut through that it's starting to wear a path through my yard, and they trample my flowers. The Hennessy lady's kid is the worst. So I put up a no trespassing sign, and next thing I know, she's pounding on my door. She said that she was a realtor, and she had proof that there was an easement on my property that gives her kid and anybody else that wants to permission to cut through my yard," Sam explained. "She is not a realtor. I called the Virginia Department of Professional and Occupational Regulation people."

"And what did they tell you?" Ron asked.

"That Lynn Hennessy is not, and never has been, a real estate agent," Sam said flatly.

"Thank you," said Ron, dismissing Sam from the bench. "No further questions."

Taking his cue from the judge, the prosecutor stood to make his closing arguments.

"Your Honor, we have a witness that puts Mrs. Patterson in the defendant's yard. This witness has absolutely nothing to gain; she doesn't even live in the neighborhood. She was just being a good citizen and coming to the rescue of a person in need. Mrs. Patterson had received proper notice to not trespass onto the Hennessy's property. She maliciously ignored that court order and trespassed with the intention of causing harm to the plaintiff. On top of that, she further insulted and humiliated the plaintiff by calling her every name in the book.

"We ask that the court find Mrs. Patterson guilty and prosecute her to the fullest extent of the law and that she be ordered to take anger management classes."

Anger management classes! Me? Julie anxiously watched the judge, looking for some kind of sign of what he was thinking, but his face was expressionless as he gestured for the defense to make their closing remarks. Ron took his position in front of the judge.

"Your Honor, Mrs. Patterson freely admits that after becoming frustrated with trying unsuccessfully to work out problems with Mrs. Hennessy that she called her a bitch, which, by the way, if you look in the dictionary, is a word that is used to describe an ill-tempered woman. So, yes, if she's guilty of anything, it is that. However, if you'll look at the law of curse and abuse, you'll find that it is described as trying to disturb the peace or using it to make someone feel threatened or vile and abusive.

"We have two witnesses, *two* witnesses, who, while they live in the same neighborhood, don't know each other, don't socialize. Both witnesses, while watching the events unfold from different angles, still tell the same story, that Mrs. Patterson at no point ever left her yard or ever threatened Mrs. Hennessy. We have proof, especially from arrest records, that Mrs. Hennessy is lacking in moral turpitude and has no trouble misrepresenting the truth, in other words, lying. I ask that the court dismiss these charges and find my client not guilty."

Adjusting his glasses, the judge glared down his glasses at Julie. Under his scrutiny, Ron stood up and nudged Julie's elbow slightly. She too stood to face the judge.

Fear had settled in the pit of her stomach, and she had to grip the edge of the desk to steady herself.

"Well, after listening to both the prosecution and defense, I am not fully convinced that Mrs. Patterson was actually trespassing. And while Mrs. Patterson does admit to calling the plaintiff the least vile of the words, they were not, I believe, spoken face-to-face in a threatening manner. According to testimony of all the witnesses, both the plaintiff and the defendant had their dogs with them, one of them being a large dog, a Rottweiler. I am convinced that the animals would have sensed the animosity between their owners. If there was as much of a threat as the plaintiff insists, then I believe those dogs would have been trying to get at each other or barking like mad, to say the least. No one ever made mention of that fact." He hit the gavel on the desk. "I hereby pronounce the defendant, Mrs. Julie Patterson, not guilty."

CHAPTER 34

"Okay, kiddo, that should do it for your school supplies," Tom said to Will as he checked the last item off the list.

"I can't believe you're going into third grade!" Julie cried mock tears as they stepped into the first available checkout at Office Depot. They'd waited to the last minute to shop, as seemed to be the story with everyone, given the line was twenty people long. "How about after this we go to the mall and buy you some new school clothes?" Tom suggested.

"Can I buy some new tennis shoes?" Will looked up at his father and asked.

"I don't see why not," Tom replied, ruffling the boy's hair. The kid was so cute; it was hard to tell him no to anything.

An hour later, the three were fighting the back-to-school crowd at Potomac Mills shopping mall. The good thing about shopping with little boys versus teenage girls was that Will was happy to go to one store. Julie would always have to walk the mall two or three times before Olivia would make her decision.

Not Will. He'd find what he wanted, and then he'd want to rush home so he could play outside with his buddies.

They only spent about thirty minutes at the mall, and while his parents were unloading the goodies from the car, Will reached inside the garage, grabbed his baseball mitt, and darted across the street where the other kids were playing baseball.

Julie picked up the new issue of *Southern Living* and sat quietly on the front porch so she could keep an eye on him.

She may have been cleared of the bogus charges, but the no trespass order was still firmly in place. There was no way Will could be allowed to play outside by himself.

"A penny for your thoughts."

"Oh hey, Anne." Julie smiled. She put the magazine aside and stood to give her friend a big squeeze. "My goodness, it's good to see you. It seems like ages."

"Well, gee," answered Anne. "You've been kind of busy trying to stay out jail, haven't you? Thanks for the phone call though. Bob saved your message on the answering machine. I was so relieved that you got through the court ordeal okay and that you were found not guilty."

"It was pretty scary," Julie said. "It's like she has no conscience at all. She puts her hand on the Bible, makes a promise in front of God to tell the truth, and then every word that comes out of her mouth is nothing but a lie. I was shocked.

"But then, I shouldn't have been. After all, she does her best with a captive audience."

Anne shook her head. "I know. That had to have been hard."

They sat in silence for a moment. Julie sensed that something was up. Anne had something she needed to tell Julie, but she dreaded it.

"Okay, Anne. Out with it."

Anne took a deep breath and rolled her eyes. "Lynn came over yesterday."

Julie put up her hand and shook her head no. "Never mind. I don't want to hear it."

"You need to know this, sweetie."

"What?" Julie braced herself. "What on earth is she doing now?"

"She is telling everyone in the neighborhood that you were found guilty of all charges and that your punishment was five years of probation and a ten-thousand-dollar fine."

Julie sat there stunned for a moment. Then she burst into laughter.

"You can't be serious," Julie said when the laughter subsided. "You just cannot be serious."

"She also said the judge issued a special restraining order, but she is still afraid that you're going to continue stalking her."

"She's telling *everyone* this?" Julie felt silly for thinking that maybe Lynn would give up on this campaign once court was over.

"She wants everyone to know that the justice system failed and that you're free to continue stalking and harassing her, and she needs everyone's watchful eye to make sure you don't come near her."

"When did she start doing this?" Julie asked quietly.

"The day she came home from the court hearing. When she left us, I watched her go from house to house. A few of the newer neighbors were asking me about it later, wanting to know if it was true."

Julie's pained expression broke Anne's heart.

"Don't worry," Anne reassured her. "I told them that it wasn't true, that you'd been found not guilty on all counts."

"I appreciate you sticking up for me, Anne. You're such a good friend. Plus, I know it's hard for you to be in the middle."

"It's all right. I just worry about you. She is hell-bent on ruining you one way or another. If she can't send you to jail, then by golly, she's going to ruin your reputation."

"I'll be all right." Julie forced a smile. "They don't call us Southern girls steel magnolias for nothing."

When Anne left, she tried to hunker down and refocus on her magazine, but it was impossible. The fact was the rumors and lies were taking their toll on Julie's business. She had lost several listing contracts due to the fact that clients were afraid to have for sale signs with Julie's name riders on them. She had explained to clients that she could simply leave her name off; no one had to know that she was the realtor. Some made the point that news traveled fast in that subdivision, and within a week it would be common knowledge. A few were afraid their homes would be vandalized by their association with her, and they just couldn't take that chance. One couple changed their mind because they didn't want to do business with someone that had an arrest record.

Julie allowed Will to play outside for an hour before she called him in. She prepared dinner for the guys, and they headed out to a movie afterwards. She decided to take advantage of a night alone and go to her office and catch up on a mountain-size stack of filing.

The office had an eerie stillness about it, but she was able to knock out several folders full of loose addendums and place them in their respective files. It was amazing how much a person could get done when she didn't have to answer nonstop phones and random visits from coworkers.

Before leaving, she stopped off at the mailroom. Her box was stuffed full of neglected mail. "Kind of like my career as of late," she said aloud to herself. Neglected.

The bulk of the mail was advertisements, credit card applications, and old, out-of-date flyers, all of which went into the big silver trash bin. The rest was made up of thank-you cards from recent clients, invitations to several upcoming events that she slid into the side pocket of her leather bag, and two commission checks that she kept inside the envelope and carried in hand to her car.

Tom and Will would more than likely stuff themselves with hot dogs and chips at the movies, so she pulled into the drive-thru for her guilty pleasure of nachos. She'd asked the young man at the checkout window to wrap the food in an extra bag, so she wouldn't spill anything on the papers and files that she had laid down beside her in the passenger seat.

When she got the food, she realized that he'd wrapped it in a flimsy plastic bag. Deciding not to argue for another bag, she simply put her Diet Pepsi in the cup holder and very carefully situated the nachos on top of the papers, placing a spare napkin underneath.

I'll just drive extra careful, she thought. She'd forgotten that she'd had those checks coming to her, so that had been a nice little surprise. As much as the court costs and attorney fees had been, not to mention the price of the private investigator, that money was definitely going to come in handy.

Luckily no one was behind her when she turned left onto Tobacco Way, as her left blinker had been busted out and she hadn't taken the time to have it fixed.

She hadn't planned on staying out past dark to where it would be so noticeable, but as she looked at her watch, she saw that it was eight forty-five. As she prepared to turn left again onto Raye Street, there was just enough light from the street lamp to see Lynn and her daughter, Hannah, standing on the curb by the Raye and Tobacco Way street sign.

That's just great, Julie thought. She'll probably report me for having the broken tail light.

She turned the corner very carefully and slowly so as not to spill her food on the papers, especially not the commission checks that totaled nearly twenty thousand dollars. She parked in the driveway at the same time her next-door neighbor, Brooke Williams, was at her mailbox.

"Hi, Brooke!" Julie called to her as she climbed out from behind the wheel. "How are you? I haven't seen you in ages. How did that big presentation go, the one you were working on back in June?"

"Has it been that long since we've talked?" Brooke asked, slowly walking over to Julie. "It went better than I ever expected. As a matter of fact, I was promoted to the head of my department very shortly after that."

"That must have been some presentation!" Julie gave a big thumbs-up. "Congratulations!"

She wanted to inquire about John and how the two of them were coping with both girls away at college, but behind Brooke, in the dark, she could just make out two small female figures walking in their direction. *No drama tonight, thank you very much.*

"I better get inside. My dinner is in the car, and I don't want it to get cold. I'll talk to you soon!"

"Don't make it so long this time!" Brooke said as she bid Julie goodbye.

Safely inside, Julie slipped in her favorite DVD, placed her nachos, drink, and a few napkins on a TV tray, and settled in to watch Meg Ryan in *You've Got Mail*.

The next thing she knew, she was waking up to Colette barking as if the house were on fire, chasing a giggling William throughout the house.

"Ouch! Ouch!" He laughed as the small dog snapped at his ankles. Julie yawned and stretched as she threw back the plaid blanket and placed her feet on the hardwood floor.

"How was the movie?" she asked.

"Well, several tall buildings got blown up, but no one was maimed or killed," answered Tom.

"So, in other words, it was just okay, not great."

Tom bent down to kiss her on the lips and then sat down beside her.

"I have an idea," he said, facing her and clasping both hands in his. "But first I need to ask you a question, and I need you to be honest with me."

"Aren't I always?"

"Before I tell you my idea, I need to know something. Do you still want to move?"

Julie sat forward and propped the pillow behind her back. Where was this coming from? He had been so dead set against her suggestion of moving a while back that she hadn't dared broach the subject again. His nasty remarks had pushed her over the edge, almost to the point of leaving. What had changed his mind?

"As your wife, trust me, I want to move. But speaking as your realtor, right now we can't afford to do it. We've already spent money out the wahoo on legal fees and court costs. And now with the way these home prices are skyrocketing? No one at the office believes me, but I'm telling you this market is going to crash, home equities will plummet, and there will be a lot of people losing their homes. We just can't afford for that to happen. We'd never recover."

"Okay," said Tom. "Then here's what I'd like to do. Let's have a contractor come in and give us an estimate on what it would cost to finish the basement and build a fence to close up the yard. We do still have some money in savings that should allow us to do that. That way, Will and his friends could play in the backyard, and we wouldn't have to worry about him. The room under the sunroom could be a home theatre room, and we could build in a little kitchenette."

It would be perfect. The basement was spacious and could be divided up into many rooms. It would be fun to decorate, and the thought of a theater room excited Julie. The best part, though, was that they'd be out of sight, out of mind, cocooned, and protected from the outside world. Julie was determined to stay positive, refusing to think about the fact that no one should have to be forced to make this decision. No one should ever have to be afraid to leave her own home.

"I'll call the contractor next week,' she said, hoping this was the solution to their problem.

CHAPTER 35

Even though it was the Labor Day holiday weekend, Julie was still able to contact a contractor she knew and had worked with on several different occasions. Ed Brown was fast, affordable, and most important, his work was exquisite.

"Okay Miz Julie, I'll see you Tuesday morning at ten thirty." Ed was a fellow Southerner, a gentleman from Louisiana.

Satisfied that the plan was in motion, she prepared to tackle her next project for the day: tending to her flowers.

She retrieved her pretty floral gardening gloves from the utility drawer then spritzed mosquito repellent on her bare arms and legs. Opening the coat closet, she reached to the top shelf and brought down her wide-brimmed straw hat. Then she slipped her feet into her yellow Crocs, the yellow Crocs that her family teased her mercilessly about wearing.

"Go ahead and laugh," she had told them. "One of these days, they'll be a major fashion trend, just you watch."

The dark clouds loomed overhead, threatening rain, but she wasn't intimidated. Standing on the front step, she took a deep breath. Mmm. It even smelled like rain. The fragrance took her back to when she was a child at her grandmother's house. Oh, how she had loved helping Grandma Millie cut flowers at the end of the day to put on the dining room table. Afterwards, they would sit on the front porch swing and sip sweet iced tea while admiring their day's work.

Julie stepped off the porch to get started before the rain settled in. She greeted old Mrs. Wilson out for her daily walk with her little poodle. Julie thought the dog must have been up there in age too, as they both just barely trudged along, Mrs. Wilson leaning heavily on her wooden cane.

As Julie put on her gloves, she waved with her free hand. "Good morning, Mrs. Wilson!" The frail woman stopped, shot Julie a look of utter disgust, and did a 180-pivot in the direction she'd come from. She looked at Julie again, gave a disgruntled harrumph, and picked up her pace, practically dragging the poor dog behind her.

Julie smiled sadly. Unfortunately, this had been happening a lot lately. She'd wave when people were driving by or try to start a conversation when they'd be outside. A few would just ignore her, some would show their disapproval, as Mrs. Wilson had just done, and still others had just outright told her they were uncomfortable being around her with all the rumors they'd heard about her. Still, others would feign busyness or make excuses for why they couldn't chat. These were all the same people who had been so welcoming and friendly to Julie before. Thank God she still had Anne and Donna.

Not only had Lynn cost Julie her reputation, but she had also cost her about eighty thousand dollars in commissions. No one wanted to do business with her now. Not to mention the court costs and lawyer and private investigation fees. She tried to erase it from her mind. She didn't want to think about that today. On this first Saturday in September, she just wanted to bask in the beauty of her azaleas and roses and breathe in their fragrant aroma. Fall would be here way too soon.

Thunder rumbled in the distant sky. Julie covered her arms with her gloved hands as she suddenly felt a chill. Goose bumps on a humid day like today? Crazy, she thought. Brushing it off, she began the tedious task of pulling those darned, intrusive weeds that seemed to grow faster than her beloved plants. On her knees, with her back to the sidewalk, she turned slightly to pick up the small spade lying on the ground next to the other tools.

Someone stood behind her. It was Lynn. She wasn't doing anything. Just standing and watching.

What will I be accused of now? Attacking her with my gardening tools?

As tempting as that mental picture might be, Julie instead picked up her things and placed them in her basket. There was work to be done in the backyard too, so she'd just work there. Behind her, the woman stood transfixed, watching, making no effort to move.

You think you've won, don't you? Lynn thought.

That day in court should have gone off without a hitch. The stupid twit had confessed to the curse and abuse. That should have made it a done deal. Lynn had to do a little extra work on her own for the trespassing charges. A few days of crying on Lois Zimmer's shoulder about the awful things she'd had to endure since the Patterson's had moved in had paid off. Even though the woman hadn't actually witnessed Julie in the yard, Lois didn't feel she'd be doing her civic duty if she didn't do all she could to protect her new friend. There was no telling what this Julie woman was capable of. Lynn herself had said so.

A few more days of Lynn showing up on Lois's doorstep and complimenting her on everything from her tacky home decorating to her K-Mart wardrobe and Lois was in like Flynn.

All Lois had wanted was someone to fawn over her. Lynn was only too happy to oblige. Afterward, if she had told Lois that Julie had grown horns and a tail and transformed into Lucifer, the old bag would have testified to it.

But none of that had mattered. That pathetic loser still got off scot-free. At least for now.

Overhead, the sky turned black. The storm clouds churned, and a loud clap of thunder jolted Lynn back to reality. All at once the angry clouds opened up and big drops of rain pelted the ground. She tilted her face upward to the sky.

Perfect weather for what's about to happen, she thought as she started to laugh.

William turned the volume down on his television. He was watching *SpongeBob Squarepants*, his favorite show, when he thought he heard someone laughing. Not the fun kind of laugh you heard at someplace like Chuck E. Cheese's. No, it was like the kind of laugh you'd hear during a scary movie. Not that he'd know. Mom never let him watch anything scary or anything over PG. The closest he'd come to watching a horror movie was an advertisement of that scary movie about the doll that chased everyone. What was his name? Chucky? Yeah, that was it. Just the thought of the possessed creature gave William the creeps. He turned the volume back up on the TV. It was hard to be scared while watching SpongeBob walk his pet snail, Gary. At least it would have been if the big clack of thunder hadn't made the whole house vibrate.

He rolled across his bed and cupped his hand over the side of his face so he could see past the glare of the window. What he saw scared him just as much as any crazy monster doll he could ever imagine.

CHAPTER 36

"Honey, what's wrong?" Julie ran to Will's side. He looked as pale as a ghost, and he was crying his little heart out.

"Hey, buddy, what's up?" Tom asked. 'Are you okay?"

"Daddy, the police are outside." The poor child's heart was about to break. He'd seen two policemen getting out of the car. He knew they were coming to take his mother.

Tom's eyes darted to Julie. All color drained from her face.

"Just wait here," he said to her. "I'll go to the door and see what they want."

Julie held Will in her arms. "Mommy, please don't let them take you."

"Shh. It'll be okay, darlin.' Don't cry." Colette was loudly voicing her disapproval as both officers stepped inside the house, so she leaned over to pick the dog up. It sure wouldn't help her cause to have the creature gnawing at their ankles. She heard muffled voices; then Tom called to her to join them.

She invited the men to take a seat in the formal living room. They politely declined.

"Ma'am, I have a warrant for your arrest." said one of the policemen, who had a name on his badge that Julie couldn't pronounce. She looked over to the other officer's name tag. *Jones*. Did the department purposely partner a 'Jones" with "What's-His-Name" so in case you were arrested you could at least pronounce one of their names? If circumstances were different she would have laughed out loud.

Instead she felt nauseated.

"Arrest me? For what?" Her exterior personified extreme calm and grace. She had to keep herself together for William's sake.

"For attempted murder."

She grasped the back of the chair to steady herself. Tom caught her before she fell, easing her over to the sofa. William started to cry again, burying his head in her lap.

"I...I don't understand." Julie's voice was almost inaudible.

"There's been a huge mistake," Tom said.

Officer What's-His-Name handed her a citizen's criminal complaint. Julie held the report with one hand and kept her other arm around William. The little boy was clinging so tightly to his mother that you couldn't tell where one ended and the other began.

On the above date and time, my daughter and I were walking our dog along Tobacco Way.

I noticed Julie Patterson driving her Mercedes from her headlights behind us as she crossed from the right lane to the left lane at a fast rate of speed.

I pushed my daughter and my dog up onto the gravel strip just as Mrs. Patterson gunned it and came straight at us. She drove over the curb exactly where we were standing. If I hadn't have pushed my little girl out of the way and jumped into a neighbor's yard, she would have run completely over us.

Signed,

Lynn Hennessy

Lynn. Of course.

"This is crazy! I simply drove past her. That's all! I just drove by her while she was standing on the corner up there. I had to drive past her to get home!"

The room was spinning. She couldn't think; she couldn't breathe. Attempted murder? When, for God's sake, was this nightmare going to stop?

"I've had enough. She's just angry because I wasn't found guilty of the other charges she brought against me." She begged the police officers. "Please go to her house and just ask her to meet us on the corner so I can ask her why she is doing this? You all will be there, so you know nothing is going to happen. I just want to know why she is doing this!"

Jones nodded. "I'm sorry, Mrs. Patterson, but we can't do that. We have to take you into custody. You'll be able to see the judge on Tuesday."

"Tuesday?" Tom almost blew a gasket. "That's three days!"

Jones replied, "I'm sorry, sir, but since it's Labor Day weekend, the judge is out until 9:00 Tuesday morning. You'll be able to post bond then."

Wait! She had a witness from that night! Yes! Brooke! They'd even talked about her promotion.

"My neighbor Brooke was there that night! She will tell you that nothing happened. She lives right next door."

"Then you'll need to tell that to your attorney," he answered. "Right now we have to take you in."

"My wife did not do this! This isn't the first time that Hennessy woman has tried to pull this off! She tried to have our son taken from us and even had my wife arrested once before. Things have gotten so bad that we hired a private investigator. Let me get the report—"

"Sir, please—" It was no use. Jones read Julie her rights while his partner placed her arms around her back and clasped the handcuffs around her wrists. Unlike the last arrest, this time the cuffs were tight. She couldn't have slipped her hands out if her life had depended on it.

The front door opened, and the officers led her to the waiting squad car. There was a light mist, and although it wasn't quite four, the dark clouds made it seem much later. In the distance was a quick flash of lightning and in the air the wail of a little boy screaming for his mother.

The loud clang of the cell door as it slammed shut stirred Julie to reality. For the next three days, this tiny 6 x 10 room would be her home. She shivered. The temperature itself was comfortable enough, but the stainless-steel interior made everything seem so frigid.

With the exception of soft humming coming from the woman in the cell directly across from her, the place was mysteriously quiet. Grabbing the edges of the blanket that was folded neatly at the foot of the bed, Julie lay down in the fetal position. It was almost 8:30. The time of night that she should be tucking William into bed. The time of night that he'd beg his mother to read "just one more story."

Every time she closed her eyes to try to sleep, she saw the child struggling against Tom, whose arms were grasped tightly around the little boy's waist. Will's legs were running in place, his arms outstretched to her as the car drove away. He was screaming, but she couldn't hear him. Before he was out of sight, she saw his little lips mouth the word "Mommy."

She rolled on her back and stared into the darkness. Every once in a while, a flash of lightning lit up the room, giving her a glimpse of her surroundings, a cruel reminder that she was somewhere she didn't belong and that she was alone. Finally, the sky broke loose, and as the heavy rain pounded on the small windowpane above the bed, her tears gave way to heavy sobs.

CHAPTER 37

The judge determined that Julie wasn't a flight risk. Tom posted her $15,000 bond and sat in the courthouse lobby consulting with Ron.

"What can we do to keep this from happening over and over again?" Tom asked.

"This is when the private investigator's report comes in handy. Take it and go see the head magistrate. His name is Douglas Sanborn. You usually don't need an appointment. Just show up and wait your turn. Plead your case to him. Show him the P.I. report. Maybe he can put a stop to this crazy woman calling the police on you every time you turn around." He pointed to Julie.

"In the meantime, I'm going to get to work on your case. I really don't think this is that big of a deal—"

"I just spent three days in jail for something that's not 'that big of a deal'?" Julie asked, dumbfounded.

"Let me rephrase that," Ron said. "I think basically the most that will happen is that we'll get to court, and the judge will say it's nothing more than a reckless/ careless driving situation. He'll throw it out, or the most that will happen is you'll have to pay a traffic citation."

"No. The arrest warrant specifically said 'attempted murder,'" She argued.

"At any rate, I'll need the number of Brooke Williams—she'll be a key witness that this never happened. I also want the numbers of the people Lynn Hennessy told that you'd been found guilty on the previous charges. I want names and numbers of anyone who has ever witnessed her stalking you and who she told that you'd abused your kid. I need it sooner rather than later. We don't have a lot of time."

Why did she get the feeling that Ron still wasn't taking this seriously enough?

Judge Sanborn was a gentle man. He settled back in his chair and folded his arms across his chest, giving the young couple his undivided attention while they spoke. He'd heard some outrageous stories in his career, so nothing really surprised him anymore. The poor woman sitting across from him was desperately pleading for his help. Her husband placed an investigators' report in his hands. It was a thick book, and as he opened it, he noticed that Chuck Bishop had been the investigator who'd gathered the information.

The fact that Chuck was a fine investigator with a stellar reputation, coupled by the statements gathered by those who had been witness to these bizarre events made Mr. and Mrs. Patterson more credible. Besides that, his gut feeling just told him that they were telling the truth.

"Julie," he spoke with a slow, soothing, Southern drawl. "Why do you think she's singled you out?"

"She is mad that she got caught in a lie," Julie stated. "She thought it was going to be so easy and that social services would just show up, take my child, and I would never know it was her. Instead it backfired. I am not the first person she's put through this, but from what I understand, and it's all there in the report, we're the first family that has stayed. I also think it makes her angry that she can't run us off."

"Here's what I can do," he said, handing the notebook back to Tom. "I will send out an e-mail to all of my other magistrates in Prince William County. They are not to let her fill out another report without talking to me first. I think that will help." He turned to his computer, and Julie could hear the clicking of his keyboard keys as he typed. Then he turned his back toward them and picked something off the printer. "Here you go. This is what I just sent to them." He handed the paper to Tom. Julie leaned over to him to see what it said.

To: All Magistrates
Subject: Frivolous Criminal Complaints

This is to affirm my guidance on frivolous complaints or complaints without legal grounding made against a Mrs. Julie Patterson. Such complaints are to be referred to the chief magistrate for review prior to issuing an arrest process.

Mr. Sanborn

Chief Magistrate

"Thank you," Julie said, but she felt little relief. This would just force Lynn to be more creative.

The car ride home was a quiet one. The closer they got to Cardinal Estates, the harder Julie's heart started to thump and the harder it was to breathe. As she gasped for air, Tom pulled over to the side of the road.

"N...no," Julie gasped. "We have to get home. Ed is coming over today to start on the basement and the...the f...fence. I want that fence p...put up as soon as possible."

"Calm down, sweetheart," Tom said, gathering her in his arms. "Don't worry about Ed. I've already called and rescheduled him for tomorrow."

He kissed her temple as she sat lifeless, staring straight ahead at the passing cars. There was no polite way to put it. She looked rough. Her face was void of makeup, exposing her splotchy, tear-stained cheeks.

For the first time in their married life, he looked at her and thought she looked old.

He didn't look much better. It had been a rough three days for all of them. He'd left at least ten messages on Ron's voice mail. The attorney had decided to take advantage of the last weekend of summer and spend it at his home in Virginia Beach. He didn't get back to Tom until late Monday afternoon.

On Saturday morning Tom thought about calling Olivia and then decided against it. Shed just returned to school a few days earlier. There was nothing she could do here, and he knew she'd cry and insist to come back home. No, she'd have to know soon enough, but not now.

Instead, he focused on the person that this whole situation was having as much of a toll on as Julie. *William.* It took him hours to get the boy calmed down after the police took his mother away. He finally cried himself to sleep. He woke up twice screaming, and finally Tom gave up and put him in bed with him. The rest of the weekend he would hardly eat or talk. He just sat in his mom's chair staring into space.

Now that Julie was calm, Tom reached over and put the car back in drive.

"When we get home, please park in the garage so I can go in through the kitchen," she said. "I don't want to see anyone."

He agreed.

The first thing she did was take a shower. She scrubbed her skin almost raw trying to get rid that dirty, dingy "jail" smell.

After getting dressed, she holed herself up in her home office, scanning the Multiple Listing System, a software that allowed realtors to view all homes for sale in the Washington DC metro area.

Saturday night, before she'd been arrested, she and Tom had discussed and decided against moving. That was before they knew just how far Lynn was willing to go to destroy her. Now Julie didn't know if a security fence and living in the basement would be enough.

She punched away at the keyboard. If she could find someplace else in the metro area to move to, she'd cancel tomorrow's appointment with Ed and immediately put their home on the market.

The doorbell rang. Julie looked out the window, saw that it was Anne, and picked up a yapping Colette before opening the door.

Julie's eyes glistened as Anne gave her a big bear hug.

"Julie, honey, what is going on?"

Julie tried to smile. "Tell me what you've heard first, and then I'll tell you the truth."

"I was unpacking from our trip Monday afternoon when Lynn came over. She said you'd been arrested for trying to run over her and Hannah. Please tell me that's not true!"

"Which one? Being arrested or trying to run over them?" Julie managed a laugh.

"Please, I know you didn't try to run over anyone! But surely you weren't arrested!"

"Oh, yeah." Julie paused for a second to gain control of her emotions. "While almost everyone I know was off celebrating the last weekend of summer, I was spending it in jail."

Anne started to cry. "What on earth is she trying to do to you, Julie? Why?"

"Your guess is as good as mine, Anne. But I give up." She pointed in the direction of her office. "I'm trying to find another house. I just can't do this anymore. I'm tired of looking over my shoulder. The police won't—or can't—help me. There don't appear to be any laws to stop her."

"I just don't know what to say," Anne said quietly. "You know I'll help any way I can. Just say the word and I'm there."

"I know that."

Donna phoned her later that evening as she was drifting off to sleep.

"Please call me if you need anything. You know I'd do anything in the world for you," she promised.

The last thing on Julie's mind before she went to sleep that night, thankful to be in her own soft, warm, bed, was how blessed she was to have such caring, dependable friends.

She would need those friends in the difficult days to come.

CHAPTER 38

The house was spotless, laundry caught up, and breakfast prepared by the time Will came down for breakfast at seven the next morning. Julie forced herself to put on a cheerful facade for his sake as she helped him get ready for the second day of the new school year.

The bus stop, coincidentally, was the scene of the crime. Julie inspected the curb. The grass stood tall and proud. No tire tracks, not even as much as an indentation in the ground. If she had driven over the curb, there would be obvious tire tracks on the grass. And what about tire marks in the street? If she had squealed her tires on the street, wouldn't there be tire marks on the pavement? But there was nothing.

She snapped her fingers as a mental lightbulb came on. *I need pictures! And fast!* Lynn was clever, and it wouldn't take long for her to figure out that she'd need to come up with her own evidence. Julie pictured Lynn waiting till early hours of the dawn when the neighborhood was pitch black and purposefully driving over the curb to make an indentation.

"Here comes the bus, Mom!" William called.

Julie waved. "I love you, babe. Have a good day now!"

As the bus drove away, she felt in her pocket for her cell phone. *Shoot! I must have left it on the table!* Without even acknowledging the other moms, she made a mad dash for the house.

She marched into the house, grabbed the phone, and dialed Janine's direct office number.

"Please, please pick up," she said aloud to herself as the phone rang and rang. She was about to give up on the sixth ring.

"Good morning. This is Janine McLellan."

"Oh, Janine, thank God!" Julie breathed a sigh of relief. "I need your help!" She quickly filled Janine in on the latest police drama and arrest.

"Can you take a picture of the area? If she sees me there, I'm afraid she'll magically come up with her own pictures. But she doesn't know you. I think you could pull into the driveway of the house that's on the corner, keep your camera hidden, and then snap away when no one is around."

Without hesitation, Janine answered, "I'm there! When do you want me to do this?"

"As quickly as possible, like, within the next hour! Please, Janine! I know you're busy, but you have a great camera, and like I said, nobody will recognize you. I need to get these pictures as soon as possible, before she gets the same idea and has somebody run her car over the curb to create tire tracks."

"Consider it done," said Janine. "You lay low, and I'll be there in the next twenty minutes."

Thank you, God, for the few friends I have left. Where would she be without the support of Janine, Anne, and Donna? She wouldn't even allow herself to think about that.

Ed Brown heard the dog before he saw it. He got out of the construction van and saw Miss Julie at the door cradling a small white dog in her arms. He had a strong dislike for the creatures—regardless of their size—and he had the scar on his calf to prove why. At least Miss Julie's dog was small. Aunt Trudie's dog, Rufus, had been a Saint Bernard. When he was six, his older brother, Roger, had dared him to ride Rufus like they'd ridden the ponies at the carnival the week before. Not only did he have to get eight stitches from the dog bite, but Mama had taken Daddy's belt to both of their back ends. That had happened over fifty years ago, but he remembered it like it was yesterday.

Ed's partner, Rob, opened up the back of the van. He snickered when he saw Ed eyeing the dog.

"Hey, at least it's just a little feller," he said and then pointed behind Ed. "She could have a great big dog like that one right there."

Ed flipped around. He didn't notice the attractive, scantily clad woman walking up behind, smiling very seductively. No, he was too rattled by the monstrous Rottweiler she had walking beside her.

"So, guys, what kind of work are you doing at the Patterson house?" Lynn was being flirtatious, ducking her head and looking up at them through her thick, dark lashes.

"We're here to—"

By the time Julie had spotted Lynn she practically dropped Colette to the floor and dashed out the front. She knew exactly what Lynn was up to.

"Ed! Welcome!" Striding right up to the men, she turned her back to Lynn as if she weren't even there.

"Good mornin', Miz Julie," Ed replied as he gently shook her hand. "You remember Rob, don't you? Rob Crossman?"

"Of course." Julie smiled, trying to appear as relaxed as she possibly could, fighting the urge to choke Lynn, who kept trying to worm her way into the conversation. Julie kept the idle chatter going as she led the two men inside the house. "The last time I saw you two was when you were finishing up Councilman Field's house, which turned out beautiful, by the way."

Once inside Julie slammed the door.

"We need to get one thing straight, guys." Her whole demeanor changed, and her voice became cold as ice. "If you're going to work for me, you are to never, and I mean never, let that woman near this house. If you talk to her while you're working for me, I'll fire you."

Ed looked startled, almost hurt. She felt awful. He had never seen her less than pleasant, but it was imperative that she lay down the rules on this. She told them why it had to be.

"Aw, Miz Julie, I am so sorry you've been goin' through all this. That woman must be off her rocker! You are the nicest person I know."

"I hate for it to be like this, guys," she said as she looked from Ed to Rob. "But if your crew is going to work for us, then you must tell them they cannot speak to her! Not so much as a good morning. She's not even allowed on this property. Trust me, if I'm not here, she'll sneak her way into this house, and I just can't have that."

Rob spoke up. "Rest assured, Miss Julie, there won't be any problems. I can promise you that."

"Thank you." She took a deep breath. "Let's go over these plans, shall we?"

"I need the fence to be up as soon as possible, hopefully by the end of the week," Julie said.

"Hmm." Rob took off his cap and scratched his head. "I don't know. Today is *Wednesday*."

"Truthfully, gentlemen, I had every intention this morning of calling you and canceling this appointment. After the weekend I've had, I'd just given up. I was going to put this house on the market and move completely out of Prince William County. However, yesterday I spent well over six hours online looking at every house in the DC metro area. You can't even buy a house in the ghetto for less than

$600,000. I've spent every dime in equity on this house for legal fees. I'm getting ready to spend another chunk of change for more legal fees. As much as I want to move, I can't afford it now. I'm paying you the last bit of our savings to do this job."

Rob looked at Ed and shook his head doubtfully.

"Can't you see why I need this to be done *yesterday*? I need this boundary. I can't step outside my own house. My son can't play outside. This boundary—this fence—is the only protection we have."

"Miz Julie, you'll have that fence by Friday if we have to work all night to get it done," Ed said. "Now where's your survey of the property?"

"Thank you, Ed," Julie said as she unfolded the document on the kitchen island. "As you see here, the Hennessy's fence encroaches on our property by about five feet. On the other hand, their fence is about three feet inside their property line, so, in turn, we'll be encroaching on their land when you connect the fences on that corner over there. That's okay. Her husband is the HOA president, and he and the board approved this, so we're good to go."

Rob promised to have the lumber delivered that afternoon.

"Thank you, guys," Julie said sincerely. "I appreciate it."

Julie's cell phone rang. Caller ID told her it was Janine, so she excused herself and stepped outside onto the deck for privacy.

"I got a picture of the grass, the curb, and the street from every possible angle," came the voice on the line. "Is there anything else you need a picture of while I'm here?"

"Why don't I sneak up there real quick?" Julie opened the French doors leading to the kitchen and walked through the house to the front door. Never mind. Lynn was still standing at the edge of the sidewalk. She had to have gone home and come back because Killer was nowhere in sight. "Scratch that. She's standing in front of my house right now."

"Doing what?"

"Uh, nothing. Just staring at my house."

"What a psycho," Janine muttered. "Okay then. I'm going back to the office right now, and I'll e-mail these pictures to you. You'll have them in about fifteen minutes."

"Okay. As soon as I get them, I'll forward them to my attorney. Oh, and Janine? Thank you. For everything."

"Don't mention it. If nothing else, it allows me to live out my fantasy of being a private investigator. Talk to you soon!"

The phone rang again. This time it was her attorney, Ron.

"We've got a problem. A big problem." He didn't even give her the chance to respond. "I just got off the phone with the prosecuting attorney. He wants to push this attempted murder to the limit. Two counts."

"I tried to tell you this!" Julie said angrily. "But no, you laughed at me and told me it wasn't much more than a speeding ticket! Well, I'm not a lawyer, but I tend to think when two cops show up at my door and arrest me for attempted murder that they're probably telling me the truth!"

Ron was silent, and Julie wondered if she had lost the call. Or worse yet, maybe her own attorney was so sick and tired of it all that he had decided to bail on her.

"Look, I know that in the past I have not taken this as seriously as I should have. I am sorry. But you have to admit that all of this is so crazy! I mean, I'm a defense attorney; I thought I'd seen it all."

"So what does this mean, Ron? What would be the worst-case scenario?"

His voice was cold and matter-of-fact.

"A minimum of five years in prison."

CHAPTER 39

"Hello? Hello? Are you still there?"

"I have a witness," Julie said when she was able to speak. "My next-door neighbor got home the same exact time that I did. We even had a conversation before we went in the house. If there had been squealing tires and someone jumping a curb, she would definitely have seen it or heard it."

"E-mail her name and number to me. We'll need her to testify. Also, I want the names and numbers of all the neighbors she told that you were found guilty in the last court case. That will also break her credibility. Oh, and one last request."

"What?" she asked, in no way prepared for what he was about to say next.

"I want you to pack up your son and leave town until your court date. It's the third weekend in October. That's a little over a month. I want you out of here so she can't accuse you of something else. My fear is that she'll do something to harm herself and accuse you of doing it. Or worse, she'll do something to harm you or Will."

Feeling as if she'd choke, Julie stepped outside the front door for some fresh air. She sighed heavily (something she seemed to be doing a lot of lately), closed her eyes, and lifted her face up toward the warm sun. Then she sat down on the front porch step, cradling her head in her hands.

"Miz Julie." Ed could see that Julie was stressed. "We're gonna have that fence up before you know it. Then I'll have the fence crew stay and help out with the basement. We'll get it done quicker that way, and no extra charge."

Tears welled up in her eyes as she tried to thank Ed, but the words wouldn't come.

All she could do was nod. Not knowing what else to do, Ed patted her on the back as he walked by her to go to the van.

Sure that the photos she was waiting on had arrived, she logged on to her computer and checked her e-mail. The pictures were crystal clear. Janine's camera had even recorded today's date on the pictures. Perfect. She clicked on forward and entered Ron's address and then attached the picture file before pressing send.

Less than five minutes later, the attorney called her and confirmed he'd received the photos.

"The pictures are great. They're nice and clear, and it looks like she has a shot from every angle.

Before the court date, I'll come out there and familiarize myself with the area. What I'm going to do now is call these numbers you gave me. I'll start with Brooke first since she's your witness from that night. Then I'll call Anne and Donna and tell them I'll need their testimony in court too."

"Yes, Anne and Donna are especially good because they don't know each other, but yet the stories that Lynn tells them match verbatim."

"Exactly," Ron agreed. "We'll get the witness on the stand first to prove to the judge that nothing happened. The testimony of the other two will show the judge that this woman has a pattern of lying and harassing you. Couple that with the fact you had to get the magistrate to call off her phony police reports, and I'll bet we can get her for perjury and filing false police reports. The stronger our case, the sooner we can get your life back to normal."

Normal, Julie thought. *That sounds nice.* She desperately tried to remember what normal felt like.

CHAPTER 40

At seven thirty the next morning, Rob and his construction crew were unloading more lumber and hauling it through the foyer and down the stairs. Ed and his men had already posted a few of the panels on the fence.

The constant commotion, pounding of nails, and whirring of saws, mixed with Colette's nervous yapping, was starting to give Julie a massive headache. She grabbed the new *Southern Living* magazine from yesterday's mail and coaxed Colette to follow her to the bedroom where she shut the door, drowning out the noise.

"Much better," she said as she hoisted the little dog onto the bed. Before she had a chance to get settled in, the phone rang.

"Hello."

'Another big problem," Ron said without even a hello. "I can't get anyone to testify."

"What do you mean?" Julie asked, puzzled. "That's ridiculous. Of course they'll testify."

"Brooke Wilson won't testify because she says she didn't see anything."

"Because there was nothing *to see*. That's perfect!"

"You don't get it. We have nothing. No one. And your good friends," he said sarcastically, "don't want to get *involved*."

"You mean Anne and Donna?"

"That would be them," Ron said. Julie wished she could reach through the phone and rip out his smart-alecky tongue. He must have misunderstood. If he talked to them the way he talked to her, they were probably just intimidated. And who wouldn't be afraid of going to court?

"I...I don't believe this!" she stuttered. "What did you say to them? What did they say to you.?" *Stay calm*, she told herself. *Don't lose it*.

"I called Anne first. I need her to testify that Mrs. Hennessy confessed that she filed a child abuse report to the school and that she also told her that you were convicted at your last hearing. She refused."

"Why?" This had to be a mistake. There was no way Anne would leave her high and dry. No possible way.

"She's scared to death," he said, "absolutely scared to death that she'll become the next victim."

"Good grief! I live closer to the woman than she does! At least Lynn can't look out her window and see inside her house."

The full impact was starting to sink in.

"Did you tell her that I am looking at five years in prison?" Julie's voice quivered.

"Yes, I did," Ron said. "She said she was sorry, but she just couldn't. It was the same story for Donna White. They're all afraid they'll be next."

"Then why don't we use the statements they made to the private investigator?"

Ron nixed that idea. "It's not admissible in court. We can only use the statements if they testify. Otherwise, it's just hearsay."

Great! So were the thousands of dollars she had spent on Chuck Bishop a total waste?

"What do I do?" She clutched the pearls at her neck so tightly that they spilled to the floor. She didn't even notice.

"Try talking to them one on one and see if you can change their mind," Ron answered. "But they were both pretty adamant about not wanting anything to do with it."

This could *not* be happening! Not this. How could Anne, her best friend, leave her out to dry? What about Donna? They'd both been there and stood by her from the very beginning. She desperately needed them now more than ever. They couldn't leave her now! They wouldn't! What was she going to do?

"If they won't come forward on their own, then subpoena their asses!" She didn't recognize her own voice.

"I can't subpoena them," said Ron.

"Why not?" she shouted into the receiver. "I know these ladies! If you subpoena them and force them to testify, they'll tell the truth! I know it! They will not lie under oath."

"I can't take a chance!" Ron shouted back. "If I get them on the stand and they cave, the prosecution will bury you! And there will be nothing I can do about it! You *will* go to prison!"

"I can't believe this is happening."

She slammed the phone down and immediately dialed Anne's number.

"Hello." Anne answered on the first ring.

"Anne, it's Julie," she said breathlessly. Her voice sounded like she'd just finished a ten-mile run. "I just hung up with my attorney. He told me that you refused to go to court with us. I need you—"

"Look, Julie, I'm sorry, but I just can't—"

"Anne! Please! I am looking at five years in prison if I'm found guilty!"

"I know, but I...I just can't," Anne stuttered. "All you have to do is tell the truth, and I'm sure—"

"She lies better than I tell the truth, Anne! You know that!"

"I just can't. I live across the street from her. Dear God, Julie, she wanted to take your child away What if I'm next? What if she tries to take Kayla or Jamie?"

"Don't you see? She can't do this again! There is strength in numbers! She can't get away with it again if we stick together!"

"Why does it have to be me?" Anne asked. "Why not the teachers? Why can't you use the private investigator's report?"

"Ron says the report doesn't matter unless everyone who participated shows up for questioning. Otherwise, it's just hearsay and not admissible. As far as the teachers and principal? Yes, that might brandish her as a liar, but it also gives me motive for wanting to run her down. So it backfires. I need your complete testimony. Anne, I'm begging you to help me."

"I just can't do it, Julie. I'm sorry. You know I wish you luck and all, but—"

"Luck? The possibility of me going to prison doesn't even faze you?"

Anne's silence was like a deafening scream.

She tried Donna next.

"Donna!" Julie was close to hysterics. "Why did you tell my attorney that you wouldn't testify? I need you to help me!"

"Julie, I can't. I just can't get involved," Donna said. "I've had problems with my heart, and I'm supposed to watch my stress levels and—"

"Stress?" Julie laughed. "I'll tell you about stress! Stress is someone stalking you day and night, trying to have your child taken from you, defacing your property! Stress is being arrested for something you didn't do not once but twice! It's spending a whole weekend in jail and having to spend thousands of dollars to defend yourself!"

"Julie", please understand," Donna cried into the phone.

"Oh, and I almost forgot!" Julie was screaming at this point. "The possibility of going to prison for at least five years for something that, once again, *I didn't do*! You might not want to throw the stress excuse at me right now!"

"My husband is begging me to not get involved. He says I always do so much for everyone else and sometimes I just need to say no."

"You picked a hell of time to start," Julie said. "As far as I'm concerned, you are as dangerous to my family as Psycho Lynn is, so stay completely away from my son! Do you understand me?"

Donna sobbed in to the phone. "Julie, I am so sorry! Please—"

By that time, Julie had flung the phone across the room.

CHAPTER 41

The next thing Julie knew, she was waking up, and Tom was hovering over her, gently tucking a blanket under her chin. Will was asleep beside her, a half-eaten peanut butter and jelly sandwich still clutched in his small hand.

Trying to focus in the dark room, Julie started to panic when she looked out the window and suddenly realized it was night. What time was it? She sat upright in bed, hurriedly throwing the covers back, her feet hitting the floor with full force.

How did this happen? When she'd hung up the phone with Donna it was only eight fifteen this morning! She hadn't meant to sleep! She'd only wanted to compose herself before she went downstairs to face the construction crew.

Oh my goodness! The construction crew!

"Hey, hey, relax," Tom said as he placed his hands on her shoulders. "Everything's okay. Wait till you see the fence; they're halfway finished."

She knew it was too dark to see much, but when she flipped the outside light on, she could see from the deck that indeed they had finished half of it.

"It's supposed to rain tonight and tomorrow, so I don't know if they'll be able to finish on time, but they did get a lot done today," Tom said.

She didn't have the energy to go down to the basement to see what they had accomplished. Besides, that would be at least a three-month project, so they couldn't have made too much of an impact the first day.

Upstairs, Tom took the now-stale sandwich from Will's hands and threw it in a nearby trash can on his way to take the little boy to his own bed. He dampened a washcloth with warm water and washed Will's sticky fingers and mouth. He leaned down and kissed him, closed the door, and joined Julie downstairs.

He gathered her in his arms and held her as she stood there limp. She looked awful. Her hair was a mess, like she hadn't even combed it that day. There were dark circles under her eyes and tear tracks on her cheeks. She had on a pair of his running shorts, a dirty sweatshirt, and mismatched socks.

This was so not like her. Even in her mid-forties, he thought she still looked as beautiful as the day she was crowned Miss Mississippi. She'd always taken such pride in her appearance, and after twenty-two years of marriage, he had never seen her like this.

When Ron had advised her to take William and leave town for a while, he had nixed the idea. It was selfish, he knew, but he didn't want to take a chance on her getting comfortable at her parents and deciding to stay for good after her court date, provided she didn't go to prison.

He squeezed her tighter, but she just stood there like a limp rag doll. When he stepped back, he looked into her red, emotionless eyes.

"I went over to Anne and Bob's tonight," he said. He hated bringing this up now. She was almost nonfunctional.

She looked at him with a glimmer of hope. Maybe he had been able to change her mind.

"Come over here and sit down." Tom tried to lead her to the sofa.

"No!" She pulled away. He was trying to prepare her for something, she could tell. "Don't sugarcoat it. Just tell me! What did she say?"

She knew it wasn't going to be what she wanted to hear. She could see it all over Tom's face.

"I tried, Julie. But she still said no. Bob was there, and by the time I was finished, they were both crying. Anne said she knew she should step up and testify, but she said just couldn't; she's too afraid."

She looked at the floor and then looked at Tom again. When she spoke, it was barely a whisper.

"Tomorrow, I'll catch Brooke before she goes to work," said Julie. "I'll get up early and I'll—'

Tom shook his head. "I went to see her first, even before I went over to Anne's. It's no use. She says she didn't see anything, so there's no reason for her to testify."

"I'm sick of hearing that!" Julie dashed across the kitchen and out the front door. Tom almost had to run to keep up with her.

She pounded on Brooke's front door. The front porch light came on, and a frightened Brooke, already in her nightgown, cautiously opened the front door. Julie didn't even give her a chance to speak.

"I know you didn't see anything!" Julie bellowed. "Because *nothing* happened! Absolutely nothing!"

Brooke started to speak, but Julie interrupted her. "That night as we were both pulling into our driveways, right at that specific moment I was supposed to be jumping the curb and squealing my tires as I supposedly tried to hit a woman and her child!"

"Why should I testify and get involved when I didn't see anything?" Brooke finally managed to get out.

"The reason you didn't hear or see anything is because there was nothing to see or hear!" Julie looked behind her at Tom and laughed hysterically. "Why doesn't anyone get that?" Tom had his hand under her elbow and tried to lead her away, but she pulled back, looking back at Brooke. "When the prosecuting attorney asks you what you saw that night, all you have to do is say, Nothing. Just that one teensy, weensy little word! What is so hard about that?"

Brooke tried to shut the door, but Julie blocked it by stepping into the threshold.

"If you harass me about this anymore, I will call my attorney!" Brooke threatened. "Do you want to be in court for harassing someone else?"

Julie backed away from the door, disheveled and quiet, like the calm before a storm.

"I didn't think so," Brooke said as she slammed it shut, making a loud popping noise. The front porch went dark. Slowly and methodically, as if she'd aged a hundred years, Julie trudged back home, Tom's arms around her holding her up. A light rain had started to fall.

Safely inside her home, Julie crumbled to the floor, sobbing violently.

'Julie, please don't." Tom tried to comfort her. "You are the most emotionally strong person I have ever known."

"No, I'm not!" She wasn't strong. She was tired, and now she was losing her sanity. She could feel it slipping away, and she couldn't do anything about it.

She tried to get up, but her legs wouldn't hold her. Tom was trying to help her to her feet when she saw Will at the top of the stairs.

"What's wrong with Mommy?" he asked, wiping tears from his eyes.

"Everything's okay, hon," Tom said. "Mom's just not feeling good; we'll talk more about it in the morning, okay?"

"Can I sleep with you?" he asked.

"No, buddy," Tom said. "Mom can't get a good night's rest if the bed is too crowded."

Julie looked up at the boy and suddenly had a vision of her family moving on without her. Olivia's college graduation, Will learning how to drive, his first date. She pictured him growing up through the years, and she was a thousand miles away, stuck in a dark, lonely cell.

"Yes!" said Julie, wiping her eyes and gathering her senses. "Yes, you can sleep with us." The fierce protectiveness in her eyes told Tom it was no use to argue.

"Okay." Tom winked. "Why don't you go ahead and get Mom's spot warmed up for her. We'll be up there in a sec." Will smiled as he bounced up the stairs, disappearing into his parents' room.

"I want to spend every single minute I can with him," Julie explained. "Every minute! After next week—"

"You can't think like that," Tom snapped.

"I think I'd better start thinking like that. And so had you," she snapped back. "It's time to face reality and start preparing this family for the inevitable."

CHAPTER 42

"I expected this," said Julie as she pointed to the fresh, muddy tire track. The fact that it had rained almost nonstop for the past three weeks made the indention even more distinct. "I'm just surprised she waited this long."

"When did you first notice this?" asked Chuck Bishop, taking a photograph of the track from every angle.

"It wasn't here yesterday afternoon when the school bus came." She nodded her head in disgust. "I noticed it this morning when I walked up here with Will, so it must have happened overnight."

Chuck, her attorney, Ron, and Al Hawley, a former FBI agent and a friend from church, had spent the past three weeks working around the clock to gather evidence for Julie's defense. These guys were the best in the business, expensive, but worth every penny. Julie affectionately referred to them as her "Dream Team", however, lately they were more of a nightmare.

From the beginning, Chuck had been offended that Ron had neither called on him to testify nor had he used his private investigator report. Ron didn't take kindly to Al's suggestion of how to handle the case strategically. Al really wasn't mad at anyone. He just drove the other two crazy by playing devil's advocate. All he wanted was to make sure that Julie had the best possible defense.

"I'm not too worried about this," said Ron, referring to the imprint. "We still have the original pictures that show there was no tire track the day after the alleged event, and now we have these, and both sets of pictures have the date on—"

"You can't rely on that," argued Al. Anyone can change the date—"

Chuck cut him off in midsentence. 'That's exactly what I told him, but no, he wouldn't—"

Soon they were all talking at once, their voices getting louder.

Julie cleared her throat. "Gentlemen."

They kept arguing. Julie was stressed to the max. She was due in court tomorrow, on the witness stand for attempted murder, and here they were wasting time over trivial facts that probably wouldn't make a bit of difference in the outcome anyway.

"Stop! I do not need this right now!" That got their attention. "I am so stressed out that my hair is starting to fall out in clumps. My skin hasn't broken out like this since I was sixteen, and tomorrow I am more than likely going to become the newest cell mate of a woman that goes by the name Big Bertha! You are supposed to be helping me, and all you do when you get together is bicker. Well, that's not helping me!"

The three men looked at each other sheepishly, muttered their apologies, and got back to work, once again talking strategy and taking notes.

Julie's head was throbbing. She sat on the tailgate of Chuck's Chevrolet Silverado pickup. She closed her eyes for just a few moments. When she opened them back up, the first thing she made eye contact with was none other than Lynn, out for a convenient stroll with her dog.

Well, well, well, what have we here? Lynn thought. Her heart started racing as that familiar excitement came over her.

What had she just walked up on? She recognized Ron, of course. And she recognized the private investigator Charles, Chuck, whatever his name was. Oh yes, she remembered him quite well. That day he'd been at the house asking questions about Julie, she'd really piled it on thick. He couldn't write fast enough as she told him stories about Julie stalking and tormenting her. She'd even managed a tear or two.

Now what were they up to? And who was this new guy? She didn't recognize him, which made her a little bit nervous. She didn't like new, and she didn't like surprises.

Careful, Lynn thought as she walked around the corner, aware that all eyes were on her. *You're just another woman in the neighborhood walking her dog.*

When she got home, she let the dog loose in the backyard. She still had this nagging feeling. What was it? She couldn't have forgotten anything. There was even a tire track right where she and Hannah had been standing that night. She'd made sure of that.

Lynn stood there for a minute. Then she grabbed one of Killer's Doggy-Doo pickup bags and marched back down to the corner.

She reached her hand through the clear plastic bag and bent over to pick up the make-believe mess, thinking they'd be none the wiser. Out of the corner of her eye, she saw them all huddled together, but she couldn't make out anything they were saying. That's okay. She didn't need to. Judging by the tone of their voices and all the pointing at the tire track, they obviously knew they didn't have a leg to stand on.

Lynn smiled, confident, as she walked with a triumphant spring in her step back to the house. Everything was set. She was sure of it.

She had coached Hannah over and over on what to say in court when the lawyers questioned her about what happened that night. She rehearsed her own dramatic version while she stood in front of the mirror, practicing different facial expressions. She had even gotten up at three that morning to drive over the curb to provide the concrete evidence. Then as soon as the sun came up, when it was still too early for the school kids to be up and about, she walked down to the corner and took several pictures.

Yes, everything was going just as planned.

"How pathetic," Julie said, watching Lynn bag imaginary dog poop. "The length some people will go to just to snoop."

"She's definitely a crafty thing, that one," said Chuck, scratching his head.

Ron looked at Chuck. "Finally, something we agree on." He paused for a moment and then said, "You know, I've been doing this for over twenty-five years. Not much bothers me anymore. I've seen it all." He paused again. "But I've lost sleep over this one. She's evil, has no conscience."

Julie couldn't hide her bitterness. "I tried to tell you that from the very beginning. If you'd taken this seriously from the get-go, maybe none of this would be happening."

Ron could feel his face getting hot, but he didn't argue. He knew she was right.

Julie spoke, "If we're done here, I have to get back to the house. Are there any last-minute instructions before tomorrow?"

"Yeah," said Ron. "I know you go to church and practice all that religious... stuff. You should pray. It's going to be a tough day tomorrow. We have the same prosecutor as last time, Bill Yarris, and he is bound and determined to prosecute you to the fullest extent."

Julie shrugged. "Why does he have it in for me? I know he's the prosecutor and that's his job, but still..."

"I don't know," answered Ron. "I asked him why this was so personal for him, and he didn't answer. He told me the best thing for us to do was plead guilty, and he'd ask for a lesser sentence."

Al said, "There has to be a reason."

"Who knows what she's told him," Julie said. "She's tried to convince everyone that I am a child abuser, stalker, and now I'm trying to kill her. She is his client, so of course he believes her. Case closed. No pun intended."

"If—*when* you come out of this tomorrow, what are your plans?" Al wanted to know. "Will you move?"

"Let me just get through tomorrow first," Julie answered. She looked at them, and her heart warmed with a genuine fondness for each man. Regardless of the next day's outcome, they had worked hard to help her. Yes, she had paid two of them. It was their job. But they had given it their all, nonetheless. And she knew they cared very much about what happened to her.

"I'll see all of you tomorrow," she said as she hugged each of them.

"By the way," Ron said to her as she turned to go, "tomorrow, you need to tone it down a bit. None of your fancy suits or handbags. Think conservative. If this goes to a jury, we want everyone to be able to relate to you, not be put off by you."

She laughed. "Look at me. I'm a wreck. Is this better?"

He looked at her jeans, shoddy house slippers, and unkempt hair. She looked like she'd lost at least ten or fifteen pounds. Her skin was pale and blotchy and she had dark circles under her eyes. Wow, had he been so wrapped up in this that he hadn't even noticed how far she'd let herself go?

Hoping he didn't sound rude, he advised, "Well, at least fix your hair a little and maybe some makeup."

"Of course," she agreed as she walked away. It had been so long since she'd dressed up and cared about her hair and makeup that it might be fun, which made her laugh out loud, considering the occasion in which she would be fixing up.

Dinnertime was exceptionally quiet that night even though the whole family was together. Tom picked up Olivia from the airport on his way home from work.

At seven thirty the doorbell rang. It was a group of about fifteen people from the church who had stopped by to wish Julie well. They held hands and prayed with her, and before leaving they vowed to be waiting for her at the courthouse the next morning.

After they left, Tom and Julie retreated with the children to the family room. Julie had full confidence that the family would cope without her, but she wanted to make sure Will had a complete comprehension of what was more than likely going to happen tomorrow. She wanted no surprises. "Come sit by me." She motioned, and he sat down beside her, enveloped closely in her arms.

"I have something to tell you, and I want you to listen very closely," Julie started. "You know what tomorrow is, don't you?"

He nodded.

"I'm going to tell you exactly what I think is going to happen," she said softly. It was very important for her to be honest with him, and she prayed for strength to lay it all out for him in as calm a manner as possible.

"First of all, I want to tell you, to *promise* you, that I did not try to run over Mrs. Hennessy or Hannah. If I had done it, I would tell you and Daddy, even the judge, that I had. I wouldn't lie about it because it's never good to lie.

"So tomorrow I am going to sit in court, and I'm going to tell the truth. I am going to tell the judge that I didn't do this. He might believe me. But I don't think he will.

"Mrs. Hennessy is a very, very good liar. She has a way of making people believe things. She will tell whatever lie she has to tell to make the court believe I'm guilty. She is so good that I think her lies sound better than my truth does."

She paused for a moment and swallowed hard. Tears were starting to form in Will's eyes, and as she continued, they started to trickle one by one down his cheeks.

"I don't think I'll be coming home tomorrow. My witnesses won't come forward. Miss Anne and Miss Donna are afraid to come to court and help me. So it will be just my word against Mrs. Hennessy's and Hannah's."

Again, she paused to make sure he was taking this all in and to give him a chance to ask questions if he wanted. As she started to speak again, she noticed that Will wasn't the only one crying. Olivia sat in the beige wingback chair with her feet tucked under her bottom, tears and mascara streaming down her face. Across the room, Tom made no attempt to cover his emotions.

'At the end of the day," Julie quietly continued, but her voice still very matter-of-fact, "it doesn't really matter what anyone else thinks or believes. God knows that I am innocent. When I meet Him face-to-face one day, I will do so with a clean conscience. That's all that really matters in the end."

His voice barely above a whisper, Will spoke, "You've always told me to ask God for what I need. I need you here with me, Mommy. He won't let you go to jail, will He?"

"I pray that same prayer, sweetie. But sometimes God doesn't always answer our prayers the way we expect him to. Sometimes things happen to us that we just don't understand. But we just have to trust Him anyway.

"I want you to promise me that if I don't come home tomorrow that you'll still put all your trust in God and that you'll remember your prayers every night. You promise? Because I'll still be saying mine every night too. Okay?"

Will wiped his tears and squeezed his mother tight. She walked with him, hand-in-hand, up the stairs and tucked him into his bed. She stayed right beside him as he fell asleep, kissing his soft, rosy cheek one last time before she went to her own bed.

As she lay her head down, she relished in the softness of her pillow, realizing all the little things about her life that she took for granted—a warm bed, the smell of clean laundry, the feel of her husband next to her, and knowing her children were safe and secure in the next room. Never in her wildest dreams had she ever thought she'd have to be away from them, especially not like this.

She closed her eyes.

Dear God, she *prayed*, please give me the strength I need to get through this next day.

She pleaded with Him to allow her to return to her family but promised Him that she'd make the best of it and to figure out what He wanted her to do if coming home wasn't part of the plan.

She thought about Brooke, Donna, and Anne, wondering if they were sleeping peacefully in their beds without as much of a thought to her. Or were they tossing and turning, racked with guilt for betraying her? How would they feel if she went to prison? Would they come forward then? Probably. But by then it would be too late.

CHAPTER 43

The folks from church made good on their promise and were waiting for her when she arrived at the courthouse. They all gathered around her in a circle, held hands, and prayed for her. Even Ron, a self-professed agnostic, joined in.

She took her seat at the defense chair, and every time she heard someone come through the door, she turned to look. In the back of her mind, she knew that either Anne or Donna or maybe both would change their minds and come to her defense. There was no way they could leave her alone today with what she faced. She knew they'd be there. She just knew it.

She heard voices near the entrance and turned to look again, hopeful, but it was Rick and Curtis. Rick gave the room a once-over and led his son to the closest seat possible to Julie. Lynn came in a few minutes later, decked out in a charcoal gray suit, thick black spectacles, and hair pulled back in a tight ponytail. Obviously someone had coached Lynn on what to wear. She looked like an old maid schoolteacher.

Hannah wasn't with them. She must not be testifying, Julie thought with relief. That relief was short-lived, however, when she saw the girl being escorted by a large, masculine woman wearing a badge and possessing an overall protectiveness of the child.

Ron could see the puzzled look on Julie's face, and as if he could read her mind, he told her the woman was an officer of the court designated to protect Hannah.

"Protect her?" Julie asked, puzzled. "From whom?" No sooner had the question left her mouth when the answer gripped her heart. The woman was there to protect Hannah from *her.* How on earth could anyone ever think she'd harm a child?

"All rise," came the order from the clerk as the judge entered the room. Julie gripped the table as she stood up. She turned and looked at the door as she saw the elderly couple that lived next door to Lynn come in and sit down. The old man shot her a dirty look, and the woman hugged Lynn as she sat down beside her. It killed Julie to know that people actually believed she had done this.

She then saw the security guard pull the huge brass door handle, knowing that the proceedings were about to begin, bringing about the realization that her friends would not be coming to her rescue. She was alone. It was all in God's hands. Even Ron, as good of an attorney as he was, had no control over what the judge would decide today. The courtroom doors closed with a thud, and at that point, she knew she was completely and utterly alone.

A few of the people in her church group made the universal I-love-you hand sign. She looked at Tom, and he mouthed the words. She wanted to jump up out of her chair and run to him. She'd never been more frightened in her life.

The judge gave his orders to start, and the prosecuting attorney rose to give his opening remarks. Julie heard him say something about proving beyond a shadow of a doubt that "this woman attempted to drive a car over the victim and her daughter," all the time angrily pointing an accusing finger at her.

She closed her eyes, and in her thoughts she sang the words to 'Jesus Loves Me," just like Mama had taught her to do as a child when she was scared. And as she sat, posture erect, she pictured Jesus looking exactly as He did in the children's Bible she'd gotten for her seventh birthday, standing behind her with His hands placed gently and protectively on her shoulders.

CHAPTER 44

Lynn couldn't have been happier. She loved this. This was her stage, *her moment*. She had never come this far with the others. Sitting in the witness stand was like being on stage. All eyes were on her. *This* was her audience.

Tears came to her eyes, and her voice quivered as she told the court what happened that September night, the night that she and her daughter were simply taking an evening stroll, bonding in the moonlight, when Julie suddenly appeared around the corner, slammed the pedal to the medal, and sped toward them.

"I screamed and pushed my daughter out of the way and threw myself on top of her. I got out of the way just in time... Mrs. Patterson was so angry."

"Objection!" Ron stood up and shouted. "How does she know what the defendant was feeling?"

"Sustained," replied the judge, a grandfatherly type with gray, thinning hair. His half spectacles were perched on the end of his nose.

Lynn didn't let the slight interruption deter her. She was the star of this show, and she was going to play it to the hilt. She continued with the drama, pausing to dab her eyes for effect, describing how difficult her life had become since Julie had moved into the neighborhood.

How she constantly had to be on guard. How the neighbors had to come together and watch over her, afraid to let her out of their sight because they feared for her life.

"We even had to switch schools because Mrs. Patterson would always be waiting at the bus stop to harass the children."

Ron had given Julie strict instructions on keeping her facial expressions totally neutral. Not one grimace, smile, and most importantly, not even a hint of anger when Lynn took the stand. It was difficult.

"Bedtime became a nightmare," Lynn continued, never skipping a beat. "Hannah slept with us for a month before she switched schools. She was scared to death about going to the bus stop because she knew Mrs. Patterson would be there. She was always there cursing and screaming threats and obscenities. The same thing with Curtis. They both were so afraid of this woman. I'm afraid of this woman. I never know what's she's going to do or where she's going to be."

There were a few gasps and whispering in the courtroom while Lynn explained the torment her life had become since Julie had moved into the neighborhood. All the things that the woman described were things that she had actually done to Julie, only this time she twisted them around to make herself the victim, except for the child abuse charges.

"Ever since someone reported her to the school for child abuse, she has blamed me." Lynn sniffed. "Although she *is* a terrible mother—I've seen firsthand what she's done to that poor child—still, it wasn't me who turned her in."

Feeling the tension in Julie's body, Ron shot her a look that told her she was in no way to show any emotion. They'd get their turn, he whispered in her ear.

Julie was doubtful. If the reaction from the courtroom and the look on the judge's face were any indication, then her fate was pretty much sealed.

William would be fourteen by the time she came home. She would miss his whole childhood. Olivia would be twenty-five. Would she be married by then? What about Mama and Daddy? How would they react? And what would her friends back home think? She'd been the golden child, Miss Mississippi. Now, she was a woman accused of attempted murder.

God, what has happened to my life?

She was so deep in thought that she completely missed Ron's cross-examination of Lynn. She heard raised voices and watched the argument over pictures that both parties had of the crime scene. Lynn's had to have been taken at a later date. It was only yesterday when the fresh tire track showed up—more than three weeks after the alleged incident. Both pictures, the ones Janine had taken and the ones in Lynn's possession, were handed over to the judge for him to study.

When everything quieted down, Julie noticed that Hannah was on the stand. Sweet, innocent, little Hannah. How old was she now? Twelve. Good God! How could anyone do this to her own child? How could Lynn want to destroy another person so badly that she'd use her own child to do it? That was child abuse!

Dear Lord, please tell me that sweet baby doesn't think I tried to run over her.

Julie listened as Hannah, in a quiet voice that one had to strain to hear, gave her version of the night in question. It was a Friday night, and they'd just come back from the mall where they'd shopped for new school clothes. Her mother had suggested they go for a walk. While they were standing at the corner, out of nowhere, her mother grabbed her and pushed her to the ground and then jumped on top of her.

"Why did your mother jump on top of you?" the prosecutor asked.

"Because Mrs. Patterson tried to run over us," the girl said quietly.

Julie's heart sank. She watched the little girl on the witness stand, listened to her testimony, when suddenly she realized that she wasn't Lynn's only victim. No, her children were even more of a victim than she was. No matter what, they could never escape her. She was their mother, and they loved her, but they must know what she was. They had to. If they didn't, they'd find out sooner or later, and their hearts would be broken.

"What did you do after Mrs. Patterson tried to hit you?"

Hannah swallowed hard as she looked at Julie, and the two made eye contact.

Hannah, she thought, as if she could telepathically communicate with the child, please look into my eyes and know that I never, ever tried to hurt you or your mother.

"We walked home as fast as we could so Mom could call the police."

"Then what happened?" the attorney asked. You could have heard a pin drop. There wasn't even a stir in the audience as the girl continued.

"I just kept asking why? Why did this happen? Why would she want to kill me?"

Ron was kicking Julie under the table and scribbling on the notepad as fast as he could write, "No emotion! No emotion!"

When it was Ron's turn, he started off gently. He'd cross-examined his share of kids and knew how to make them feel comfortable with him before he went in for the kill. He asked her what grade she was in. Did she like school? What has her favorite subject?

Not understanding the value in those questions, Julie allowed her mind to wander. Would the judge sentence her today, or would this go to a jury? If he decided to sentence her today, would she be allowed to go home first to get things in order, or would she be taken straight to prison from here?

The intensity of Ron's deep baritone commanded Julie's attention. His next question left her on pins and needles.

"Hannah, did you see Mrs. Patterson try to hit you?"

Without missing a beat, Hannah replied, "No, but my mom did," not realizing for a moment that she had just blown a hole as big as an eighteen-wheeler in her mother's testimony.

Julie closed her eyes. Bless your heart, Hannah.

The girl was dismissed from the witness stand, and Ron called on Sam Watkins. Julie wasn't sure if his testimony of Lynn's character and the fact that he had witnessed her stalking would be of much benefit, but it sure wouldn't hurt, she supposed.

When it was her turn to testify, after being sworn in and taking her place on the witness stand, she, for the first time, had full view of the courtroom. She hadn't realized that Blanche and Janine had been there. They were sitting with the church crowd. Blanche gave her a quick wink. Janine smiled and nodded. Tom sat in the back of the room in a chair off to the side. He was in plain view. He'd picked his seat carefully, knowing that if Julie could just see him, she'd be all right.

The prosecution went first.

"So, Mrs. Patterson, I am curious to hear your story about that night in question."

"Nothing happened," Julie said calmly. "I simply was driving home from the office. I had about twenty thousand dollars worth of checks in the front seat and a plate of food on top. I was driving extra slow, not even the speed limit, because I didn't want to spill the food. I drove from my office to the drive-thru at Taco Bell and then into my own driveway with nothing happening at all."

"And do you have any witnesses to the effect?"

Before Ron could object, Julie said, "Yes, I did have a witness, but she refused to come forward because she said she didn't see or hear anything."

The prosecutor smirked. "Of course. I'm sure."

He mocked her as he turned to the audience and then back to Julie. "So I can only imagine you were completely shocked when the police came," he said to her, using his fingers as imaginary quotation marks.

"This isn't the first time she's had me in court over false charges. I wasn't exactly shocked, per se, just surprised."

No matter how hard the prosecutor tried to trip Julie in her defense, it wasn't happening.

"Look," Julie said at one point during his nonstop grilling, "this is a nonevent. It. Did. Not. Happen. If you would really look at these pictures, and I mean really take a close look, you will see that logistics make it impossible to speed down the street, jump the curb, or squeal the tires without someone or something actually getting hurt or being damaged."

She took the picture that he had thrust in her face, looked at the attorney, the judge, and the audience, and pointed. "See here! There isn't enough room to do all of that without driving into someone's yard, leaving tire tracks in the street, which there aren't any. See? Or without leaving a tire track on the curb. And look at my picture. No tire tracks on the street or the grass. Her picture has a tire track on the grass, but that wasn't there until a few days ago. But if you'll see right here, there isn't a tire track from squealing tires on the pavement!

"Once again, I am telling you this didn't happen! A complete fabrication."

"No more questions," the prosecutor mumbled.

The judge looked over at Ron. "Do you wish to question the defendant?"

"No, Your Honor," Ron said as he tried not to grin, thinking to himself that she had done fine. Just fine.

Julie felt her strength completely renewed as she sat down. She still didn't have high hopes about going home when it was over, but she had told the truth, and for right now that was good enough for her.

Ron was allowed to make his closing remarks first. He talked about the complete differences in the testimony between the mother and daughter. He drove home the fact that the plaintiff had once tried to pass herself off as a realtor in an effort to intimidate Sam Watkins, had been a convicted criminal, and had done jail time for felony shoplifting. Lynn Hennessy had also brought false charges against his client earlier in the year, in which his client had been found not guilty. As a matter of fact, the Prince William County magistrate had finally had to intervene to keep Mrs. Hennessy from filing frivolous and false charges against his client.

Ron took his seat beside her as the prosecutor rose, buttoned his jacket, and made his way to the front of the room.

"*Something* happened that night on that corner."

Don't listen! Julie willed herself as the prosecution made his closing arguments. *Do not cry; do not cry. They may carry me out of here in shackles, but I will not give that woman the pleasure of seeing me shed a tear.*

She cradled her head in her hands as she blocked out the words and prepared for the inevitable. She was so entranced in her thoughts she didn't even hear the cries of joy from her church family when the judge pronounced the defendant, Julie Patterson, not guilty.

CHAPTER 45

A week after the hearing, life began to settle down. Olivia returned to Mississippi, William was starting to sleep in his own bed again, and after three and a half days of no rain, Ed and Rob were going to finally finish the last half of the fence.

Things were even quiet on the Lynn front. She was still up to her old tricks, following Julie, watching everything from the deck, and spreading lies, but since the Patterson's trip to the magistrate there had been no more visits from the police.

Julie hadn't seen Anne, and she'd avoided the bus stop for a few days so she wouldn't have to encounter Donna. But today she told Tom to go ahead and go to work. She could handle it, and besides, she couldn't avoid the woman forever.

Julie was prepared for some awkward moments. What she wasn't prepared for was Donna's emotional outburst. The woman was a complete mess.

'Julie!" Donna cried, grasping Julie's hands and squeezing them tight. "Oh, thank God you're all right!

I saw Tom, and you weren't with him and I thought you were, you know, had gone—"

"To prison?" Julie sardonically finished the question for her. "Sorry to disappoint you."

She walked to the other side of the street, but Donna was right behind her.

"I'm so sorry, Julie. I am begging you to forgive me! I haven't been able to live with myself—"

"Please just leave me alone!"

"What can I do to make this up to you? I'll talk to the judge or the lawyer, anyone. Just please forgive me."

Where is that bus? Julie thought nervously stepping from one foot to the other. Donna's visible anguish was making her uncomfortable and angry, mostly at herself because she could feel her own resolve begin to crumble. It was evident to Julie that Donna was remorseful. But how, how could she forgive a betrayal like this? Good God, this woman was willing to let her go to prison!

"How could you turn your back on me like that? I thought you were my friend." She felt a tear trickle down her cheek as she quickly wiped it away. "You knew what was at stake. You knew that I could have been torn away from my family, and yet you refused to come forward."

Neither said a word for what seemed like an eternity. Donna continued crying. In the distance, Julie could hear the school bus a sit shifted gears and headed toward them. She knew the children would be there any moment and didn't want them to be a witness to any kind of confrontation.

The hurt was so fresh, so new, and Julie didn't think things would or could ever be the same between her and Donna. On the other hand, she could hear Mama's voice in her head quoting Scripture.

... forgiving one another even as Christ has forgiven you ... Colossians 3:13

She turned to face Donna. "I forgive you, Donna, but you are going to have to be patient with me. I am heartbroken beyond belief, and it's going to take a while. I don't know if we can ever be friends like we were, but I do forgive you."

Donna suddenly grabbed Julie and hugged her tight, thanking her profusely, which only made Julie even more uncomfortable. She wasn't sure in her heart if it was really all that easy to say you forgive someone and then do it, but she would definitely try. She had to if she was going to be the person she used to be before all of this. And that's really all Julie wanted: to be who she was before she moved here.

The significance of his mom being at the bus stop that day was not lost on William as he bounced off the vehicle, rushing to her open arms. She had been groggy the past couple of days, but he had snuck in to her bed twice and lay beside her, stroking her hair and patting her back like she did whenever he was sick.

"I love you, Mommy," he said, hugging her tight, not caring one bit if his friends were watching.

Julie's heart felt so warm as she hugged him back, burying her face deep in his blonde head. "I love you too, pumpkin."

"I've been meaning to ask you," Julie said as they walked hand-in-hand toward home, "what are you going to be for Halloween?"

"I'm going as a motorcycle guy," he said without hesitation. Obviously, he'd given this quite a bit of thought. "Robbie said I could come over after school today and get one of his dirt bike helmets. Can I go get it now?"

"Sure," Julie said. "But I'll go with you. Here, set your backpack down on the porch." There was no way she was letting him out of her sight. Plus, she wanted to make sure it was okay with Shelley for him to borrow the helmet. They could be rather expensive to replace if something should happen to it.

"Sure, take it," Shelley said. "We have way too many of those around here anyway. Besides, I think everyone's outgrown that one."

Then she pulled Julie aside and asked her how she was coping.

Julie smiled. "I'm doing pretty good, actually. Once we get back to a routine and the fence is finished, I'm really praying everything will be back to normal."

"I hope you're right," Shelley said doubtfully.

Satisfied that he had all he needed to complete his costume, Will thanked Robbie.

"I'll catch you later, Shelley," Julie said as they stepped out to the sidewalk. "Be sure to bring the kids by our house on Halloween. I make the world's best popcorn balls, I'll have you know."

"Oh, I love popcorn balls," said Shelley. "But I can't eat them."

"Are you allergic to popcorn?"

Shelley laughed. "No. It's just that once I start I can't stop and I end up eating the whole thing."

"Then wait until Mike is at work and the kids are in school. That's what I do. In the South we have a saying, 'If no one sees you eat it, then it doesn't count.'"

Will took his mom's hand, and they instantaneously started skipping down the sidewalk. *Oh, thank you, God!* Julie thought for the umpteenth time that day. Her heart was running over with love for her family, her new lease on life.

Suddenly, Will came to an abrupt stop. All color drained from his face. His body went limp as he grabbed his mother around the waist. Confused at the sudden change in his demeanor, Julie looked down at him as he started to cry. She tucked the motorcycle helmet under her arm and dropped to her knees.

"Honey, what's wrong?"

He pointed behind her. "Mom, look. She's videotaping us!"

Julie whipped around. Lynn was at the end of the sidewalk and coming at them with a video recorder, the flashing red light indicating that the tape was rolling.

What should she do? Confront her or ignore her? Her heart raced, but she had to hold it together for Will. *Think fast!*

"Quick! Strike a pose! Let's pretend we're movie stars, and she's the paparazzi!"

Julie laughed as she put one hand on her hip and flung the other in the air and gave a big, toothy grin to the camera. Then she did a cartwheel, landing on her knees with both hands in the air, belting out a triumphant, "Ta-da!" William started laughing and followed his mom's lead, making all sorts of crazy faces and poses.

Lynn flipped them the bird, turned off the camera, and stomped back to her house. While Julie laughed and hammed it up for Will's sake, inside she was seething.

In Julie's backyard, Ed was having problems of his own. He and his men were putting up the last panel on the fence, connecting to the Hennessy's corner post.

Rick had watched, waiting patiently for the past hour until they got to his property line. He waited until they dug the last two postholes that would complete the job before he went out to deal his blow.

"You're trespassing," he snapped.

Ed wasn't fazed. He had really kind of expected this. "Let's be fair here, sir. Your fence encroaches onto their property by five feet back there. These homeowners' association documents address that and give us permission to connect to your fence."

"I don't care what the homeowners' association documents say."

"But as president of the HOA you signed the documents," Ed argued. "You agreed to this!"

"Well, looks like I've changed my mind, huh?"

This was getting nowhere, so Ed called for Tom.

Rick wouldn't budge. "My fence is two feet inside my property line. If you connect your fence to mine, you'll be violating the no trespass order. All I have to do is pick up the phone and your wife, and you, will be arrested."

"So are you going to pull up your part of the fence that's five feet into my property?" Tom asked coolly.

"I'm not movin' *shit*," Rick replied as he stomped away.

"You're the HOA president!" Tom called after him. "Why did you sign off on this and then wait to the last minute to come out here?"

Rick kept walking. He didn't have to answer a damn thing. Yeah, he did sign off on it. He knew when he had signed the form along with the other HOA officers that he'd nix it at the last minute. Sure, Patterson would probably be within his legal rights to go ahead and connect the fence to his, but Rick knew that all he'd have to do was threaten to have that beautiful wife of his arrested, and Patterson would run away like a puppy with his tail behind his legs. Mission accomplished.

CHAPTER 46

The fence issue remained unsolved. Tom requested a meeting with the HOA board, including Rick. He said he'd paid his dues recently, although Tom doubted it. A call from Julie to Cecile at the HOA office confirmed those doubts. Still, Rick remained president, and still, he wouldn't allow them to connect to his part of the fence. He did, however, after being pushed by the other two board members, agree to pull up his part of the structure that encroached on Tom's Property. He was given a time limit of ten days.

For ten days there was a gaping hole from Tom and Julie's unfinished portion, hanging in limbo. Every day for ten days Lynn stood there and took pictures or videos of the family every time they stepped outside. Now William couldn't even play in his own backyard, nor would Julie let Colette out the back door to use the bathroom. She was scared to death that if they were in the backyard Lynn would accuse them of being on her property. While the magistrate had curbed her from making false police reports, the fact was the no trespass order was still active. Incidentally, that tiny piece of ground she stood on was her property.

"There's really nothing we can do," the police dispatcher told Julie over the phone. "That is her property and technically she can take a picture or video anyone or anything she likes. There's not a law against that."

"I understand that." *Here we go again.* "But last week she was in the middle of the street videotaping us. There has to be a limit to how close she can get to us and—'

"Ma'am, she can get as close to you as she wants and take as many pictures as she wants. As long as she doesn't touch you or harm you physically, she is within the realm of the law."

Julie was angry. *That woman has to kill me before anyone can step in and help.*

The phone rang. It was her new neighbor, Mrs. Kirkpatrick.

"Julie, I remember you telling me at settlement that you had a spare key to the house. May I pick it up sometime? I'd like for our daughter to have it."

"Sure." Julie knew right where it was. "I've been meaning to bring it over to you. I'll do that now."

"You don't mind?"

"Of course not. I'll be right there." She welcomed the distraction.

"William, I'm taking this key next door to the new neighbors. Stay inside. I'll be right back."

"Please let me know if you need anything," Julie offered as she slipped the key to Mrs. Kirkpatrick.' And if you know of anyone else that needs a realtor, will you please give them my name?"

"Of course," the lady said. "You did such a wonderful job for us. I'd be more than happy to refer you to someone else."

They seemed like such a nice couple, although she missed the Lopezs. Sometimes she wasn't really sure if she was sad about their actual leaving or just jealous because they were getting out of the neighborhood. Maybe a mixture of both.

She was almost in front of her house when she heard a clicking noise followed by a bright light. Dazed, she turned around and saw Lynn right on her tail with a camera, clicking away as fast as she could.

She jumped in front of Julie and they almost tripped over each other. The sudden bursts of flash in her eyes were blinding. Lynn was showing a new aggressiveness, and it frightened her.

She hoped that the Kirkpatricks weren't witnessing this and wondering what in the world they had gotten themselves into by moving here. As for her, she was coming to the realization that Lynn would never, ever give up until she destroyed her or drove her crazy, whichever came first.

"Don't freak out when I tell you this," Janine said when she called Julie a few hours later.

"No promises."

"Your favorite neighborhood psycho just called me."

"What did she want?" Julie asked, surprisingly calm.

"She wanted to file a formal complaint against you."

"For what?" She sure was glad she hadn't made that promise not to freak out.

Janine sighed. "Fair Housing Violation. Supposedly you made disparaging remarks about her to the new neighbors. Are they by any chance nonwhite?"

"They're African American," Julie replied, wondering what difference it made.

"Ah, that explains it," Janine said. 'Apparently, you warned them that the Hennessy family was racist, and they needed to, and I quote here, 'watch their back.' She also says she has a witness."

"Janine, you know I did no such thing. At this point, they don't even know she exists! I, on the other hand, have scarred retinas from her shoving a camera in my face. I swear that woman just keeps getting crazier—"

Janine huffed. "I know that and you know that. Richmond, however, doesn't know that."

"What does Richmond have to do with anything?"

"She said that if I didn't fire you that she'd call Richmond and report you to the Fair Housing Board."

Julie flipped out. "Where does this woman get her information and knowledge on the legal system? How does she know what to do?"

"Beats me." Janine shrugged. "You know I've got your back as far as your job is concerned, but I can't protect you outside the office. Just be careful out there."

Violation of fair housing was a serious complaint, and the real estate board always investigated every single one. It was illegal for a realtor to make a comment, whether positive or negative, regarding a neighborhood, including the neighbors. *Just what I need*, thought Julie, *more lawyer fees.*

Much to Will's excitement, Halloween arrived. It was a crisp autumn day with no wind and plenty of sunshine. The family took a few pumpkins on the deck to participate in their yearly tradition of carving jack-o-lanterns. They would be used later to light a Pathway to the front door for trick-or-treaters.

Tom was carving out a wide-toothed grin on the second pumpkin when a voice came from the corner of the lawn toward the Hennessy home.

"Smile for the camera!" It was Lynn herself in that same familiar spot snapping away.

Will was so rattled by the sight of the woman and her camera that he fell out off his chair, catching the corner of the tablecloth with him. The pumpkins crashed to the ground, bursting into pieces, completely ruined.

He started to cry.

"Get outta here!" Tom said as he stood up and started to walk toward her.

"Tom, no!" Julie grabbed his elbow.

"This is my property!" Lynn stood defiantly. "I'll stand here as long as I want!"

Julie picked Will up and sat him on her lap. The child was shaking.

"We can't keep living like this, Tom," she whispered.

She'd thought the basement and the fence would be an answer to their problem. Especially the fence. But it was already past the ten-day mark, and Rick had made no effort to move his part of the fence so they could finish theirs.

Tom approached Henry Stottle, one of the board members, about it on the eleventh day. He told them his hands were tied. They couldn't *force* Rick to actually do anything. The twelfth day Tom paid a visit to the county government office. One of the board of supervisors told him he was well within his rights to pull up Rick's fence without his permission. He decided to be smart about it and have a policeman there to supervise, but the chief of police advised against it. They could always hire an attorney, of course. They'd win the court case, but lawyer fees would eat up the construction money and then there wouldn't be a fence anyway.

"I can't take this," Julie said to Tom when they were alone. "Lynn Hennessy controls every aspect of our lives. *Every single aspect.* It's like we're prisoners in our own home."

Tom ran his hands through his hair, a nervous habit.

"We won't wait for them to pull up their fence." Tom was matter of fact. "I'll talk to Ed tomorrow and I'll have him go ahead and finish and build it around their part. We'll lose five feet of property line, but hey—" He threw his hands up in the air. Right now property line was not high on his priority list.

"Where are your gloves?" Julie asked Will. It was about an hour before dark. Temperatures had dropped significantly, and the forecast called for a cold, windy night.

"Oops, I left them at school."

"Hmm, it'a going to be pretty chilly. You really need gloves. It wouldn't hurt to wear a t-shirt and a flannel shirt under your costume, either." She snapped her fingers. "7-Eleven! They have gloves. I'll send your dad up to get a pair."

As requested, Tom walked up to 7-Eleven and bought the gloves. Walking back home he admired the creativity that some of the neighbors had used in decorating their homes and yards for Halloween. But what he saw next made him stop dead in his tracks.

"Julie!" He tried to sound calm so he wouldn't alarm Will, but he was fuming inside. "Come here a minute!"

"What is it?"

"Come with me. I want to show you something. And bring the camera." He called up to Will. "Hey, buddy. Your mom's gonna step outside with me for a sec. We'll be right back and then we'll go trick-or-treating!"

Julie didn't bother to grab a jacket. The cold air smacked her in the face as they rounded the corner on Frostman Court, and she was glad she'd sent Tom to buy Will gloves.

Tom stopped in front of Lynn's house. "Look." He pointed.

Very neatly in a row loomed four large tombstones. Each stone had its own inscription. *Tom Patterson. Julie Patterson. Olivia Patterson. Will Patterson.*

"...*I wish you were dead...!*" Julie had a quick flashback.

While Tom took pictures, she fought the urge to vomit.

"Trick-or-treaters already?" Julie asked when the doorbell rang an hour later. She kept her mood upbeat. The last thing she wanted to do was spoil this night for Will, or worse, scare him.

Excited, Will ran to the door as fast as he could.

Jamie Mumfort, dressed as an Indian chief, stood in the doorway with a big chocolate grin on his face. Obviously someone had gotten started on the Halloween treats a little early.

"Hi, Miss Julie," the Indian chief greeted her. Then he raised his right hand and put on his best Indian chief face. "Oops! I mean, 'How,' Miss Julie."

Then transforming back to his regular voice,

"My mom wants to know if Will can go trick-or-treating with us. Can he? Please?"

Over my dead body, Julie thought bitterly.

She looked over Jamie's head, and there was Anne, standing on the sidewalk, smiling sheepishly, managing a half-hearted wave. *The nerve of that woman! She didn't even have the guts to come up here and ask me herself.*

"Sweetheart," Julie said to Jamie, cupping his face in her hands, "why don't you go on in the house and get some candy off that table right there by the door? I'm going to go down and have a chat with your mama, okay?" That was all Jamie needed. He grabbed two fists full of candy and shoved them in his bag.

Julie marched down the hill to the sidewalk and stood face-to-face with the woman she'd once considered a close friend. She put her face as close to Anne's as she could get without bumping noses.

"Are you kidding me? You were willing to let me rot in prison without as much as batting an eyelash! And I'm supposed to trust you while you take my little boy trick-or-treating on a dark street while that woman has a headstone in her front yard with his name on it? You don't have the guts to do the right thing, but I'm supposed to trust you with my child? Not on your life!'

The expression on Anne's face was priceless. Julie turned and walked away.

"Jamie! Come here! We're leaving!" The obviously disappointed little boy trudged down the hill to his mother. "I don't have time for this!"

"You might need me someday, Anne. Who knows? You may wake up one morning and discover that you're her new sport. I sure hope I can muster up the courage to be there for you."

It was dark, but just enough light reflected from the porch light for her to see Anne flinch.

CHAPTER 47

She tossed to one side and then the other. She closed her eyes, but still sleep wouldn't come. She turned on the radio to soft, elevator music, but still she was wide awake. She glanced over at Tom. He was out like a light and sawing logs.

Then a thought occurred to her. Throwing the covers back, she tiptoed downstairs to the computer. Maybe there was a support group for people like her. She typed in google.com. But what were people like her called? Okay, so she'd been a victim of a stalker, she knew that. But it wasn't the kind of stalking you read about or heard about in the news. That's what was so frustrating. You couldn't really explain what was happening. Whenever she'd tried, people always wanted to believe she'd done something to deserve it.

For a lack of a better term, Julie typed in *reverse stalking*, wondering if there really was such a term. Several articles popped up. They discussed the type that she had read about or seen on the news. None of that really pertained to her though. She wasn't a celebrity or a victim of spousal abuse.

Wait, what was this? She scrolled down. *False victimization syndrome.*

> In these cases, the stalker holds the victim in very high regard and will imitate the victim's style of speech, dress, habits, etc. Some stalkers go as far as buying a house with the same floor plan, trade in his vehicle for one like the victim's, or even make a career change to the victim's chosen profession. This type of stalker is very manipulative and convinces others (often authorities) that the victim is the one at fault when in reality the victim probably would not have known what was going on until the stalker started a campaign against him. Often the victim is reported to the authorities for defending himself from the stalker. (www. counseling.pitt. edu/pdf/stalking. pdf)

She read it again. And again.

She almost giggled. Wow. I'm not crazy! There is a name for this. An actual name!

She kept reading.

> The stalker wants, in a nutshell, to be like her victim, and when she feels like she doesn't measure up, her motive is to bring the victim down. Sometimes this means merely ruining the victim's reputation. Other times, this means murder.

Murder? Would Lynn become so desperate that she'd resort to murder? Julie didn't want to be melodramatic, but she honestly couldn't say for sure that she wouldn't.

She slowly trudged upstairs and back to bed. Tomorrow she would show Tom what she'd found. What was happening had a name, and for some reason that gave her great comfort.

CHAPTER 48

She couldn't remember when she had slept so soundly. No bad dreams, no tossing, no turning, just peaceful, unadulterated sleep. She couldn't wait to tell Tom what she'd discovered. He was still sleeping, and she fought to resist the urge to wake him. It would be best to wait until he was fully awake and she had his full attention.

She slipped on the robe and house slippers the kids bought her for Christmas last year and went into the bathroom to brush her teeth before going downstairs to cook breakfast. In a few minutes, the smell of bacon would waft through the house, and everyone would gather around the kitchen table before heading off to Sunday morning Bible class.

She loved this time of year. The sun had an amber glow, illuminating the foyer, making it seem warm and cozy even though there was a crisp chill in the air.

Julie looked out the window as she passed through to the kitchen. She stopped. *That's strange.* She backed up and looked again. *What?* She quickly grabbed the doorknob and flung the door open so hard that it hit the wall and bounced. She rubbed her eyes. Her sunny mood turned to shock.

It looked as if a twister had gone through and ripped up the yard. Every single one of their plants and shrubs, about fifty in all, had been pulled up by the roots and strewn throughout the yard. Her beautiful rattan furniture had been thrown from the porch and scattered throughout the grass, the cushions thrown about, some landing in the neighbor's yard.

The mailbox had been pulled up out of the ground, and the Victorian yard light was busted and laying in a million little pieces all over the lawn into the driveway.

Her eyes darted to John and Brooke's yard next door. Their bright colorful mums stood at attention in the morning sunlight. Across the street, Salena's autumn flower garden was perfect. So was every plant, every ornament in every yard. Perfect. Untouched.

A chill ran up Julie's spine.

"Tom!" she screamed, grabbing the phone to call the police. "Come look! Quick!"

The yard was Tom's pride and joy. In a matter of weeks, he had brought what once looked like a fescue field to a prize-winning English garden. Now, in one swooping act, it was destroyed.

Somberly, he began the task of picking up each and every plant and putting it back in its proper place. Thankfully, most of the roots were intact and would be able to be replanted with no problem.

Slowly, neighbors were starting to trickle into the yard. A few were sincere about what they could do to assist. Most, however, were just there to get a front-seat view of the latest drama.

"Did you see or hear anything in the middle of the night?" Julie asked Reed Kirkpatrick. He hadn't.

Blanche began picking up the furniture, setting each piece back on the porch in its proper place. She then sat on the sofa, placed her hands over her face, and wept.

Within five minutes, the police were there. The saga was familiar to them by now. They interviewed Lynn, and of course she knew nothing.

"I'm going to tell you something totally off the record," the officer said to Tom and Julie. "You know this will never stop, don't you?"

He pointed to the backyard, to the unfinished fence.

"You will never be able to build a fence high enough to keep this woman away from you. We can't protect you until she harms you physically, and by then it will probably be too late."

Ron was more blunt and to the point.

"Pack up and move. Get out of Prince William County. Don't tell anybody in this neighborhood where you're going. And until you're out of here, you need to have someone parked outside this door at all times. Don't leave this house without someone that can offer you protection. Basically, what you need is a full-time bodyguard."

CHAPTER 49

The "For Sale" sign was ordered first thing Monday morning. By two that afternoon, she watched silently from her living room window while it was being installed firmly into the ground. Ed, Rob and the crew finished the fence and then worked overtime to get the basement done.

Julie could have listed the house at a higher price, but they just wanted out of there, so they did everything they could to make the house more attractive for a potential buyer. Even though Tom made a six-figure income, the cost of their legal fees had pretty much eaten their savings. Now she wished they hadn't spent the last bit they'd had on fixing up the downstairs or building the fence.

The cost of 24/7 security also cost a bundle. Julie tried to get out of it. Now that the fence was done she didn't worry about Lynn so much, and besides, she and Will could hide out in the basement until Tom came home. But Tom wouldn't hear of it.

Chuck Bishop referred them to a company that he used quite often. Within two hours someone was beside Julie at all times. She had to admit that she did feel more relaxed, but she missed her privacy immensely. She couldn't step out to the mailbox or even take the dog out without this person. A trip to the toilet was accompanied by someone standing outside the door. Still, she was a prisoner in her home. Lynn didn't stop with the picture-taking or videoing, but at least now she stayed a good distance away.

Within twenty-four hours of the for-sale sign going up, there was a viable contract on the house. The buyers were from El Salvador. Their realtor took them through the house, where they spent almost an hour before offering a contract. Acting as an interpreter their agent asked if they could borrow her dining room table while they wrote the contract.

Another hour later and Julie had a contract in her hands, though for far less than what Tom and Julie actually owed. The contract also asked for possession within thirty days, as well as the antique buffet, a few expensive paintings, her living room suite, and all the furniture in the sunroom.

Yikes! That's half my furniture, and we really can't afford to sell for less. She started to say no. Then she remembered the first time she'd looked at this house. Barbara McKinney had left most of her belongings, and she'd wondered why. Looking back she knew she'd even been judgmental. Now she totally understood. Tom and Julie would have to use what little money was left in their savings to pay off the rest of the mortgage. It would sting, but their family would be free.

"Deal. But if I need more time to look for a house, can we do a rent back for another thirty days?" Julie crossed her fingers.

"¿Si ella no puede encontrar una casa en treinta dias, sera posible que se pueda quedar treinta dias mas?"

"No, no." The woman shook her head profusely and then started speaking very quickly to her agent.

No and the shaking of the bead, a universal language, Julie thought.

"Thirty days doesn't give us enough time," she complained to Tom, remembering how long it had taken them to find *this* house. "It's not a good idea for us to buy in this market right now; but there aren't any rentals out there either."

"Don't worry about it," said Tom. "You're the realtor. Just do what you have to do to get us out of here."

Three weeks later, the moving van was loaded, and Julie patiently waited outside while the buyers and their agent did the final walk-through.

Her protective detail waited outside with her.

"You can go ahead and go now, Eric," Julie said, reaching out for his hand. "I'll be fine. In a few minutes, I'll be locking this place up and leaving for good. Thank you for everything."

"No problem," he replied. "Good luck to you guys."

After about thirty minutes, the realtor gave the thumbs-up and told Julie that he and his clients would meet her at RGS Title in Lake Ridge to finalize the sale.

"Sure, let me lock up, and I'll be right behind you," she answered, more than ready to leave this place, these people, and these years behind her.

When she and Tom had left their beautiful home in Jackson, she had taken her sweet time, pausing to emotionally relive the cherished memories of each and every room, the day they brought Olivia home from the hospital as a newborn, Will's first steps. Not this time. She didn't even look back. She pulled the door as tight as she could, as if trapping the memories inside so they couldn't escape, couldn't follow her.

She shoved the key in the door, locked it, and almost ran to the car.

She stopped dead in her tracks. Rick.

"This should be a happy day for you," Julie said bitterly as she opened the car door. "Or maybe not. After all, what will your wife do for sport now that I'm gone?"

He didn't move. He stood so still and silent that for a moment Julie was frightened. Maybe she'd been too hasty in dismissing her security. Fear gave way to disgust when she saw tears welling in Rick's eyes.

"Too little, too late, Rick," Julie said, starting the ignition.

"I *love* her," he finally spoke, his voice quivering. "I'm sorry for all that's happened, but I love her."

"If you really loved her," she said before pulling the door shut, "you would have gotten her help a long time ago."

Julie put the car in reverse and backed out of the drive for the very last time. As she drove down Raye Street, she stared straight ahead to the future, never once looking in the rearview mirror.

EPILOGUE

Two years later
Old Town Alexandria, Virginia

"Sold!" cried the auctioneer as he slapped his gavel for the final time. The hutch had been Tom's grandmother's, and now it was going home with the highest bidder, along with most of their belongings. The home was going into foreclosure. Everything was gone, indicative of any and all semblance of the life they'd once known.

How many times had they been given advice to just pack and leave Prince William County? She'd tried, in vain, to explain that moving wasn't that easy. They wouldn't be able to get the money for their house to accommodate the skyrocketing prices of a new one, and they'd spent every last dime on Julie's defense and court costs. Besides that, she could feel in her gut that the housing market was getting ready to take a big tumble. Then they'd be left with a house they couldn't afford. One person, and she couldn't remember which one, the police chief maybe, had even laughed at her when she had predicted the housing market would crash.

"This is DC," he'd scoffed. "We always have a housing shortage, so that will never happen here."

But it did. And of course, in the end, the Pattersons had had no choice but to leave anyway. Foreclosure was better than physical harm to you or your family. Or prison. Julie tried not to be bitter, but sometimes it was so hard not to be. Two years later, twenty miles farther away, and they were still paying the price for what Lynn had done.

At least she'd had the good sense to put the cottage in her name only. Tom's good name wouldn't be affected by this at all.

In an effort to redirect her thoughts, she took one last walk through the cottage. It was no longer theirs, but this place had served its purpose. Within these walls they had found peace, tranquility and healing.

These things that strangers are packing in their cars and hauling off are just that, Julie thought. Things.

Yes, she'd have to start over. Her career had come to a complete standstill with the real estate market. She had no clue how she was going to repay her incredible debt. Janine was kind enough to let them rent one of her properties inside the District for as long as they needed.

"Are you okay?" Tom asked, slipping his hand into hers. He bent down to kiss her cheek.

"I will be." She smiled, trying not to let him see how scared she was. What would they do? How would they get themselves out of this mess? And when would life go back to being what it was before they moved here?

Tom looked at her, stood closer, and put his arm around her shoulder. He could feel the tension in her body. That tough exterior wasn't fooling anybody, least of all him.

"We'll work this out," he said to her, taking a sip from his coffee cup.

"How?" she asked, not really expecting an answer. "My real estate gig is pretty nonexistent right now, and I have no job prospects."

"Hmm." He took another drink of coffee, swallowed, and then nonchalantly planted the seed. "Then it sounds to me like you have plenty of time to start that book that you've been meaning to write."

"You mean the one I've been putting off because I couldn't come up with a good-enough plot?" she asked, still not catching on to what he was hinting at.

"That would be the one," Tom said with a half grin.

Julie looked up to meet his gaze. Suddenly, the reality of what he was saying hit her smack between the eyes.

Wait a minute! Would it work? She hadn't sat down to write anything in years, not since she'd been a reporter. Okay, she'd had an article published in

Jackson's Clarion Ledger, and she'd written a few things for a realtor trade magazine, but a *book*?

"Well, I definitely have a good plot now." She smiled. Yes! She could do this. She'd *make* it work. "What do you think?"

"What's that old saying about truth being stranger than fiction?" Tom said. "You couldn't have made this one up if you'd tried."

About the Author

Kathie Truitt grew up in the tiny Ozarks town of El Dorado Springs, Missouri. She started her writing career as soon as she could form sentences, spending hours journaling stories in the Big Chief tablet provided her grandmother. By 6th grade she was writing and producing plays for her class.

After graduation she attended Missouri State University - for about 2 minutes - before running off and marrying her high school sweetheart.

Kathie thought they'd settle down in El Dorado Springs, raising farm animals and babies, but instead travelled the world living in Texas, Mississippi, England and back to Missouri.

She spent over 20 years as a radio personality and when her show first became an Arbitron-rated number 1 show, she publicly thanked her teachers who said she'd never amount to a hill o' beans because she couldn't shut up in class. In 1996 she received the honor of being crowned Mrs. Missouri—in which afterward she promptly went up to her hotel room and changed a dirty diaper.

One spring day in 2001, Kathie's husband Jay announced he'd accepted a position on the East Coast and a few weeks later, he dragged her kicking and screaming to that den of iniquity some call Washington, D.C.

Those first few years were more than rough when the Truitt's moved to their neighborhood. After being the victim of a crazy neighbor lady that stalked them for 5 years, they were forced to move to another county for their safety. This was the basis for Kathie's first novel, "False Victim" in which she not only sold the movie rights, but it was also a featured segment on Investigation Discovery.

Kathie's second book, "The Hillbilly Debutante Cafe" is a much lighter, more fun novel that has been compared to 'Fried Green Tomatoes'.

Kathie maintains a blog, aptly called 'Hillbilly Debutante: Adventures of an Aging Beauty Queen'.

Kathie now makes her home in the beautiful lakeside town of Rowlett, Texas.

You can follow Kathie at:

hillbillydebutante.blogspot.com

CPSIA information can be obtained
at www.ICGtesting.com
Printed in the USA
FSHW022010240120
66470FS